PRAISE FOR VIVIAN AREND

"Vivian Arend does a wonderful job of building the atmosphere and the other characters in this story so that readers will be sucked into the world and looking forward to the rest of the books in the series."
~ *Library Journal*

"Steamy and sweet complete with a whole host of colourful side characters and enough sub-plots to get your teeth into. A fab read!"
~ *Scorching Book Reviews*

"There's a real chemistry between the characters, laced with humor and snappy dialogue and no shortage of steamy sex scenes to keep things lively. The result is an entertaining, spicy romance."
~ *Publishers Weekly*

Silver Mine is an outstanding story. The author creates a world that invites readers for the ride of their lives."
~ *Coffee Time Romance Reviews*

Arend offers constant action and thrills, and her characters are so captivating and nuanced that readers will have a hard time guessing who the villains really are.
~ *RT Book Reviews*

MOON SHINE

TAKHINI WOLVES #4

VIVIAN AREND

This is a work of fiction. Names, characters, places, and incidents either are the product of the author's imagination or are used fictitiously, and any resemblance to any persons, living or dead, business establishments, events, or locales is entirely coincidental.

PART I

Wherefore, the wolf-pack having gorged upon the lamb,
their prey,
With siren smile and serpent guile I make the
wolf-pack pay—
With velvet paws and flensing claws, a tigress roused to slay.
One who in youth sought truest truth and found a devil's
lies;
A symbol of the sin of man, a human sacrifice.
Yet shall I blame on man the shame? Could it be otherwise?
"The Harpy"—Robert Service

Evan Stone shot off the couch and scrambled to the window, clutching back the living room curtains as he stared into the darkness. His heart continued to rattle hard enough his hands shook.

It took a long time to blink away the images, for the echoes of screams to fade from his ears. To admit it was true. The flames were only in his mind. His dreams.

Instead of red and gold fingers consuming everything around him in destructive heat, outside his second-storey apartment window the streetlights of Whitehorse flickered. Their pale blue glow a faint defense against the chill of night.

As the fog in his brain cleared, the ache in his belly arrived, silent pain striking deep. The gaping hole in his soul became his single focus point. Far more than the dreams of his past, the unknown cut him apart and shot his concentration to hell.

Life as he knew it was over—but his future refused to arrive.

Somewhere out there was his mate. He'd scented her,

following her trail from his hotel until she'd vanished without a trace. He'd dedicated every spare moment since to the search, but all his attempts had come up blank. Frustration led to restless nights pacing before passing out wherever he ended up. Restless sleep led to nightmares made of tortured memories.

He was past ready to move on.

A quick glance showed the clock on the counter had failed. Evan pressed his watch to check the glowing numbers. Time clicked over to twelve-ten as loud pounding sounded on his front door.

"Evan, wake up. Wake *up*."

Bloody hell. "Shaun?"

Wolf-pack hierarchy said Evan was *numero uno* and Shaun second in command. Evan tried to maintain a light hand on the reins—he'd witnessed too intimately what happened when men and beasts allowed power to go to their heads. But laid-back ruler of his Takhini-pack kingdom that he might be, unless this was a real death-and-dying emergency?

He would happily take out his frustrations on his Beta.

Evan jerked the door open. Shaun stood there, his usual "what the fuck" attitude noticeably absent. Instead his dark hair and broad shoulders were covered with a thick layer of black and green...stuff.

"What the hell happened to you? Whoa..." Evan stepped back in self-defense as the first wave of putrescence hit him smack in the face. "Crap."

"Not crap, it's garbage." Shaun knocked a handful of what looked to be half-decomposed road kill off one shoulder.

"Get a new hobby," Evan snarled, his eyes watering. "Jeez, you reek. Stand downwind, I'll come outside."

"You need to get to the hotel," Shaun insisted, even as he inched farther back on the landing. His face twisted into a horrified expression. "I can barely breathe, I stink so bad."

Evan wasn't sure what was going on. Their livelihood was based on the hotel, and over the past couple weeks, strange shit had been happening. He strode back to his bedroom, shouting at Shaun through the open door. "Stay there while I pull on some clothes. Tell me what's wrong, and why the hell you look like a zombie."

"Power is out at the hotel. *Only* the hotel—none of the other places on the block are affected, and the pack house three streets over is fine as well. I was in the middle of shutdown at the bar when everything went black. None of the usual fixes helped, so I thought I'd try you. But your phones are out, both your landline and your cell. And the shortcut between the hotel and your place was booby-trapped."

Shaun grimaced at the muck-coated fingers he raised skyward as Evan joined him on the landing, fully clothed. They both turned and headed down the stairs to the street level. "Thanks for getting me. Did you turn on the generator?"

"Busted."

"Bullshit," Evan snapped. "I serviced that myself last week."

Shaun stopped beside him, bits and pieces of debris falling off to the ground as if he truly were a zombie on his final legs. "Don't go snarly at me. I know engines too, dude —it's busted. No bullshit."

"That makes no bloody sense," Evan complained. "Plus, there's no reason for an outage this time of year in the first place."

They skirted the area where Shaun had hit the booby

trap. Evan was too keen to get to the hotel to do more than give the setup a quick glance, but even that was enough to make him whistle in admiration. "Damn, the trick-or-treaters are out in full force already. Look—"

He pointed to the neatly assembled buckets hanging empty above their heads. Shaun grumbled. "They were hidden behind the board. That's why I didn't see them."

"Must have sealed the tops to stop the smell from warning you off as well." Evan shook his head, his stomach protesting the stench wafting off Shaun. "You must be dying. I'm dying standing next to you. God, you stink like... Hell, I can't think of anything nasty enough, actually."

"Fuck you. You want my help tonight?"

Evan made a snap decision. "No. Go home. Get a shower. Try not to freak your mate out too much, or she might decide to light you on fire and get a newer model."

"Har-har." Shaun stepped away as Evan pulled open a side-entrance door to the hotel. "Seriously, though. Call if you need me."

"We'll be fine." Evan waved his Beta off before turning and entering the darkness.

He strode down the hallway with no hesitation as he paced the black-as-coal passages. He was familiar with every inch of the hotel he'd turned into one of the centerpieces of the Takhini pack resources. Plus, he was a wolf. His senses were sharp enough to warn him not only of his surroundings, but that he was rapidly approaching a group of upset people who'd gathered in the lobby.

Dim light greeted him as he rounded the corner to the open foyer. Swinging flashlights sent golden beams dancing off rock walls, the wet surfaces all that earmarked the impressive waterfall that usually graced the entrance to the hotel. The feature wall was silent. Even the voices he heard remained low, although their dismay and concern carried clearly enough, echoing in the darkness.

Evan shoved behind the desk and laid a soothing hand on the shoulder of a very agitated young wolf who was supposed to have the simple task of night clerk. "What's up, Dale?"

"Thank goodness, you're here." Dale didn't get another word out before the mixed crowd of humans and shifters in the lobby all started talking at once. Demanding the power be restored.

Demanding refunds.

Evan took a deep breath and used as much of his wolf power as possible to send out calming vibes. The mystical mojo wouldn't work as well on the humans as his pack, but there was still a noticeable effect. "We'll do our best to get things up and running ASAP. There must be a line down that services the building. Let me look into it. In the meantime, do you all have flashlights? Good—now return to your rooms, and I'm sure you'll find we have everything fixed by the morning."

His smooth promises didn't erase all the grumbling. Dale and the other pack members on staff seemed to have gotten the most good from Evan's reassurances. They worked quickly to restore peace and quiet to the entranceway.

Evan answered the summons of one of the maintenance staff who'd popped out from the basement stairwell.

"You figure out what's wrong?" Evan asked.

Toby shook his head. He'd tilted his oversized flashlight up beneath his chin, and the resulting shadows turned his face into the feature creature on the late-night horror channel. "I've checked the connections. Nothing is shorted out, and there's nothing obviously wrong inside the hotel."

"Then we must have a problem outside." Damn. It couldn't be simple, could it? "There's no one on shift with you, is there?"

Toby straightened, his attitude darkening. "I can do an exterior check by myself."

"You know the rules. Potentially hazardous situation, you take a backup."

"It's stupid to wait. I'll be fine—"

Evan jerked the flashlight forward so it shone straight at his own face to make sure Toby spotted the displeasure there. More than that, his wolf rumbled in displeasure, and Toby's eyes widened as he caught the sensation of power rolling from his Alpha.

Evan grumbled the words softly but clearly enough he knew Toby would not ignore him. "Call for backup, *then* you can do the exterior check. No forgetting or ignoring the rules just because you feel like it. Do I make myself clear?"

Toby swallowed hard and backed down. "Yes, sir."

The bit of attitude wasn't unexpected. Toby was the age and strength where he wanted to impress his Alpha, but even as laid-back as Evan could be about some issues, safety wasn't one of them. He would never deliberately put one of his wolf's lives on the line—his own life would be offered up first. "Good man. Do what you can then call me. I'll work on the other possibilities."

He patted Toby's shoulder for a moment, sending the young man off with a dose of acceptance and encouragement. All in a typical day for an Alpha.

Typical, if it weren't after midnight and pitch black.

Evan cut through the Moonshine Pub to the side door to his office. His cell phone lay on the credenza where he'd forgotten it. He used the light of the screen to spotlight the emergency-phone-number list his previous office assistant had tacked to the wall with a heading *IMPORTANT, Look Here First.*

Damn, he missed Caroline. The human had been part of the Takhini pack for years, only she was off gallivanting with her bear-shifter hubby. While he wished her nothing but the best, he could have used her ability to troubleshoot.

"Night office, Whitehorse Power and Water, Riverside Station. How can I help you?"

Thank goodness. Not a "click one if you have a rash" answering service. "Evan Stone from the Moonshine Inn. There's a power outage here. You got squirrels committing hari-kari on the transformer lines again?"

"No. That's weird. Moonshine Inn? On Fourth Ave?" The kid on the other end of the phone, who must have been all of sixteen, clicked his tongue before responding with far too much "didn't give a shit" for Evan's taste. "According to the grid, there's nothing wrong at our end. Full power to the entire city."

"Oh, come on." Evan aimed the flashlight he'd found toward the corner of his office, where an enormous pile of oversized boxes was stacked precariously halfway to the ceiling. Who the hell had made a delivery since he left at nine? "That can't be true. The power was also off at my apartment. Third and Caribou."

"Nope. Not us. Check with your direct power supplier."

The kid hung up.

Fucking hung up.

"Damn customer service." Evan strode back to the phone list, dragging his finger down the paper until he found the one labeled *utilities.*

Of course, this time he got an answering system and spent the next ten minutes punching numbers and pounding keys, cussing until he got a live person. While he answered her bazillion security questions, he grabbed a knife from his desk and sliced through the tape sealing one of the mystery boxes.

"Does that sound correct to you, Mr. Stone?"

"Yes, that's my account information, my date of birth, mother's maiden name. Unless you need more, like my blood type and a skin sample, tell me why my power is out."

"Looks as if your service has been cancelled, Mr. Stone."

Evan lifted the top layer of bubble wrap from the box, wondering who the heck had sent him a container full of sand. "Bullshit. I didn't cancel it."

"No, we did. I see a note on your account you received three warnings that your bill was overdue. There was no response, so as of midnight, your services were disconnected."

"Wait—what?" Evan debated flinging a few choice words her direction. He opened the next box, and found this one contained row after row of Ziploc bags full of beef jerky. "You can't cancel my service. I have the proof of payment in my bank statements. You've made a mistake."

"If you have receipts, we'd be happy to look at them in person at the customer desk during regular office hours of nine through five, weekdays."

Good grief. Evan fought to keep from shouting, which made his voice lower and his tone turn glacial. "It's twelve-thirty a.m. on Saturday, and I'm running a hotel. What do you suggest I do until Monday morning?"

The perky response he got back was enough to make his skin crawl. "I can give you the number of our manager if you'd like."

Unbelievable. He dragged a hand through his hair. "Yes. Do that." A pale light blinked in the corner of his office, and

Evan instinctively turned toward it. "Give me a second to grab a pen."

He stomped to his desk, grumbling under his breath the entire time. "Bloody weekends off. Turn off the power. What the hell is going on...?"

He was writing down the number when the computer screen flashed again, this time turning all the way to bright. It was his laptop computer—the one he hated with everything in him, but Caroline had insisted he needed. The little black arrow on the screen moved to the right, and Evan jerked in surprise.

What...? He pulled his hands back to make sure he wasn't accidentally triggering anything.

"Sir? Did you get the number?" his tormentor on the other end of the phone asked.

"Yeah, thanks." Evan hung up, distracted by his haunted computer. How was it running with no power? Oh, right. Those things had batteries.

But why had it started?

The arrow moved to the top of the screen, and a new picture appeared. This one stated "Hotel Safety Controls". Under the bold lettering were orderly boxes. Electric. Water. Cooling system. Sprinkler system. Fire alarms.

The arrow moved unerringly to the sprinkler label, and the box moved as if pushed. A schematic of the hotel appeared, with thick lines showing the different runs for the fire system. The arrow shifted again, pausing over the teeny picture of Evan's office, and his confusion turned to utter dismay.

In the ceiling above him, discreetly hidden nozzles poked their silver heads into the room and extended little fanlike arms. A blast of water descended, instantly drenching him, his desk and his computer.

He slammed the top shut in some misguided idea that might reverse what had just occurred. Water wasn't good for demon-spawn computers, was it?

The door burst open, and a half-dozen high-beam flashlights hit his face and torso, damn near blinding him.

"Freeze," the order rang out. "We have a search warrant for these premises."

"What the—?" Evan jerked to a stop, blinking madly to clear his vision. Why the hell were uniformed RCMP officers pouring into the room? He raised his hands skyward. "Someone want to tell me what's going on?"

Men pushed past him to reach the mysterious boxes. "There they are, Captain, just like we were told."

Water continued to spray everywhere, droplets sparkling in the flashlights as a crew rushed to open the cases. Two officers laid hands on Evan's shoulders, pinning him in place. "I don't even know where those came from," he insisted, peering through his wet hair and the steady deluge running down his face.

"Take him to the station." The captain held a Ziploc bag in front of Evan. "It's illegal to transport sand and/or unlabeled meat products into the country, Mr. Stone. We'll discuss details once you're in a holding cell."

This wasn't happening. "You're not serious. You're *arresting* me?"

"Looks that way, doesn't it?"

Moments later there were cuffs on his wrists. Firm hands gripped his upper arms as Evan was guided from the Moonshine Inn and stuffed into a police cruiser.

Confusion. Anger. Frustration. He wasn't sure which emotion was the strongest, not to mention the sheer discomfort of being soaking wet. Evan stared out the window as they pulled away, glancing back toward his beloved hotel and ignoring the noise and questions being tossed his direction. He'd talk once he had more information.

Now? Something was hugely off, and he was damned if he didn't figure out what, and soon.

A lone figure stood on the sidewalk, watching intently. A slim, feminine form with her arms folded over her chest. She wore a coat with a hood, so her hair was covered, but for one second they made eye contact, and Evan jerked back at the intense anger reflected there.

What the hell?

Then she gave him the finger, and Evan's brain fogged over.

After everything he'd had thrown at him that evening, some random stranger on the street was telling him to fuck off? *Alrighty then.* As if he didn't have enough to deal with. He eased back onto the car seat and sighed.

It was going to be a long night.

2

———

*A*my Ryba stumbled into the kitchen, bleary-eyed and foggy-brained from too little sleep. She grabbed a coffee from the preprogrammed machine, leaning against the counter for vertical support until the first sips of her high-test espresso cleared the cobwebs.

Plenty of time to check what was happening in the world before she headed across the Yukon River to begin her day. She settled onto her overstuffed couch, coffee mug balanced on a book, cereal bowl in her hand, then clicked on the news. National updates. Weather reports. She was spoon deep into a big bowl of Cocoa Puffs by the time they hit the good stuff.

"In Whitehorse-area news, local businessman Evan Stone spent the night at the RCMP station before being released on bail this morning while they investigate further charges."

The blond behind the microphone wore a typical reporter expression of "this is serious, serious business", his good looks saving him from crossing the line from mysteriously intense to comical. Amy waited until the bitter end of the news bite, the words of the report fading into the background as she fixated on watching Evan walk down the steps from the station more rumpled than usual. His clothes were creased as if they'd dried on him after a good solid soaking.

No one should look that attractive after a night behind bars. A layer of dark scruff covered his jaw, and between that, his dark hair and handsome eyes, he could have been strutting along some movie-debut red carpet instead of escaping incarceration.

After a year spent spying on the man, Amy knew him far too intimately. What she'd discovered lined up well with the information she'd pulled from hidden files. He was cocky. Arrogant. Above the rules.

She wouldn't deny he was eye-catching, but evil lived in the hearts of good-looking men as well as ugly ones.

Amy piled her things into her backpack and slung it over her shoulders. She jogged the trail behind her house that led inconspicuously into town. Taking precautions against a direct route to and from home was second nature —the instinct to hide her presence built into every move.

But once she'd reached the outskirts of the park she slowed. Found a bench at the edge of the trees and waited.

Calm. At peace. Her early-morning time spent in the quiet green space was another ritual that had unexpectedly entered her life during the past year, but one she had learned to enjoy. A brief moment of regrouping before heading into the demands of her day. She put aside the rushed thoughts triggered by the morning news. Lifted her face to the sunshine and closed her eyes to breathe deeply.

She didn't make it to the park every morning, but as often as she could, Amy took the time to pause. Most days she was rewarded for her patience.

Ten minutes of silence had passed before she felt a gentle nudge against her knee. She opened her eyes, pleased to see the wolf who had risked coming forward to sit at her feet, his chin resting on her thigh. His body language and actions revealed his trust. Amy leaned forward, stroking a hand over the grizzled white fur on the old wolf's head.

He stared up, eyes blinking against the harsh sunlight, the undiminished intelligence of the man hidden within the wolf sparkling back at her.

"Good morning. I hope you've been well." Amy petted him, offering respect and comfort at the same time. "I haven't seen you for nearly a month."

A wolfish shrug was all she got in response. Matthias stayed there for another five minutes before brushing his warm nose against her palm. He turned and faded into the trees, gone back to wherever it was that retired, partly feral wolf shifters hid during the day.

Amy's heart ached a little as she rose to her feet and headed to work. The moment of contact had been as much for her as for him. In the middle of everything else that had brought her to Whitehorse, she'd never expected to find a pack of wolves who needed her so badly.

She'd never expected to end up not only wanted, but loved.

Slipping through the doors of her computer shop, Bytes Unlimited, was like entering a safe zone. The front-room staff she employed snapped to attention as she moved briskly toward the service desk, past pristine laptop displays and wall racks full of the latest Bluetooth tech.

"Mail's on your desk." Tom waved a greeting from behind the counter. "I opened your computer and did the weekly update. The morning member reports from the pack are in. Everyone is fine, although you might want to check with the Lands for a follow-up on their son."

"And we have one job you need to take a look at," Braden added, turning from the other counter, his shocking red hair sticking every direction. He made a face. "I admit defeat. I can't figure out what bugs are mucking up the system."

Amy nodded. "Not a problem." She paused, then shared a secretive smile with them. "Thanks for your help on the booby trap last night, guys."

They'd been surprised by her request the previous day, but eager to help. Now Tom returned her smile, as did Braden, pleased with her praise. "Simple, really. Other than gathering the materials. Did it work the way you hoped?"

"Exactly like I hoped."

Braden looked nervous for a moment. "Takhini isn't going to be mad and come gunning for us, are they?"

Amy made soothing sounds as she shook her head. "No. No, of course not."

"Because it was pretty close to their territory," Braden muttered before backpedaling. "I mean, not that I'm saying you don't know what you're doing, because you do. I'm sure."

"You're fine," Amy promised. "No one knows we set it up. It was just a little...test, of a sort."

"I don't like Takhini." Tom's expression had gone black.

When she paused to let him finish, he refused to share anything else. Old history, undoubtedly. She stopped to give him a hug, and then one for Braden, aware of how much the brief contact calmed them. A flash of anger hit, quickly suppressed so they wouldn't notice.

How many times had she walked into a room and felt that longing sensation? The unbearable hunger of lone wolves who craved physical touch from another of their kind.

Meanwhile, it seemed Evan Stone sat on his high horse in the Takhini pack house and let the more needy wolves in the area rot. It wasn't right. It wasn't the way wolves should act. So she was doing something about it. Her wolf wouldn't allow anything less.

The door chime went off, and she hurried to get out of the main shop area in case it was a shifter from the Takhini pack.

Secrets had to be maintained, at least for a little longer.

Her second-storey office window faced the Riverside Park on the banks of the majestic Yukon River. Positioning the computer repair shop in one of the prime locations just off downtown Whitehorse had been deliberate, not only from a business point of view. The nearby wooded path allowed her to shift whenever she wanted to escape into the wilderness, even though the opportunities to get away were rare. Between work, and the pack, and plotting revenge, her calendar was pretty full.

If she was lonely at times, it wasn't for the first time, nor the last. It also wasn't without a purpose. As far as she could tell, the members of the Miles Canyon pack who she'd fallen in with deserved far more than they had gotten over the years, and if she had to make sacrifices along the way to make their happiness happen? So be it.

She dove into her work, planning her day. Considering who of her pack she should visit and give a little extra attention to.

Not even five minutes passed before there was a knock on her office door.

"Sam? Someone to see you."

She glanced up from the debugging program, surprised

to discover the handsome reporter from the morning news entering the room.

He held out a hand. "Colin Wheeler. CBC News."

Amy stood and came around her desk because she was too short to reach his hand from behind it. "Samantha Ryba. Call me Sam. Are you looking for a news story regarding computers?"

"Perhaps." His fingers slipped into hers, and as he shook her hand firmly, he also dropped his eyes with respect. "More important matters first. I'm new to town, unaffiliated wolf. Wanted to let you know I've been transferred to the area. I hope that's not a problem."

Amy paused. Considered the best way to deal with his out-of-the-blue announcement. "Well, that's...unusual."

She gestured to the chair opposite her desk, and he sat obediently while she found a comfortable perch on her desktop. The position gave her a height advantage, which was stupid, really. She was a hell of a lot stronger than Colin in terms of wolf mojo—she didn't need to tower over him physically as well.

"Why not announce you're here to the Takhini pack? They're the ones controlling Whitehorse."

"They're the ones who are noticeable, you mean," Colin commented.

"What are you suggesting?" Amy crossed her arms, pushing down the gut sensation of uneasiness. Just because she didn't like surprises didn't mean Colin had an agenda. "You hiding something, Mr. Wheeler?"

"Not much use if I was—you're an Alpha wolf and I'm not," Colin admitted. "You could order me to spill the beans."

She tested him. Reaching out with the part inside her that was connected to the wolf side of her soul. It wasn't like extending a hand, but more like sensing with her heart, and what she read gave her another reason to pause.

The man was no weakling when it came to wolf mojo. "Modesty is not a wolf trait. You're pretty powerful yourself."

He remained motionless, though, submissive and friendly, and Amy made a decision. Whatever his game, he seemed determined to at least appear innocent and she refused to second-guess herself at every turn.

"You've come to me, announced you're in town for a while. That kind of puts you under my protection, doesn't it?" Amy picked up a pen from her desktop. Played with it, rolling it through her fingers. "And now that you've aligned yourself with me, it would be rude to go all wolfie and ask how you even found out I'm in charge of the *other* pack here in Whitehorse."

"And you don't do rude." Colin smiled, the expression enhancing his good looks. Made him rather dashing, in fact. "I did my research before being assigned to Whitehorse. Let's just say I'm not a fan of the loud and showy parts of shifter pack-dom. I might spend time in front of the camera, but I'm a private man. I don't want to be involved in a noisy pack house with everyone trying to one-up each other all the time, and the rest of the games wolves play. Miles Canyon seems a lot more like the type of pack where I'd fit in. For a while."

"We call ourselves Canyon, by the way. Simpler."

"I like simple." He leaned back and relaxed. A slow sense of "other" drifted from him. Amy watched for a moment, taking in the nonverbal cues as well as the things she could discover from his wolf side.

Colin had secrets he wasn't sharing—that was crystal clear. But he was right, she didn't do rude, and unless his secrets impacted the pack, he was welcome to keep them.

What he wasn't hiding was his attraction. It scented the air, a powerful ego booster mixed with aromatic libido kick-starter.

Male attention of a sexual nature was something Amy had been avoiding, mostly out of necessity since she was too busy with other things. Still, the flat-out physical lust pouring off the reporter turned this into a different kind of conversation again than what she'd expected.

"I'm not looking for a lover, Mr. Wheeler," she announced, adding a little twist of shifter power to make it clear she wasn't joking.

Colin dipped his chin, pulling away from direct eye contact. "Sorry—didn't mean to be so forward. I was serious, though. I did some research once I got here, and you… intrigue me."

"And you find *intriguing* sexually titillating?"

"Doesn't everyone?"

Amy muffled her amusement.

"But I've received your message, loud and clear, and will keep my hero worship at the distance you require." Colin stood and took two steps toward the desk. Casually pinning her in place with a hand on either side of her body. He lowered his voice, and his next words came out deep. A verbal caress. "Unless you decide you'd like some up-close and personal worship. In which case, I'll state again, I'm more than happy to oblige."

Conflicting urges tore through her. The first told her to grab hold and kiss the man senseless before enjoying an invigorating session of desktop jockey. The second urge demanded she lift a knee and temporarily render him soprano for daring to be so cocky as to flirt after being denied.

Unfortunately, she had to go with door number three.

Amy planted a hand on his chest and prepared to push him away. Today she had things to do.

Her wolf nudged her. There was nothing wrong with a little physical satisfaction in a time and place that was more convenient.

Amy paused, her fingers softening on his firm chest. It had been a long time since she'd had the pleasure of an attentive wolf in her bed. None of her pack members were the type who enticed her to sexual escapades.

Temptation whispered.

A flash of hope rose in his eyes.

She tapped him with her fingers, allowing her nails to scratch lightly through his pale blue cotton shirt. "What are you doing for lunch on Monday?"

A devastatingly attractive smile shone just for her. "Picking you up and going somewhere?"

Two days from now. With that much warning, she could arrange for a bit of time off. Amy returned his smile. "Go, make mischief in the reporting world. Stop by around ten-thirty on Monday, and we'll see what we feel like for lunch."

Colin grinned wider as he stepped away, pausing with his hands on the doorframe. "If you change your mind and want to speed things up..."

He flipped her a card, and she caught it in midair, smiling as he vanished down the stairs. She hopped off the desk and returned to her computer-repair task.

Once the job was done, she'd stop for lunch. By then she should safely check in with Evan. See how he'd enjoyed his time behind bars. Find out what his next plans were.

He'd be happy to receive a concerned IM from his "secret mole" in the Canyon pack. It had taken her months to set up that bit of finagling. The woman working as Evan's assistant had been a tough nut to crack at first, but now the prep work was proving priceless.

Her fingers flew over the keyboard as she entered the code needed to begin the diagnostic, her subconscious taking care of the details.

Her gaze might be focused on the screen in front of her, but her mind was daydreaming about the moment she would look Evan Stone in the eye and see him broken.

Everything was falling into place.

3

———————

*E*verything was falling apart.

Evan had made it home after one of the most uncomfortable nights he'd ever experienced. He changed quickly then returned to the hotel to find the power restored, but an exodus of customers vacating the lobby, and there was nothing he could do to convince them to stay.

The kitchen informed him they would be running a limited menu as half their supplies hadn't shown up, again. It was the third time in as many shipments the order had been mucked up.

And to top it all off? His Hummer had four flats.

His escalating bad luck was no longer strange, it was freaky. The situation had moved beyond what could be considered coincidence, by any stretch.

It took until noon before things were borderline back to normal. At that point, Evan abandoned the hotel to his subordinates, fed up with just about everything.

He returned to his apartment, where the power had also been restored, accompanied by Justin Cullinan. The least expected of allies, the man was assistant-slash-sometimes-bodyguard-slash-friend to the new husband of Evan's recently married office assistant. Evan had found the enormous bear shifter waiting for him after he'd gotten bail.

Which, it turned out Justin had posted. And that was just the start of his involvement in Evan's affairs.

"How the hell did you get power restored to the hotel and my apartment so fast?" Evan slapped the papers he'd been handed against his leg.

Justin folded his arms. Tilted his head. Waited.

Evan cussed under his breath. He was grateful the big bear shifter had stayed in town, and even more pleased the man knew a thing or two about dealing with emergencies.

Still burned his britches to have to fawn over anyone.

"*Thank you* for getting the power restored," Evan gritted out. "I have no idea how the mistake in payment history happened."

"Your lawyer has been alerted, and your accountant. After I called them this morning, they both promised to do some digging. Said they might have some ideas." Justin eased onto Evan's sofa and waited.

Damn bears. Far too patient. Evan wanted to do something immediate and physical, like finding an appropriate neck to wring. Instead all he had were more questions without answers.

He hauled his temper back into line. Last night had been a hell of a trip, but the time in the cell had allowed him to plan. Evan knew what he needed to do. He plopped himself down onto the coffee table, resting his elbows on his knees as he faced the bear. "I appreciate you getting me out of jail. Shaun tried, but they didn't listen."

"Shaun doesn't look as impressive in a suit as I do," Justin pointed out. "And it's no problem. If you were in jail and Caroline heard, she'd be upset. That would make my boss upset, because they'd have to cut their honeymoon short, so for the next while keeping you on the straight and narrow is my job."

Oh, hell to the no. This wasn't going to turn into some kind of let's-take-care-of-Evan deal. "Look, I said I appreciated being bailed out this morning. Don't push it. I don't need a nanny."

"You won't even know I'm around," Justin promised.

The six-foot-six, dark-haired bear shifter who sat on Evan's couch wore a thousand-dollar suit along with polished black shoes and a watch that probably cost more than Evan's shiny red Hummer. "Right. Because you're so inconspicuous and shit."

"Like a fly on the wall." Justin lifted his hands to shoulder height and fluttered his fingers, and Evan burst out laughing, the tension piled on his back vanishing for a moment in much-needed levity.

"Between you and Shaun, I'm going to get nothing done."

"Oh, you'll get stuff done, because I'll keep the problems out of your hair."

"You're a bear. What do you care?"

Justin waited again.

"Caroline, Tyler, honeymoon, I understand that part. But is that all?"

"If you're looking for some deep confession of love, nope. Not getting it."

Evan made a rude noise, even though he was amused. The wolves he took care of were hilarious at times with their antics, but this bear hit a different part of his funny bone.

There was something other than amusement on his mind, though. He was no charity case. "I'll pay you. Hourly rate to match whatever Tyler gives you."

"I don't need money." Justin leaned forward and lowered his voice. "And you can't afford me."

"Bullshit." Evan straightened up. "I've done all right for myself."

Justin raised a brow. Held up a hand and twisted it so the gaudy oversized ring on his oversized finger caught the light and damn near blinded Evan.

"Fine. I don't own a diamond mine."

The bear shifter winked. "It's okay, honest. I'm on salary with Tyler, and while he's gone there's not much for me to do. You wolves are entertaining."

A familiar bark of laughter sounded from the door.

"That phrase gets said way too often around here." Shaun stepped into the room. "You got a minute, Evan?"

Evan stood to greet his Beta, who looked, and smelled, far better than the previous night. "For you, always."

"Your tires were stabbed with a knife. Something long, thin and not usually used on vehicles." Shaun paused. "Not that blades are typically used on cars anyway, but you know what I mean. My contact thinks filleting knife."

"For fish?" Evan dropped into his favourite chair, throwing a leg over the arm as he attempted to breathe out his tension. "Who the hell would take a filleting knife to my tires?"

"You piss anyone off lately?" Justin asked.

"He's the Alpha of Takhini." Shaun stomped to the side of the couch to glare at Justin. "Anyone he pisses off can take a hike."

"Well, someone didn't take a hike, instead they pulled off some well-executed and perfectly timed mischief. Which means someone else, probably from around here, made more than a few mistakes over the past couple days to allow that kind of trouble to go unchecked." Justin eyed Shaun, judgment written all over his face.

Shaun bared his teeth at the enormous bruin. "If you're accusing me of fucking up—"

"Guys. Stop." Evan's command snapped like a whip. Shaun straightened as if he'd been zapped with a Taser, and even Justin looked wary.

"I'm not blaming anyone, I just want solutions. Who is behind the things that have gone wrong?" He stared at the ceiling as he test-drove ideas, discarding them one after another.

For the past six months he'd been focused on a financial takeover of as many properties in the Whitehorse area as possible. The recent big bear gathering that had threatened the city had briefly sidetracked him, but for the most part, he'd thought he was in control.

Well, except for the charming little fact he'd sniffed his mate but had zero luck tracking her down. That hadn't disturbed him at all.

Bullshit.

He couldn't dwell on it, not only because her absence would drive him mad, but because there were no easy solutions. Obviously, he was missing some information. Now was the time to put aside his distractions and get to the root of the most demanding troubles.

He shot to his feet and paced the living room.

Shaun cleared his throat. "Suggestion. Don't worry about who, yet. Worry about how."

"Figure out how these seeming coincidences happened and put my butt in jail for the night? Sounds logical." Evan glanced at Justin. "Since you're planning on sticking around, grab some paper and take notes."

Justin pulled a pad from his briefcase. "Fire away."

"Bills supposedly went unpaid, and shipping orders are being changed, both for the kitchen and the hotel, that much is certain. The power is one example, but lots of recent deliveries have been cancelled." Shaun wrinkled his nose as he concentrated.

"Bookings got messed up. We've had complaints about that as well," Evan noted.

"Sometime in the past week? Month? ...well, it can't have been for very long or Caroline would have noticed." Shaun's eyes widened. He glanced at Justin before crossing the room to Evan's side and whispering, "Is it safe to talk around Booboo?"

Evan nodded. "He's got our back. I trust him."

Shaun narrowed his gaze, giving Justin the evil eye. "I don't know that I do, but fine." He spoke louder. "All these weird things are happening around the hotel, your apartment or the pack house. Which means it's got to be someone on the inside."

Evan shook his head. "Impossible."

"Why?" Justin asked. "There's no one in the pack upset with you for any reason?"

"Doubt it. Also, the hotel profits go into funding the pack's activities, and their retirement funds. It's unlikely anyone would mess with things that affect their livelihood just to get at me." His pack members were wild at times, but not stupid. "Plus I've talked to all of them over the past week. If someone was *that* upset, I'd know."

Justin lifted the pen from the pad, watching Evan closely. "The wolf thing? Really, you'd just know?"

"The pack connection is an important part of us." Evan leaned a hip on the island counter as he considered. "No. I'm positive, everyone I talked to is doing great. Maybe some of the women I turned down are disappointed. The ones who hit on me since it looks as if I'm single again."

"Women." Shaun and Justin exchanged knowing glances instead of being at loggerheads.

Shaun hummed. "Could be one of them. I mean, woman scorned, and all that."

"Jeez, Shaun, grow up. You prove to me any of the females were upset enough to screw over the entire pack because I said I was taken, and I'll quit the damn job right now."

"You can't quit. You quit, and that puts me Alpha, and no way do I want the pack when it's this fucked up." Shaun ducked under the halfhearted fist swing Evan tossed.

He growled at his friend through his frustration. "You're lucky I like you, or I'd burn off some of my irritation pounding your ass into the ground."

"You can try. Anytime, anywhere, *mon capitaine.*"

All their debating wasn't finding solutions. "This is the trouble with doing things the sneaky, undercover way. I might want to amalgamate the two packs in Whitehorse, but it would have been so much easier to march in and take over territory after ripping out a few throats."

"You want me to get some friends to look into your troubles?" Justin offered. "I know you've got your own people, but the ones I deal with shift through dirty bear accounting all the time."

"*Duuude.*" For the first time, Shaun sounded impressed. He was damn near bouncing with excitement as he faced Evan. "Take him up on it. I was talking with a couple bear shifters last week, and you should hear some of the nasty shit they try to get away with. I bet his guys can find the trouble, no matter how deep it's hidden."

A quiet *ping* sounded in the silence that followed

Shaun's approval. Evan paced a few more times back and forth across the floor, considering hard.

Ping.

Ping.

Justin tilted his head toward the desk. "You going to answer that?"

Evan frowned. "Answer what?"

"You got an IM." Shaun pushed him toward the desktop computer Caroline had set up in the apartment to allow basic hotel tasks to be completed without having to go into the office.

Evan eyed the thing with suspicion. Great. More technology.

"Do I have to?" He turned back to see both guys examining him as if he were an alien creature. "Look, last night I swear my computer turned on the sprinklers without me. I don't want to do anything to piss off the evil techno-overlords again."

"Come on. Computers don't work without you." Shaun laughed. "Don't be a scaredy-cat. You can do it."

Evan's fist hit Shaun's shoulder with a resounding smack as he reluctantly passed his Beta en route to the desk. "Shuddap, you jerk. Justin? Go ahead and find out what information your people need. I want answers as to what's going on, and I want them yesterday."

Justin rose to his feet and pulled out a phone. "I'll do this outside. Then lunch?"

"Sure." Evan found the mouse and answered the summons. Ahh. This conversation was worth risking contact with a computer. His secret connection within the Canyon pack.

Amy?

Hi Evan. You okay?

Oh hell. She must have seen the news. I'm fine. Just a mix-up. Everything is straightened out

Not really, but that was as much as he was willing to admit.

Amy had been sharing bits of information about Canyon, and her intel was vital to his goal of merging the packs.

Can I help with anything? she asked.

I'm more worried about you, Evan admitted. *You've been risking too much, getting in contact with me so often. I don't want you in trouble. There's always a risk your Alpha will find out you've been talking to Takhini*

Amy paused for so long he thought the Internet had gone down.

I'm positive Sam won't do anything

Which was not an answer, because there was no way she knew for sure how her Alpha would respond. If the shoe were on the other foot, and he discovered one of the Takhini pack had been discussing secrets with someone else, he'd be extremely pissed.

Evan grew more uncomfortable by the minute with the entire situation. Having access to information was important, but damn if he wanted to put an innocent wolf into harm's way. He'd found out about Amy a couple weeks ago, and the longer the deception went on, the more unsettling the idea became.

"Anything good?" Shaun stepped behind him. "Oh, your Canyon contact." He leaned down to read over Evan's shoulder. "Sweet. There's one thing. Confirmation this Sam guy we keep hearing rumours of is the one in charge."

"Great. Now go find me the right Sam in all of Whitehorse so I can challenge him and take over his pack."

Shaun's chuckle turned to a low questioning hum. "Dude. I think... Yeah, I know her."

"My informant?" Evan's heart thumped like a pile driver into solid rock. "Seriously? What are you looking at? Where?"

"You are worse than useless with computers. Stop staring at your fingers when you type." Shaun pointed to a small picture in the corner of the screen. "Right here on the contact list."

"That entire list is like one inch square," Evan snarled, leaning in to peer closer.

"Get some bifocals, old man."

Evan backhanded Shaun without looking away from the screen.

His Beta laughed evilly as he rubbed his chest. "Seriously, I know her. She works at the place that fixes all the computers you manage to bust. I haven't seen her often, but I've caught a glimpse or two of her hiding in the background."

Evan could have sworn that picture hadn't been there any other time he'd IMed with Amy. Another *ping* dragged his attention back to the computer as she poked him.

You still there?

Evan focused on the screen. On the small picture showing a delicate-looking woman with enormous eyes. Amy seemed far too small to be hiding the burden of deceit from her pack, and his protective nature kicked into overdrive.

We have to stop this, he wrote, desperate to assure her she wasn't alone. *It's not right for so much pressure to be on anyone's shoulders. I want you to come in. Come to the Takhini pack house, and let me protect you*

I don't need protection

Her response was instantaneous, and totally the wrong thing to say.

Damn. She was going to be stubborn? She hadn't met the king of stubborn. He was about to try one last chance at diplomacy when a wonderful idea blossomed. *Fine, but if you get worried, I expect to hear from you. Anytime you need a hand, you call me, and I'm there. And no more contacting me via IM.*

That little warning message, the one stating *Amy is writing* appeared. Vanished. Appeared again, as if she were writing and erasing a note a few times. Probably planning to protest.

All he got was a final *Okay*

This conversation was over, anyway. Now that he knew where to find her? He was going to bring his informant into protective custody for her own damn good.

One quick trip to the computer shop, and she'd be under his wing and then he could get back to the business of straightening his pack affairs.

Because only once that mess was cleaned up could he concentrate on the aching pit inside demanding he drop everything else and look for his missing mate.

Another frustrated battle of wills raged within as the human side and the wolf pulled him in different directions. His wolf couldn't understand why they weren't off doing a house-to-house search of Whitehorse if that's what it took to find her, damn the time and energy it would take.

The human side sympathized and sort of agreed, yet the truth sucked. Alpha wolves didn't get the chance to do what they wanted. The pack and its well-being came first.

He soothed the wolf the best he could with promises of another nighttime search through the city.

In the meantime, he had a different quarry to track.

Evan rose to his feet and slapped Shaun on the shoulder. "Hold down the fort. Feed Justin, and make sure he has everything he needs. Oh, and could you ask your mate to help at the hotel front desk if she's got the time? A little of Gem's social savvy could go a long way to soothe ruffled clients."

"Where are you going?" Shaun asked as he pivoted out of the way.

"I'm going to have a one-on-one with a certain secret who needs to become un-secret for her own good."

4

<hr>

*A*my leaned back in her chair, annoyance rising. Well, that hadn't gone nearly as well as she'd hoped. Evan had clammed up, and she hadn't had a chance to set up the next sting.

Losing the ability to drop leading hints would have hurt a lot more a few weeks ago, though. Now she just about had everything in place.

She rose to stare out the window, the nearby leaves trembling in the slight breeze. Her skin itched, as if she'd been too long in a hot tub and was badly in need of cream.

Her wolf nudged her. Hard.

It wasn't a trip to the spa she needed, but a good long run. Everything she did for the pack drained more of her energy. She loved each of them, cared for them deeply, but they were a group of individuals who required a unique kind of attention. Plus, there was the computer shop that was a real business even though she also used it to hide her presence.

Add in the extra time she'd put into planning surprises for Evan?

Screw it. A run would refresh her so she would have more to give. Amy pulled off her clothes and folded them carefully, stacking the articles to one side of her desk. She pushed open the sliding door behind her that led to the second-storey balcony, and drew in a deep breath of fresh air.

The sound of an email alert stopped her in the middle of taking advantage of her usual route to freedom. She stared longingly at the slim ramp built along the outside of the building at a narrow incline, stopping just far enough off the ground her wolf could make the leap but wild animals didn't access her domain uninvited.

Amy took a quick glance at the email in the hopes she could blow it off, but this one needed attention ASAP. She left the door open, though, even as she sat, bare-ass naked in her computer chair and put out the pack fire.

But as soon as this was dealt with? She would take her cranky butt into the bush and work off her lingering aggression. The power of her wolf side hovered in the background as always. The beast made her strong and drove her nuts. One of the downfalls of being an Alpha female— she rarely had someone to work out her itch without them caving to her superior wolfie vibes.

The date with Colin on Monday was very much needed. He seemed strong enough to give her some physical relief without her wolf becoming pissed off or bored by a weaker partner.

Solitude and frustration had become her constant companions, and she didn't expect that to change. She'd been alone for years, and she always would be alone. Expectations of anything more had long ago been burnt away. Her heart was devoid of all but two things—love for her pack.

And vengeance.

She bent her head and put her fingers to work composing a reply, the fire burning up her spine balanced evenly with the ice that had trapped her heart.

~

EVAN STARED at the computer-shop signage, every nerve in his body on high alert. This neighbourhood wasn't his usual stomping ground, and a computer store? The last place on earth he'd ever go for shits and giggles.

But the closer he got to Bytes Unlimited, the more agitated his wolf became. He paused across the street in the shadows to scope the place out. Make sure there wasn't a hidden assault team from the mysterious Canyon pack waiting in ambush.

Amy might have thought she was safe, but that didn't mean her Alpha wasn't checking up on her. Evan needed to get the woman out of danger, his sensation of uneasiness rising by the second.

Damn the risk to himself, this was happening now.

Evan strode across the road, jaywalking between moving vehicles. He was at the door in no time, jerking the glass open. Somewhere deep in the shop, a gentle buzzer sounded.

From the back of the store, two males turned to face him, welcoming smiles melting into rigid grimaces. Before Evan could say a word, the men vanished.

Gone. Completely.

It was like the coolest magic trick imaginable, only Evan was more pissed than impressed. He stepped into the shop and closed the door behind him, glancing past shelves that were loaded with computer thingies and plastic packaging.

"Hello?" he called into the silence.

And that's when it hit him.

Peaches. Sunshine. The aroma of a wind that had crossed miles of seemingly empty tundra—wilderness at its rawest yet full of hidden life. All mixed up into one unique package.

It was a full-on dose of the scent he'd caught a hint of nearly two weeks ago. His stomach tightened, his heart rate kicked into overdrive. Instinctively his legs carried him forward as he tracked the scent that grew stronger and stronger.

His mate.

His *mate* had been in the computer shop. More than once. Often enough that as he moved toward the cash register and the counter, his head was so full of her he had to work hard to remain alert.

What was the deal with the missing staff? Evan kept his gaze moving as he silently padded forward. To one side, he spotted a couple of doors that explained where the men had gone, but not the why.

Until he hit their scent. Wolves.

Two unfamiliar wolves who vanished when they spotted him? Had to be Canyon pack. He'd deal with them later, though. Spend a little time explaining he wasn't the enemy.

The enticing trail led him to the back of the shop and a narrow set of stairs. He moved like a wolf, noiseless and invisible. Sensing which treads to avoid stepping on to maintain absolute silence.

Easing his way upward was brutal when everything in him demanded that he run. Rush forward and swoop in on the woman who had to be at the top of the stairs.

His wolf clawed at him, eager for the hunt. Evan wrestled that part of himself under control for long enough to reach the top landing and step through the doorframe.

The room was filled with her, the open door pushing her intoxicating scent toward him like a sledgehammer to the brain.

He got a quick glimpse while she was unaware of his presence. Impressions struck like lightning bolts. Short dark hair worn in a simple style that suited her. Smooth creamy-brown skin, similar in shade to his own.

Lots of *naked* skin as she sat behind a desk and stared at her computer, and he wasn't even going to ask why the hell she was working in the nude because she was his mate, and if she chose to wear nothing but skin for the rest of her life, he was oh-so-fine with that.

Then she looked up, and their eyes met. Pupils widened against her dark brown irises. Her nostrils flared, and if possible, her eyes widened farther.

"Amy?" Evan moved cautiously.

His naked goddess didn't answer. Just blinked, hard, as if in total shock to see him in her office, which made sense.

He lifted a hand to reassure her—

She bolted. Twirled and shot through the open door, naked skin transforming in a flash to midnight-black fur.

He cursed even as he leapt after her, scrambling onto the balcony. The lithe body of a wolf ran full-out down a narrow ledge on the side of the building. Evan stripped his clothes off as quickly as he could, but she'd already hit the ground before he was able to make the shift.

Chasing her wasn't a good idea. She'd obviously been shocked enough to flee, and having an Alpha on her tail wasn't a very nice thing to do to any wolf, especially to one who was afraid.

But hell if he could let his mate get away again.

SHE WASN'T THINKING. Wasn't plotting. Wasn't doing *anything* but trying to get the hell away from him.

How had Evan found her? Amy twisted between the trees, ducked under a low bush. She considered doubling back to hide her trail in case he chose to follow her, but that would take time she didn't have. Her best bet was to lose him far behind before he was able to track her.

She knew these paths, heading north and east on the straightest route possible to the bridge over the river.

Once on the other side, she had a dozen places where she could vanish. Even as she considered her options, she chastised herself.

How had everything gone wrong in just the past few hours?

Her wolf wasn't cooperating either. The edge of adrenaline she usually got while running was dull this time, as if her wolf had a different agenda. Two parts in one whole, she was the wolf and the wolf was her, but the human mind and the animal's could and did disagree about what they thought was important.

Now was not the time for a lengthy internal self-debate.

Muscles burning with exertion, she tore up the trail, cutting into a clearing where she could choose one of four escapes. She headed to the right in the hopes of disappearing when she was tackled to the ground by the weight of a far heavier wolf.

Her first response of panic was washed away by an entirely new emotion as she slipped from under him and whirled to face him.

Evan's scent wrapped around her, and for a second she

froze in utter shock. Comprehension slid in and ensnared her in its icy realization.

Oh, *no*. No. No. *No*.

He was *not* her mate. She slammed her lips together to hold back the howl of frustration and fury she couldn't give voice to. Not without baring her throat, and that was one thing she would never willingly do. She'd *never* give him a chance to see her defenseless.

Evan sat back on his haunches, head tilted to the side like a puppy. Confusion at her response was written into his posture.

Had he known they were mates? Amy wondered.

Frustration filled her, yes, but even stronger was bewilderment, and sorrow, then all-out emotional-anger hit, and she did the only thing she could think of to stop herself from leaping at him and swiping her claws across his defenseless throat.

She shifted, letting her rage escape in a shout. "Damn you, Evan Stone. Damn you to *hell*."

He was on his feet seconds later, his muscular human form so pleasing to the eye and such a knife to her heart. "Amy? What's wrong?"

She planted her fists on her hips and stared about four inches over his head, fighting for control. In her worst nightmares she could never have imagined this. "Everything is wrong. *Everything*. Oh my God, you're my *mate*."

The final word escaped in a choking gasp, and her guts twisted as if someone had reached inside her, wrapped their fingers around her heart and were slowly tearing it out.

She folded her arms around her torso and held on tight in the hopes of stabilizing her shaking world.

He didn't try to touch her, which was good. He *looked*, though. Looked as if his heart was breaking as well, and it was beyond annoying that she instantly cared what she'd said had hurt him. She should have been rejoicing, but instead the conflict threatened to rip her in two.

"This is wrong. All wrong." Amy swallowed hard, fighting tears of anger. Fighting the need to lash out and plant a fist into that perfectly formed muscular six-pack.

He shook his head. "I don't understand what's upset you, but we're mates. We can fix it. We can fix it together, Amy. I know we can."

She took a deep breath and ignored the tone in his voice, the one that was oh-so-reasonable and oh-so-logical, because this had nothing to do with reason or logic, and everything to do with pain and sorrow. "You can't be my mate. It's impossible," she whispered vehemently.

"It's true. You sense it. Can taste it on the air." Evan inched closer. Only one step, but enough she shot out a hand to warn him off. "Why are you denying it?"

She pulled back her shoulders and lifted her chin. Stiffened her spine to brace against the coming battle. His dark eyes were pools she could fall into, but that way led to madness and regret. "I have to deny it. I can't be mates with the man who killed my brother."

5

Evan's ears rang with her accusation. "What?"

There was no mistaking Amy's full-out conviction in the verbal grenade she'd tossed. Only she didn't go on to explain the impossible statement. Instead, she folded her arms over her chest again and looked away.

The list of what Evan wanted was pretty basic. He wanted to take his mate, find out what she was talking about and make things right. He needed her to look at him with something other than an ice-cold glare.

He needed to touch her. To hold her. To make her his, but none of those things could happen until they'd put this insanity behind them.

And he doubted they could figure it out here and now. Not in the middle of the woods. This wasn't a conversation he wanted interrupted, and it really wasn't something he wanted to get into while naked.

"Amy. Look at me."

She twitched before reluctantly glancing his way.

"We need to talk."

"Right now talking is the last thing on my agenda.

Kicking your spleen through your back would make me happier." Every muscle in her body had gone taut.

A body that was exactly the kind he wanted to lick and explore until she screamed in ecstasy. There was no way to avoid admiring her nakedness as his wolf's mating urge flashed to maximum, but he forced his human side to the foreground, shoving all baser instincts aside. "You've had a shock. So have I. I had no idea my contact in the Canyon pack was my mate."

"You and me both." Bitter laughter escaped, and she paced away, her hips swaying as she stomped across the forest floor. She lifted her hands, fisted palms pressed to her temples. "My God, my brain is going to explode. And my heart."

One hand dropped to her chest, utter agony on her face as she half curled into a ball.

Evan was going to break in two if they didn't do something soon. "I can't make it better until you tell me what's wrong."

"Maybe it can never get better." Amy whirled away. "Damn you. And damn you, fate. This isn't some cosmic joke, because I'm not laughing."

Her last words were shouted heavenward, her fists clenched tight at her sides.

"Calm down." Evan pushed out the words accompanied by a nonverbal command. Hysterics weren't the solution, and while the last thing he wanted was to overpower his mate with the mystical side of his wolf, using some of his power seemed his only choice.

What he got was an instant backlash, and he was the one to waver on his feet.

She lunged at him, an undersized ball of fury and energy. Evan ducked her swing but still ended up on his ass on the ground, Amy looming over him like an avenging vigilante. "Don't you *dare* try that on me." Her words were a whisper of fury.

The power of her wolf side had literally knocked his feet from under him. "Holy shit."

She backed away, light on her feet, hands rising to a defensive position. "Did you expect your mate would be a quiet woman who'd roll over when you told her to?"

To be honest, he hadn't really thought it through that hard, but...she was right. His mate had to be someone powerful and strong and perfect for him. And because they were perfect for each *other*, if he actually turned on his brain instead of allowing shock to rule his actions, he knew what she needed, crazy as it seemed.

They needed to talk, but first she had to get her rage under control. Evan rocked to a standing position and looked her over. Testing her signals, reading her body language. There was too much aggression and fury to deal with in any other way than the good old wolf one. "You want to hit me? Go on. Try—"

Her foot made contact with his chest before he'd finished speaking, the powerful blow rocking him backwards as he worked to remain on his feet. She retreated so quickly his grasping fingers slicked over her skin.

Amy watched cautiously from a few feet away, circling to one side. Intoxicating power rolled off her, and his wolf all but howled with excitement.

She was so strong, his mate. Together, they'd have the ability to do so much for the pack. But here and now, it wasn't about the others. It was about her, and him, and somehow getting past the enormous roadblock she'd thrown between them.

Evan held back as she darted forward, taking the blow to

his torso. She growled. Struck him again, this time knuckles rasping hard against his jaw, snapping his head. He raised a block between them, but refused to actually hit her.

"Stop pulling your punches," she demanded, the command whipping him with enough compulsion his head lifted. "You think you can tame me? You're not worth tak—"

The move felt so wrong, but he did it anyway because it seemed his only option. He pivoted and slapped a hand downward as she aimed a blow at his kidneys. Wrapped his fingers around her fist and pulled, twisting her off balance and tumbling them both off their feet. He made sure he brought her over him, preventing her from smacking hard against the ground.

Instead every inch connected, naked skin to naked skin. Amy's face hung over his, and those enormous eyes of hers were wolf-wild and needy. She might be fighting their mating, but her wolf was on board. Sexual tension ensnared them in a tight embrace the second before she tore her hands free and slammed rock-solid fists against his chest.

Evan rolled, pinning her to the grassy ground. A second later his hands held her wrists firmly on either side of her head, his legs locking her lower body in one spot.

A low rumble escaped her throat as his hips settled over hers. "Get off me," she demanded.

"No." He lowered his head, and with his nose tight against her throat, took a deep, deep breath.

An entire evening spent getting inebriated was nothing compared to taking a single shot, one hundred proof, of his mate. She filled his senses and made his body ache with unanswered need. He stayed there for a good minute, forcing her to breathe him in. Her squirming protests died away. Every attempt she made to buck him off just rubbed them together intimately, and she stopped, a shiver rolling over her from top to bottom.

"Damn you, Evan," she repeated, but this time it wasn't so much a curse as a lament. Aching and raw, and he pressed up on his arms, separating their torsos far enough he could stare into her eyes.

All that was there was hopelessness.

"I'll make it right," he promised. The words were softly spoken but clear as they cut though the quiet of the wilderness. "I swear I will. I don't understand yet, but I swear I'll find a way to prove I'm worthy to be your mate. Give me that chance."

A single tear trickled from the corner of her eye. "I've hated you for so long. And I hate myself for how easily my body wants to accept you as my mate."

"Don't hate yourself. It's your wolf. She knows we belong together, and that we can do this. She senses it, even if your human side is hurting too much to hear."

"I kind of hate her right now as well," Amy whispered, her eyes focused on his so intensely he was in danger of burning up.

Evan released her right hand and stroked her face with his knuckles, wiping away the streak of moisture that had trickled down her cheek. "No matter how long it takes for us to figure things out, we'll take it. I won't let you go."

She closed her eyes, body shaking under him. He matched her breathing, synchronizing their motions. Silently stroking her with the affection of his other side while holding the wolf at bay.

"Give me a chance," he repeated. Damn near begged if he was honest.

Finally her tension melted away and she softened under him. He waited, barely breathing. Even without moving, their desire heightened, an edge of fire that was a constant presence between mates.

The temptation to taste her lips was there, but that was his wolf side urging him on. That side could willingly roll over, ignore her fears and anger, and convince her to satisfy the physical craving that rose like molten lava.

If they gave in to their animalistic desires, she'd be a willing participant. She'd take him into her body, accept him, but hate him later. His human side knew this, and the wolf unhappily acknowledged his guidance and retreated.

Evan rolled them partway again, rising to his feet and bringing her with him. "We need to go somewhere private to talk."

Amy brushed leaves from her backside as she sighed heavily, then nodded. "Yes, I suppose so."

He risked it. Caught her fingers in his and tugged her to face him. A wild crackle of attraction passed between them.

"Somewhere safe. Somewhere we won't be interrupted, and where I'm not worried about your Alpha charging in." She opened her mouth, but he cut her off before she could offer him an off-hand comment about not needing to worry. He fucking *needed* this. "I'll deal with Sam later. This isn't about our packs, it's about us. I'll call my Beta. You talk to whoever you need to at the computer store. The world won't explode if we're gone for twenty-four hours."

She raised one brow high as she stared him down. "You're awfully cocky. You might want to turn off the assumptions for a while."

"I'm your mate. I'm trying to make things go quicker and easier. I hate how much you're suffering."

A hard rock shook her again, and she gasped even as she agreed. "Okay, but I'll explain later why you're a jackass. Back to the shop for our clothes?"

"Yes. Do you know a place we could go?" Giving her charge of that decision might ease open the door she'd slammed shut between them, and he didn't care where they went as long as he was with her.

Her emotional pain remained the strongest sensation, and every time she looked at him, her anguish spiked. Deep and intense, heavy enough he wondered how she'd carried the burden, no matter how strong she was.

Amy nodded slowly. "I know a place."

Evan squeezed her fingers. "We'll figure this out," he reminded her. "I promise."

In the second before she shifted back to her wolf-form, her eyes reflected the haunting hurt inside her. He joined her, his mind racing as she led him back to the shop.

It was barely noon. The past twelve hours had more than shaken him. His world had turned inside out and too many questions remained. How much more would happen before the earth settled, and where would they be in the final standing?

One thing he knew for certain—he'd found his mate, and he wasn't letting her go.

She insisted she would drive. Evan was smart enough, this time, to let her have her way. Of course, she knew his Hummer was out of commission at the moment, although he didn't know that she knew that.

The tangled web she'd woven drew tighter.

Part of her desperately needed to get away from him and think through the implications of their discovery. Finding out Evan was her mate wasn't just having a rug pulled out from under her, it was having the roots of her existence torn away.

She'd told the truth. At this moment she pretty much hated everyone involved in the mess. Him, herself, her wolf. The only creature she'd give a break was Evan's wolf because the beast hadn't fucked up yet, although it had come close.

Amy pulled in front of the Moonshine Inn and waited for him to arrive. Maybe to a casual observer this trip would appear all wrong. Heading into the bush with the man she'd been systematically working to destroy for nearly a year? Yeah, not a move worthy of the brightest crayon in the box.

But they were wolves, not humans, and that changed everything.

Mating instinct made the trip both less and more dangerous. She was safe—he'd never in a million years hurt her. Not physically at least, and she was strong enough to defend herself from an assault.

Emotionally, though? The situation was a ticking time bomb. Her strength meant she was capable of rejecting him, but that would tear them both apart. Far more violent than any vengeance she could have planned—ripping their wolves apart forever would be the ultimate revenge.

And yet as hot as her anger burned...she hesitated to take the final step. She wasn't a fool who would continue to guard the safe once the treasure was stolen. The situation had changed, and until she had all the facts, she'd put her retribution plans on hold.

If part of her hoped for a miracle? She'd blame such romantic sentiments on her wolf. On the part inside her that *wanted* on a far more visceral and instinctive level.

Her wolf rode close to her skin. Aching for contact with

Evan's wolf—the beast wanted to roll in his scent and wallow at having found her mate.

Amy slapped her down, the internal battle between them nothing new, and yet this time subtly unique. Her wolf was stronger than ever, and Amy worried she could be too easily swayed from human logic if she wasn't careful.

Human vengeance made no sense to a wolf.

Evan tossed a canvas bag in the backseat and got in, adjusting the shoulder strap as she took off. He glanced in her direction, but she refused to meet his gaze.

"Any troubles getting time off?" he asked.

This was one issue she had struggled through already while packing her bag. They had so much to share, she wasn't going to lie to him. Not ever. This was the first of many secrets she'd have to share. "I own the shop."

Evan's body language changed. "Impressive."

"You've been a great supporter. Thanks for crashing your computers so often."

It was unfair that his soft chuckle amused her, the deep sound sending goose bumps rolling up her arms. Damn the man. She didn't *want* to like anything about him. She wanted him to be the evil, self-serving bastard she'd tracked to Whitehorse.

Her wolf snapped at her, and Amy jolted in surprise.

"Whoa, careful." Evan caught the steering wheel, pulling to correct their dangerous sway into the oncoming traffic lane.

Amy adjusted her handgrip. Ten and two positioning, fingers curled so tight her knuckles showed white. "Sorry."

He didn't answer her, and the car went completely quiet as she headed out of town and down a logging road leading into the mountains. The gravel was well maintained, but she had to stay alert, the narrow switchbacks taking them toward the mountain peak.

She turned down a side road, crossed the final one-lane bridge over the creek, and rounded the corner.

"Sweet mercy, that's gorgeous." Evan leaned forward and peered out the window. "How come I didn't know this was here?"

"Canyon pack land."

"Ahh. That makes sense." Evan pointed into the trees. "Company."

A wolf stood at attention on the rocky ridge to the south of the cabin, allowing himself to be seen. Amy dipped her chin, and he vanished.

She understood why her pack was watching, but she'd left direct orders none of them were to contact her unless she gave approval.

"Sentries. They'll leave us alone, but they maintain a constant patrol in the area." Amy put the car into park, leaving her bag in the trunk. If this didn't go well, they'd be back on the road in the next hour.

The cabin *was* beautiful. One side had been built against a stand of towering spruce that guarded the log structure from the bitter north winds. The west windows faced over the expansive valley rolling for miles before them while the tiny back porch looked toward the mountain. When the sun finally rose over the tall peak in the morning, the entire sitting area flooded with colour and warmth.

Fixing up the old cabin had been her contribution to the pack—a place to retreat when needed. Somewhere for souls who craved quiet to find it, only a short distance from Whitehorse, and there were a lot of those quiet-craving souls in her pack.

It was her time to take advantage of the isolation.

Evan stood on the path and took a deep breath, eyes closed as he enjoyed the fresh air and wildness of the place. His bag in one hand, coat in the other, he was this living statue right where she didn't want him. Right where she had to deal with him, whether she wanted to or not.

There was no retreat for her.

6

———

*B*umping too close as they entered the front door only made her wolf more antsy. "Please, keep your distance."

"I'm trying."

"Try harder." Drat. Amy took a deep breath to regain control. "Leave your things at the door for now. You want juice, or something stronger?"

Evan dropped his bag to the floor, set his coat over top, then stepped into the cabin, looking up at the open rafter system. "No alcohol. I want a level head for this conversation."

Amy paused in the middle of pulling open the refrigerator door to examine his expression. It was far more solemn than usual. Arms folded over his chest, feet spread wide. Another rush of attraction hit, and this time she admitted he was exactly her type. Dark, muscular. Sexual overtures in his every move.

Except for the fact that until an hour or so ago, she'd hated his guts.

She ignored everything but the mundane for the next

two minutes. Poured drinks, brought them to the living room. She slowed to a stop in the middle of the room as she debated where she wanted to sit while they did this. Put the kitchen table between them as a barrier? Sit in the easy chairs that looked over the valley? She certainly couldn't pick the couch or the loveseat where the buttery-soft leather was all about comfort and decadence.

Stupid things to be worrying about when her brother was dead, her world had been torn apart, and the man responsible for everything stood less than five feet away.

"You look as if you're holding a bomb in each hand." Evan pulled one glass from her and gestured to the table. "Come. We may as well start at the beginning. This isn't going to work like any conversation you've had before, so don't bother trying to anticipate."

"I don't like surprises." Only she obediently dropped into the chair he pulled out for her.

"Seriously. Wait until I tell you about my night."

There was another secret that would soon be out—that she was the organizer of most of *his* surprises.

One step at time. She wouldn't rush. Just do what had to be done and evaluate each move.

Evan eased his chair back, one arm resting on the table, his strong fingers wrapped around his glass. "You want to explain what you meant back there? About your brother?"

That block of ice encasing her heart seemed to cool her entire body. "You've killed so many people you don't know who I'm talking about?"

His eyes went cold. "I've killed a few wolves and a few humans. I never did it impulsively, maliciously or without a great deal of thought. That doesn't make me a cold-blooded murderer, and it doesn't answer the question. Who was your brother?"

Amy linked her fingers in front of her, staring at her hands for strength before lifting her gaze to pin Evan in place as she spoke. "Philip de Lorne. Hudson Bay pack."

The colour drained from Evan's face, and his jaw tightened. A furrow appeared between his brows as he looked her over more carefully than before. "I don't remember you."

"I was too young to be on your radar. I was eight when it happened. You were one of the up-and-coming youth. Seventeen, like my brother." As she thought back, the knot in her throat only grew bigger. "You remember Philip, though?"

A slow nod. "He was a good friend."

His words hit like a knife strike to the heart. "Right."

"I'm serious. I mean, he was very private about his family. I never went to his home, which is probably why I don't remember you and I meeting. But Phil and I did things together with the youth all the time." Evan shot to his feet, dragging a hand through his hair as he paced away. A sound of frustration and anguish escaped. She couldn't see his face, couldn't read his wolf as he twisted his back toward her, shoulders rigid. "I... It's complicated."

Amy stiffened her resolve. "I know what happened. I looked into it, a few years back. What I want to know is why."

Evan rotated slowly. "You looked into what? The human media reports of the accident? Newspaper accounts?"

"Deeper. I know computers, and I know pack. I found trails...and they led to information that the shifter community had buried deep. The media got the whitewashed story about a mine collapse that killed nearly twenty men. But that wasn't the whole truth, because it wasn't a mine that collapsed and trapped them underground. It was an explosion, wasn't it? An explosion you caused."

The hard lines of his face and body could have been etched from granite. "Yes."

The icy sensation in her veins returned in a rush. The one she got whenever she'd planned another moment of her revenge, only this wasn't how the confrontation was supposed to go. Her wolf moved restlessly, uneasy with her inner stillness. Would Evan deny it? "Philip died in the accident you were responsible for."

Evan nodded. "You're right."

The light faded from the innermost part of her that had hoped she'd made a mistake somewhere along the way. "Then there's nothing more to discuss."

"Wait." He crossed the room and knelt beside her chair. His nearness like a cage closing around her. His power, his presence. His wolf. "We're not done, because while I understand what you must think, you don't know the full truth."

Amy nodded. This was the only reason she'd agreed to meet with him alone. "Tell me."

He was staring. Not at her face, but her hands. "Two weeks ago. A security tape at my hotel caught video footage of a hooded person with your hands snooping around in the kitchen while no one else was there. That was you, wasn't it? What were you doing there?"

He'd find out soon enough. "It's...complicated."

Evan lifted smoky eyes to hers. The dark centers matching his pupils. "Hudson Bay pack went bad from the leadership down. It was a slow growing rot. As soon as I sensed what was happening, I tried to make a change. The first time I challenged the Alpha, Kirk Gatlann broke my arm. The second time he didn't even try to fight fair, he simply set his Betas on me. I ran out of time before I could make a third attempt, and it came down to triggering the explosion that killed him or watching him systematically destroy the pack I was desperate to protect."

She listened, she really did. His words were logical, they weren't enough to break her free.

"I was eight. I have few childish memories of the pack, and none of the Alpha." Amy wasn't ignoring what he'd shared, but her reality had been completely different. "All I know is that one day Philip didn't come home, and neither did my parents."

"What? That's impossible." Evan's shock punched forward, heavy and weighted like a falling anvil.

She was too numb to do anything but continue. "Is it? You know everything that happened during the chaos caused by the explosion, and the shifter cover-up that followed?" She stared out the window, over his shoulder. "One moment my family was there, the next my brother was gone and so were my parents. They were never very attentive—Philip was more of a caregiver to me than they were. I don't know if they went feral, or had some other reason they bolted, but I was abandoned. I rambled around in our house in the bush for two weeks until social services finally came by and picked me up."

An agonized growl rumbled up from Evan's chest. "I'm so sorry."

"And now..." If Evan was telling the truth, he might have been justified in causing the explosion. She knew how much sway an Alpha held over their pack. How much the leader's attitude set the tone for how the rest of the members behaved. The hurt and fury she carried inside remained, but it was wavering. Broken, like her. "I don't know what to do."

"Amy." He touched her carefully, his fingers sliding over hers. "Your brother was my friend, and his death was an accident. There's more I need to tell you, but we're too raw. Too tight from the shock of finding each other, and the mating urge, and everything else we're facing."

The point of contact between them was like a livewire. Sparking hot, a steady pulse with a pounding rhythm, but even that wasn't enough to cut through her misery. "I feel cold. In spite of the mating attraction, I'm frozen."

"I understand."

"Do you?"

Evan's grip tightened on her fingers. "I'm ripped up inside as well. My wolf wants to claim you, but my human side tells me to back the fuck up and give you space. I can feel your agony, and your anger, and both are tearing me apart."

"I've spent years hating you, Evan. *Years.*" Her claws itched to escape so she could slash out at him, and yet with the mating urge riding her, the last thing she wanted was to hurt him. So torn... "How do I let go of the pain after nothing but a short conversation? Even if you were justified in what you did?"

"You can't. Switching convictions like that would make no sense." He hooked the nearest kitchen chair with his foot and pulled it over so he didn't have to release her fingers as he sat. "It's going to take time. It's going to take time for trust to develop between us, and we can't force it to happen. We have to allow it to grow."

"Damn wolves," she muttered.

Evan stroked her fingers as he pulled back. "The wolf side is right about so many things. Like choosing mates— knowing who is our best partner."

Fear shot through her again, more intensely than before.

Evan as a mate... The *idea* of having a mate made her crazy with longing, yet every part of her wanted to deny the hope. The need to control the new hunger was bigger than her thwarted revenge.

The situation was so much bigger than she'd expected to have to deal with. Amy already missed the physical contact between them. She scrambled for a temporary solution that would cut the pain. "A run. I need to run, and your wolf could use it as well."

The tension pouring off him was as powerful as the frustration binding her limbs. The fact she could sense his need so strongly—she wasn't sure if that pleased her, or just made her angrier.

Evan nodded. "Great idea. You can show me around." He paused. "Will your pack mind the Takhini Alpha roaming their territory?"

She shook her head. "You're my guest. No one will bother us."

It wasn't her fault he hadn't caught on to who she was, and after his snippy order back in the forest when he'd cut off her confession, she didn't feel like enlightening him yet. Maybe she was being stubborn, but in light of everything else she was giving him slack on, letting him stay ignorant for a little longer seemed justified.

But before their time of talking was over, she would have to explain so much more.

EVAN TOOK his bag to the second bedroom, barely aware of his surroundings. His hands damn near shook as he stripped off his clothes.

So. The ghosts from Hudson Bay had returned, no

longer satisfied to haunt him, but determined to intrude with enough impact to destroy his future like they'd savaged his past.

He hadn't lied. Philip's death had been an accident. The only people who were supposed to have died in the explosion had deserved to rot in hell. But with how delicate Amy's soul was, Evan was going to tread lightly before telling her the rest. Before having to face his own nightmares all over again.

The only good part was they were moving forward. The potential for them to be together was closer than an hour ago.

"We can shift in the cabin," Amy informed him, calling through the closed door. "The back door is rigged to allow us to go in and out in our wolves."

Evan took his time. Folded everything with far more care than he'd usually take back at his place. He was in the middle of warning his wolf to behave when the door cracked open, and Amy stood in the doorway.

"Ready?"

Nudity was commonplace among wolves. Between shifting, and sex being enjoyed for fun far more than even in the human population, Evan had seen his share of skin.

Only this was his mate, and that changed everything. He couldn't seem to avert his eyes. It proved physically impossible to do anything other than to leisurely admire her, starting at her toes.

The petite package before him was all kinds of perfect. She'd painted her toenails a bright green polish with flecks that sparkled in the sun shining in the window.

Slim but muscular legs—he already knew she had the ability to use them. The bruise on his chest proved that.

Her hips flared nicely, waist curving inward. Smooth

brown skin over delicate breasts that were round and firm with dark nipples and...

Evan stabbed his nails into his own thigh to force himself to move past fixating on the woman's chest. Instead he got as far as the swoop of her throat and the flickering pulse visible there, both erratic and heavy. Mesmerizing. He wanted to touch. To press his lips against her soft skin and soothe away her fears. His body ached with anticipation.

She moved, bending her knees ever so slightly so their eyes met. She spoke surprisingly softly. "Hey. Time for a run."

She shifted. That in itself was an act of trust, he realized. To be the one to take her other form first, and let him truly see *her*.

It was powerful. Humbling.

Oh, she'd been in her wolf form when he chased her, but that had been a different situation altogether. That had been born of impulse and instinct. This? This was about revealing herself.

Her fur was dark and lush. Intelligent eyes stared at him as he squatted, bringing their heads on a level plane. Evan reached out slowly, uncertain how Amy would take his touch.

He wasn't sure what he would do if she rejected him.

That first touch, the first caress, nearly rocked Evan to the floor. His wolf howled, eager to come out and meet his mate. But first Evan wanted this moment. He smoothed a hand down Amy's back as he admired her. Thrilled to know that she was there, and his resolve firmed to iron.

They were going to get through this. They would find a way. Somehow he would tear aside the walls that were threatening them. It was what he did. It was who he was.

He shifted right beside her, their bodies so close that not

only their fur but the heat of their bodies made contact. Her scent enveloped him. Her presence.

Her power. For a split second Evan wondered...

Amy nudged him in the side then headed for the door. She was only a step away when the heavy wooden planks swung upward, the entire lower half of the door rising skyward on a hinge. Evan was fascinated, but his wolf was far more interested in following Amy as she paced down the stairs and onto a narrow path between two towering spruce.

Evan turned his back on the cabin and followed his mate.

She began by leading him along the winding trail through the trees. He was surprised when they went neither up nor down the mountain, but in a steady line on a vertical plane. He racked his brains to think of the terrain in that area, but it grew harder to use his human reasoning. All the wolf wanted was to run with his mate. Evan acknowledged the beast's wisdom, put aside his questions, and instead concentrated on keeping up.

She had a new agenda, this one far clearer than any previous. Her pace was rapid enough Evan had to push to keep up. Even though he was following, the new terrain made it difficult for him to move at his highest speed. She seemed to delight in taking last-minute corners, using small trails off the main path, especially ones passing under low bushes or other obstacles that challenged his larger form. It was a game of one-upmanship, and he had no difficulty in accepting the challenge.

When they broke free of the trees, the world had changed. Instead of looking down on the city of Whitehorse, they were in the valley on the far side of the mountain. The horizon seemed so far away, with nothing but wilderness stretching before them.

Amy rested beside him, both of them breathing heavily from their exertion. Evan lowered himself to the ground, relaxing and allowing himself the luxury of just being. The wolf was at the foreground. The wolf was pleased.

And when Amy settled beside him, close enough their haunches touched, a tiny seed of hope germinated.

There was so much to decide. So much forgiveness to work through. Having Amy with him made everything inside that was wolf stand up and cheer. Bringing forward the pain of the past was going to be nasty, and his human heart feared hurting her irrevocably.

The tightrope between the two paths scared him the most.

7

─────────

*A*my rocked her easy chair, the view from the wide deck of the cabin almost as spectacular as the one that she and Evan had enjoyed on their run.

She sipped from the glass of wine she'd poured to help steady her nerves. It had felt incredible to be able to run with a fellow wolf, one as strong as she was. She often spent time in her wolf form taking care of others in the pack, but it wasn't the same. Then she was the one in charge. She was the one constantly looking for clues of what was needed in the pack.

Today?

Running through that door with Evan at her side had been different from anything she'd experienced before. She wasn't sure how it was possible to feel affected on so many levels.

Inside her chest was a hard, heavy spot. For the last five years, ever since she had begun to seek the truth about what had happened to her family, that layer of rock and ice had been building around her heart. Evan said he still had more to explain, and that was true. But what he'd already shared made sense. His brief summary made a difference, and now she wondered if she'd been chasing, not justice, but a nightmare.

She hated being wrong. She hated the thought she might have spent time and energy seeking to punish someone who didn't deserve it. Guilt heated her inside and began to melt the ice and anguish.

Evan pushed through the door and joined her. His hair was wet from the shower.

"It's all yours," he said.

She rose, stepping to the left to get around him. He moved at the same moment, unintentionally blocking her path.

Twice more they shifted position, twice more they jerked to a stop mere seconds away from making full physical contact. Evan rotated his shoulders to the side and opened a path. "Please. Go on."

Stepping past him was incredibly hard. Amy's wolf had been content while they were in the forest, but now that they were back at the cabin, the creature was no longer as patient. What her wolf wanted was to halt in mid-stride, curl up against him and rub all over.

And that was just to begin with—the beast had a very vivid imagination, and she used it mercilessly. Amy made sure the shower was icy cold, and she scrubbed as hard as she could, but even then his scent lingered. Wrapped around her.

Tonight was going to be hell no matter what.

She wasn't in the shower for long, but by the time she got out and dressed in a comfortable pair of sweats, she discovered Evan in the kitchen digging through the fridge, a pot of spaghetti boiling on the stove. He glanced over his shoulder. "I'm starving. I thought you might be as well."

Amy nodded. "Did you find the spaghetti sauce in the freezer?"

They worked together to make the meal, and it was far too casual. There was something wrong, Amy thought, about standing beside the man and teetering between confusion and lust.

Her wolf couldn't understand why they weren't moving on to the next stage of mating, i.e. jumping his very delectable bones. Her fully human heart was still working on letting go of the thought that this was the enemy who she was bumping into as they made a salad. As Evan ripped chunks of lettuce from the head and her gaze fell to his strong hands, her sense of guilt strengthened even further.

She had to find a way to deal with this dilemma. She was a strong individual, but the conflicting desires between her two parts would pull her world apart if she wasn't careful.

If it were only her life to worry about, Amy would let chaos run its course, no matter what the end result. Only she wasn't free to take that route. Her situation meant too many others were relying on her. Too many plots had already begun that she had to make a decision about, and quickly.

"Eat outside on the deck?" Evan asked once the meal was ready.

"Great."

They balanced plates and drinks. Evan pushed open the door with his shoulder and let her go first.

"Do you want to tell me what happened to you after the accident?" Evan spoke quietly after they'd settled in their chairs. "Or do you want to talk about what you're doing here in Whitehorse? Or do you want to ask me questions?"

The idea of going back through the hell her life had been for so many years would make her lose her appetite.

And telling him why she'd come to Whitehorse—that burden could wait until after dinner was over. "Tell me something about yourself. Your education, or what you did after you left Hudson Bay."

Evan's expression grew a touch lighter as he twirled spaghetti on his fork. "I traveled for a while. Ended up in Europe, which was a complete surprise, both getting there and how they do things. I spent a few years working in Germany and Russia with a paramilitary organization."

Well, now, that was unexpected. "Para, as in shifters, or semi-legal mercenaries?"

Evan tilted his head from side to side. "In a way, both. We were all shifters, and while not all of our activities involved working in shifter-only communities, a lot of the assignments did. The roughest ones were in Russia. Most West and Central European shifters tend to be more civilized, at least on the surface. What I've come to think of being the norm in the shifters found south of the forty-ninth parallel. Our wolves tend to be rougher."

"The wolves in the Yukon are a different lot," Amy agreed.

"Caroline said it's not just the shifters. She said the humans who come North tend to have a different attitude than folks from the South. Something about wanting to do things their own way and loving the isolation."

A new and unwelcome sensation struck as Evan casually mentioned the other woman's name.

Amy stabbed a piece of salad with her fork. "Oh, right. The human."

Evan stiffened ever so slightly. He glanced at her, concern the strongest emotion she sensed. "You don't have to worry about Caroline."

"Who's worried?" Amy could've kicked herself for even

responding to his comment, but her wolf's hackles were up. Damn her world.

Evan put his plate on the small table beside his chair. He knelt before her and placed both hands on her knees. "From the moment I discovered you were in Whitehorse, I haven't touched another woman. I know we have more to discuss but, Amy, even if you need to learn to trust me on other things, trust me on this. You are the only woman I want."

Her wolf preened, and Amy wanted to smack the beast. "I believe you."

She believed him as well because she'd been watching him, closely. There was no scent on him more than what would have been caused by casual interactions. And wasn't that mucked up? That she didn't know where this conversation was going, but she was fanatically happy to hear no other female had gotten a piece of him recently.

Evan remained on his knees in front of her, fixing her with a dark intense stare that drove straight into her soul. "I'm dying here, Amy." He set her plate to the side so he could take her hands in his. "Tell me something. Give me hope we'll get through this."

She shook her head, hating to do it, but unwilling to lead him on with an untruth. "I can't promise anything yet. Part of me wants to remind you we're both damn strong, so of course we can get through this. But there's so much you don't know. There's so much you have to tell me."

He nodded slowly. Sat back in his chair and picked up his plate. His expression going more determined, if anything. "Your turn. What have you been doing? You own the computer shop. That's cool."

"When I finished high school, I headed into computer programming. By the end of the first year, I'd realized getting a degree wasn't going to work. The classes were too easy." Amy stared into her wine glass, swirling the liquid gently. "It was the other parts of going to school that intrigued me. Since I could solve the computer-programming assignments in my sleep, learning to deal with the people around me became far more fascinating."

"You've spent years learning how to read people?"

"Shifters, humans, the usual set of misogynists involved in computer sciences," she admitted. Amy took a deep breath and prepared to make her confession regarding her position in the Canyon pack.

He didn't give her a chance. "When you join Takhini, that's going to help you a lot."

Amy guessed Evan was attempting to be reassuring, although it was hard to tell as her blood pressure spiked again.

"I have no concerns about being able to fit in just fine wherever I go." She might have offered the statement with a little too much sarcasm.

Evan observed her carefully for a moment then stared over the view. The sun was beginning to set behind the western mountains, and golden-yellow rays streaked across the sky. "It seems at every turn I say things that upset you. I don't know what I'm doing wrong."

"That confession is a step in the right direction," Amy commented. "Finish eating. I can hear your stomach rumbling from here, and I don't need a testy wolf on top of everything else. We'll talk once we've done dinner."

The setting was far too idyllic considering the tension between them, but Amy took it. She ignored the pressures they still had to face and focused on the beauty of the world around her. Guiltily allowed her wolf to enjoy the presence of the strong, alpha male at her side.

The clouds were backlit with brilliant colours when the

sentinels surrounding the cabin started to howl. Their wolf song was full of respect and appreciation. A shiver raced over her skin as she met Evan's eyes.

His focus narrowed, his concentration tightening as the pack continued to serenade her. It wasn't just because she was there and finally taking a rare night off, it was their way to show they cared.

The homage was humbling and strengthening all at the same time.

Evan stood and walked to the edge of the deck, staring into the trees as he listened intently. The position left his face in profile, and she couldn't take her eyes off him. Admiring the sharp features of his jawline, a hint of silver beginning to show in the black hair at his temples. Her wolf nudged her and again confirmed its interest in taking this man as a mate.

He turned to her. "I'm an idiot."

Amy's lips twitched. "If you say so."

He leaned his elbows on the railing, his long muscular body stretched out facing her and highlighted by the fading colours of sunset glow. His eyes gleamed, a hint there of both his amusement and his continued caution. "So. When did you intend on letting me know that you're the Alpha of the Miles Canyon pack?"

Busted.

HE WAS PLEASED to see she didn't look guilty at getting caught, but instead tilted her chin upward and for the first time offered him a grin.

"I did try to tell you. More than once."

Evan thought back, nodding slowly as he considered.

"You did. Thus my admission I was an idiot."

Amy lifted her feet into the chair and wrapped her arms around her shins. "I suppose this starts a new conversation."

"I know we're not done answering your concerns, but what the hell?" If Evan had thought his world had become twisted before, this only made it worse. What the fuck was going on? "First question—all the rumours I've heard said Sam runs Canyon. Your name is Amy. Which is right?"

She sighed. "Both. My name is Samantha Amy Ryba, but for many reasons it seemed better to go by Sam when I took over Canyon. A masculine-sounding name stops a lot of bother before it even starts. Unfortunately."

"But you used Amy as your code name?"

"It's the name I used in college, and it hid my identity from your pack when I made contact with Takhini."

Hidden in plain sight. "Congrats, it worked. But why have you been sharing pack secrets when you're the Alpha?"

When she didn't answer him, instead staring at a spot over his shoulder, Evan's respect for her went up and his sense of *oh-shit* grew exponentially.

"You were pulling a fast one," he guessed.

"I was gathering intelligence," Amy suggested. "I didn't share anything about the Canyon pack that wasn't actually common knowledge."

Evan grinned as another thought occurred. "Oh man, I don't believe it. Perfect, efficient Caroline made a mistake. You duped her into taking you under her wing! I'm going to razz her like crazy when she gets back."

Her eyes darkened. "I thought she was moving away."

Oops. He exercised a little more caution. "She's not living full-time in Whitehorse, no, but she will be around every now and then. Her sister Shelley is part-time with the pack. But again, you have nothing to worry about. She's just a good friend, and she's thoroughly married. She'll be thrilled to meet you in person."

Amy shook her head, the motion somehow very wolf-like. "Don't mind me, I feel as if I'm jacked up on Red Bull and caffeine tablets like during exams week at college. I have no beef with Caroline."

Evan looked her over carefully. He understood her hesitation, but there was no reason they shouldn't move to the next part of their relationship. To the part where they could trust each other and work together.

Not to mention all the lovely physical interactions he was longing to bring to the table.

"You realize my number-one goal for the past year has been to merge the Takhini and Canyon packs. There is no need for more than one pack in Whitehorse."

"That's what I believe as well," Amy agreed. "I'm pretty sure I said that to Caroline, in fact."

Hope flared brightly. "Then at least one fact is pretty simple. Now that we know we're mates, we join the packs. Done. One united pack under Takhini."

Her response wasn't as enthusiastic as he'd hoped. In fact, she faced away, her body tightening. She paused for a moment before turning back.

"I told you before you're making assumptions. Let's see how smart you really are." Amy lifted her eyes to meet his. "The packs should merge, but I'm ninety-nine percent sure that means Canyon pack takes over."

His instant response was to laugh, but in light of her comment regarding assumptions and how smart he was, he resisted the temptation.

"Even though Takhini is in control of most of the activities in Whitehorse?" Evan shook his head. "I personally know a half dozen members of the Canyon pack.

There's maybe, what? A couple dozen more? Even if you have members hiding in the woodwork, what makes you think Canyon could control Takhini?"

"Control isn't always about the number of bodies in the room. Power comes in many forms." Amy rose from her chair and stood next to him, arms resting on the railing. She was close enough her warm upper arm brushed his. Her scent tangled around him, stirring fingers into his brain and messing with his thought patterns.

He fought to concentrate on something other than the smooth skin caressing his. "That's true, but it still seems to me that if the packs amalgamate, Takhini will lead."

She didn't budge an inch. "This is another area we'll have to figure out. First, of course, is deciding if we'll work together, or fight to be in control."

The idea of fighting with his mate was not only ridiculous, the mere suggestion made him crazy. He held back from saying anything, though. At least about the thoughts racing through his brain that said no way in *hell* was she going to turn him down.

The possibility of her taking Takhini from him didn't even register.

He risked lifting a hand to stroke back a hair that had fallen across her cheek, tucking it behind her ear. "I don't want to fight."

Amy laughed, and the sound broke around him like a spring breeze, melting some of the fear in his heart as echoes bounced off the mountain. Bright and joyful for the first time since he'd met her.

She lifted her face toward him, her smile real. "Did you hear yourself?" she asked. "Did you, a wolf, just admit you don't want to fight? I call bullshit."

"How about I don't want to fight *with you*."

One brow went up. "I want to fight with you. In fact, I think it's exactly what we need."

Evan considered her words, and the truth hit like a two by four. They were both craving contact, but their human sides weren't ready to let go of their inhibitions yet. A fight would allow them to give into their animal appetites without really admitting it to the human side.

Even being a wolf had layers of deceit to it.

"You are rather brilliant. I like that in a woman."

"Thank you. You don't mind if I fight dirty, do you?"

The light chuckle that escaped him felt amazing. "I'm pretty sure I can handle you."

They stared at each other for a moment, tension rising again, this time of an entirely different nature. Sunset glow lit the area. Amy motioned with her head toward the living area. "Follow me if you dare."

It was a challenge Evan had no intention of turning down.

8

—————

The hatred Amy had nourished for years was no longer strong and growing. Enough doubt had been planted, but she wasn't free of it yet. The roots went too deep, no matter how much she wanted to move forward.

The craving for revenge was fading but...

When one of the first things Evan had focused on had been joining the packs? A bit of her hope had faded. Was he really excited to have her as a mate, or pleased because she had power he wanted?

Would anyone ever want her for herself, or was the tradition that had started that horrid day of her childhood going to continue? Abandoned. Alone, even when surrounded by others. Unloved, even with a mate.

Now she had was the additional problem of having an animal side growing more insistent with every minute that passed. Her sexual cravings increased. This man was her mate, and her wolf *wanted*.

Demanded.

She couldn't give in to her desires, but she could soothe it in the basest way possible. Evan was as desperate as she was, the tension in his body enough to make her sense his attraction even without physical contact.

"Where do you want to do this?" Evan stepped into the living room a body length behind her, unmistakable eagerness in his voice.

Amy moved like lightning. She stepped onto the nearest chair seat, up to the tabletop then twirled to leap full force into the unsuspecting man at her back.

Her momentum toppled him to the floor. He sprawled under her, a lazy grin spreading across his face as he gazed upward. "You do fight dirty."

He looked far too delighted, and Amy ignored the contented rumble rising from her wolf as she lay spread over his muscular body, heat passing between them. She rolled and regained her feet, dodging between the chairs of the kitchen and the living area.

"You want to take this outside?" Evan asked. "Not that I have any issues tangoing in here, but it might be safer for the furniture if we go elsewhere."

"Sure, I got the jump on you because of the furniture." She backed up, keeping her eyes on his torso so she could react at a moment's notice. "I don't mind, though. You'll look good with grass stains on your ass."

"Or you might end up wearing pinecones."

She turned her back on him and boldly walked out the door, leading him to the grassy area between the deck and the trees. The entire time she walked she was intensely aware that only a few steps away an alpha male in his prime stalked her.

This wasn't about revenge, or finding a solution. It wasn't about any of the human reasoning side of their brains. This was about the wolf, and Amy shoved all logic to the side and prepared for the coming battle.

She had one foot crossing from gravel to grass when he made his move, hurling himself at her with a twisting motion that should have ended with her on the ground, his arms wrapped around her lower limbs. She sensed it coming, ducked to the side and narrowly escaped.

Evan rolled to his feet, an enormous grin stretching his cheeks as he nodded with approval. "Nicely done."

"Save your breath," she teased. "You're going to need it."

She darted forward, striking with an open hand toward his chest. He blocked the move easily, but failed to anticipate her leg lift. Her knee connected with his hip and rocked him backwards.

Evan crowded forward, his larger size and stronger muscles dangerous if he chose to give one hundred percent. But Amy was stronger than she looked. Her deceptive softness had fooled others, and her wolf was almost disappointed it appeared he too would be an easy target.

Evan swung, obviously looking to tumble her to the ground rather than land a blow. Amy grasped his hand and rotated her body, curling in and surprising him as she moved into his body space. Her back made contact with his chest hard enough to rock them both on their feet.

She dropped to her knees to escape the iron band of his arm that attempted to close around her body. The motion brought them into intimate contact for a moment, and her wolf sighed contentedly, a little cocky at having successfully tricked her mate.

Evan retreated a couple paces, legs spread wide as he warily watched her regain her feet. "You have some good moves."

Amy smiled, then attacked. One strike after the other shot toward his torso. Evan blocked them all, his forearms and hands moving in a blur of motion. She stepped in closer, and this time he caught her, pinning her hand against his chest. She twisted, trying to break his hold, but that only resulted in him capturing her other hand.

She struggled, and the motion rubbed them together.

"Damn, I knew I forgot something." Evan set her free, pushing her away slightly. Amy twirled to see what he was up to, but he wasn't preparing for an attack from behind. Instead, he grabbed the bottom of his shirt, peeling the fabric over his head and exposing far too much gorgeous, muscular chest and stomach muscles. Her fingers twitched with the urge to touch. To trace the intricate tattoo on his right biceps.

She hesitated for a second before copying his move. Her shirt hit the ground to one side, but he wasn't watching the fabric, his gaze pinned on her body.

"No bra. I like that. I like that very much." Evan licked his lips, heat rising in his eyes as he admired her.

Amy had plenty to admire as well, looking across the small distance separating them. Evan wore a faded pair of jeans that sat low on his hips. Solid muscles flexed and extended rhythmically, one foot crossing over the other as they circled.

"Less clothing makes it easier when it's time to shift," Amy pointed out. "Besides, I don't really need one."

"You're perfect just the way you are."

She didn't fight the sensation. Satisfaction that her mate found her attractive rushed in, and for one second she preened.

Didn't stop her from making the next move. She leapt, and as expected, his eyes remained on her torso. Amy took total advantage and slung out a leg, aiming for his side.

Evan seized her foot and hauled her with him as he tumbled to the ground. Arms and legs scrambling to escape, she was nevertheless trapped as he caught both her wrists and slammed them into the ground on either side of her head. His larger body pinned her in place.

Once again they were skin against skin, and a sense of satisfaction rolled over her. She had an itch she desperately needed to scratch, but only with this man. Evan moved his head to the side to capture her earlobe in his teeth and nip lightly.

"You're fast, strong, and my God, you're sexy." He breathed deeply, and a low, sensual grumble started at the back of his throat. Her wolf reacted instantly, moving against him. She wasn't even sure when she opened her legs to allow his hips to settle between them. The hard heavy length of his cock rested over the aching core of her body.

He rocked, and the aching pressure inside changed to a tingling alertness. Need and desire rocketed.

Only she wasn't ready to give in. "Next time you won't be able to use that move with me," she warned.

"Then I'll try something new." Evan stretched her arms overhead, transferring her wrists until he held her trapped in the fingers of one strong hand. With his second hand free, he reached down and drew a finger along her arm.

If he'd moved in a rush, taking that hand and placing it against her throat or her chest, Amy would've continued to struggle. But the bastard moved so slowly, and so cautiously, she was mesmerized. His fingers traced from her wrist along her forearm, lingering for a second on the inside of her elbow.

By the time he passed over her biceps to where her arm and torso connected, Amy was struggling to breathe. "Let me go," she whispered.

"No."

Two fingers now ran along side of her torso, pausing on

her rib cage. He pressed his hand to her skin and caressed. Small circles at first, getting larger until he skimmed the edge of her breast. Amy closed her eyes and fought the shiver that rolled over her.

When he settled his full palm on top of her breast, his hand possessive for all that it was a light contact, she took a deep, deep breath.

As good as his touch felt, she couldn't go any further. Her wolf was ready for more. God, the beast was ready to all-out fuck in the middle of the field. But her human was waving a white flag and demanding they retreat and consider terms.

This time? The human need was far stronger.

"Evan."

Her tone said it all. Her desperation, her confusion. Evan removed his hand from her breast, bringing it up instead to cup her cheek.

He didn't say anything, just looked into her eyes. The contact had a continued calming effect. That, and the adrenaline fading from her system.

She had been right about a fight being a good thing. She was still turned on, still wanting more, but not nearly as desperate as she had been fifteen minutes earlier.

They lay on the hard ground, her back on the solid earth and his warm body over hers. For a good five minutes that's all they did. Satisfaction soaked into her bones. The kind of peacefulness she hadn't expected.

But the longer they lay there, the more the injustice of the entire situation burned. It was annoying as hell she couldn't simply accept him and know that everything would work out.

Evan leaned in close and brushed his cheek against hers,

the gentle caress intimate and yet not overwhelming. "Challenge you to a game of chess."

He let her go and helped her to her feet, and she nodded. "You're a glutton for punishment."

A cocky grin reflected back at her. "You'll find I'm good at all sorts of games." He scooped her shirt off the ground and handed it over. "Not that I'd argue if you spent the rest of the evening naked, but your choice."

Naked for shifting? Fine. Naked without being able to touch him and know it was the right thing? She wasn't ready for more. Amy returned the favour and passed him his shirt. "I don't want to win because I distracted you."

He raised a brow in the air. Then he reached his hand out. Held it there, steady. Firm. Amy stared for a moment, considering hard.

She slipped her fingers into his. The contact wasn't sexual. It wasn't about who was more dominant, or trying to move faster than they should. It was about connection, and who they were at their core. Wolves.

He grasped her fingers a little tighter, holding on. Letting her know he was there. "Come on. You can show me your worst."

HE DIDN'T WANT to let go, but it would be far too difficult to spend the rest of the evening with one hand clutched around hers. Not that he would've minded. Not at all, but so far they'd kept moving forward, and he wasn't going to do anything to jeopardize that fragile momentum.

So, they took an entirely different tack. Amy squeezed his fingers and he released her.

"You really want to play chess?" she asked.

Evan settled on the couch opposite the coffee table. "I'm not ready to leave you. I think my wolf would go insane if I tried, so you're stuck with me for the night."

Amy made a face. "Damn wolves."

"Yeah," Evan agreed. "I know we've got more to figure out, but I don't want to talk about any big issues tonight. And since spending hours making you scream during hot, sticky, satisfying sex is out of the question, no matter how much I want you, we need to do something else to pass the time."

She'd swallowed hard when he'd mentioned sex, her eyes gone wide as silver dollars, and for one second he hoped, before logic rushed in and slapped him for being an ass.

"I just meant are you sure you want to play chess," Amy muttered, not meeting his eyes. "There's a whole cupboard of other games here as well. I stocked it so when families come out they have other things to do in the evenings."

Okay. That was awkward. He made himself busy while she grabbed the game. He needed another cold shower. Damn him for making a smart-ass comment regarding sex. Now he had another hard-on from hell.

He adjusted his position on the couch in an attempt to ease the pressure. Then he looked around the cabin again and focused on changing the topic, not just with her, but with his own damn libido.

No television. No electronic games.

"Does the cabin see a lot of use?" Evan asked.

Amy shrugged. "Off and on. Some of the Canyon pack have their own retreats. I fixed this one for those times I needed to get away, and for those who like the idea of a place they can call their own for a short while, but can't afford it."

Interesting. "The Takhini pack has the house in town, but nothing in the wilderness. When we go out, we tend to go farther afield from Whitehorse."

Amy placed the chessboard on the coffee table and settled on the floor. "Yes, but the Takhini pack is different than Canyon. Your people don't need the same kind of space my people do."

She set up the board quickly and efficiently as Evan considered her comment. "Wolves don't tend to need a lot of space."

He made the first move.

Her countermove came immediately. She leaned on an elbow as she glanced across the table at him. "It depends on the wolf. You stick people with lone-wolf tendencies into a pack house, and that's the surest way to drive them mad."

Evan frowned. "Lone wolves don't tend to congregate in packs in the first place."

"Right."

That's all she said, as if *right* was any kind of answer. Silence followed as he concentrated on the board, but it was no use. She had made all of four moves, and already Evan was sweating. "Damn, you're a chess master."

"Just really good at long-term planning," Amy deadpanned. She slid her bishop into line with his king. "Checkmate."

Evan sat back on his haunches. "Huh. Do that again."

Fifteen minutes later Evan had been defeated three more times. Amy crossed her legs and sat back, a contented smile on her face. "Ready for something more your speed?"

"Checkers?"

"I was thinking snakes and ladders."

Evan grabbed the cushion off the seat behind him and tossed it at her.

Amy ducked to one side, smiling as she stood. She lifted the board to put it away. "Go Fish?"

"Strip poker."

She whimpered, a look of pain crossing her face as Evan's wolf lunged upward in hope. "Be nice," Amy muttered.

Evan was instantly contrite, especially since the suggestion had made his cock react far more than it should have. "Sorry."

Her butt wiggled nicely as she strode to the cupboard. "Here, strategy and physical dexterity. Maybe it will distract us enough to forget...the other things we're fighting."

The game she placed on the table consisted of stacked blocks of wood. Evan was familiar with this one. "I'm the pack-house Jenga champion," he warned as he got to his knees.

"So I've heard. That means you might have a sporting chance against me."

Her dare warmed him. There was a challenge in it, yes, but none of the aggression she'd been tossing his way ever since she'd discovered he was her mate.

Proximity was easing things along, and that was all he could hope for at this point. "Ladies first."

Absolute concentration reigned for the next twenty minutes as they alternated moves, slipping the thin rectangular pieces of wood free from the tall tower and carefully placing them back on top. Evan made sure to focus while it was his turn.

But when it was Amy's? He was all about watching her.

Her dark hair was messy from their outdoor romp. Her eyes sparkled as she concentrated, the merest bit of her tongue poking between her lips as she steadily pushed a block free. There was a rosy glow to her skin, and a freshness and vitality about her that made Evan long for the moment he could put the games aside and take her in his arms. Take all of that energy and enjoy it to the fullest.

She smiled with satisfaction as she held a block in the air. "You're in trouble."

"We'll see." Evan didn't care at this point who won and who lost. Spending time with her was what he was interested in.

His competitive spirit wouldn't allow him to lie down and let her win, though. He leaned over, carefully checking the tower that was stacked precariously enough he wanted to hold his breath. A single sneeze would send it tumbling.

There were no simple moves left. He reached for a block, momentarily distracted by the faintest hint of delight that crossed Amy's face.

He checked again, and spotted the trap. Removing that piece was guaranteed to send the entire tower crashing. Instead he went for the only other possible move. Evan delicately placed a fingertip and nudged ever so slightly.

The tower swayed.

Forget about breathing, this was all about concentration now. One tiny motion after another the block inched free from its position. He pulled the final inch and a quarter straight to the side, sighing with relief as the tower settled.

He held the block in the air and beamed at Amy.

"I'm impressed."

"Anything can be accomplished with enough patience."

She took a deep breath then let it out slowly. The conversation was suddenly not about the game at all. Tension rose again in a rush, and urgent need and desire swooped around them like dive-bombing eagles. "I think I'm going to call it a night."

Evan looked pointedly at the tower, but didn't say anything.

Amy rolled her eyes. "You're such a wolf."

"You know it."

She tipped her chin. "You win." She raised a hand to the fragile structure and sent it tumbling into dozens of random pieces scattered on the floor.

They cleaned up the mess together. She carried the game away while Evan turned to the sink to wash the dishes. Silence, but this time far more comfortable.

He was drying his hands when she came up behind him. "Evan?"

He rotated, facing her with only inches separating their bodies.

She stared, those enormous eyes like magnets pulling him forward. "I... I'm not ready. God, I could rip your clothes off and fuck you right here if my wolf side got control, but then I think about what—"

He pressed his fingers over her lips. "I know. I understand. So I have a suggestion."

"What?"

Did she realize her fingertips were brushing his chest? "Sleep in your wolf. She needs it."

It was a way to give both of them what they were craving without pushing too far.

The faintest hint of a smile appeared. "I'll wash first."

Five minutes later he caught himself debating if he should wear a pair of boxers to bed or not, which only proved his logic centers were totally fucked up. Who cared what he wore? She wasn't *sleeping* with him. His wolf howled in frustration, and the human side muttered in agreement.

He exited the bathroom and stepped into the room she'd given him.

Amy was already curled up on the bed. She lifted her head, her unique personality shining from wolfish eyes.

A shot of something close to obsession struck, and he hid the yearning under a teasing quip. "I hope you don't snore."

She growled.

Evan didn't bother to pull back the quilt. Just lay down, one hand slipping into her fur. He stroked her, thoroughly enjoying the chance to pet her until she rumbled with pleasure.

"You're a beautiful wolf," he said as he admired her. "Your wolf and your human, both of them are amazing, and I can't wait until we're truly together."

Amy rose on her front paws, head tilted to the side as she studied him.

"I'll be patient," he promised. "But I won't give up."

Something changed, just slightly, but enough to make his wolf sigh contentedly. Amy turned in a circle, moving closer. She settled, her nose resting on her tail, body tight against his chest like a furry furnace.

Maybe it wasn't the typical first night for mates, but all things considered?

He'd take it.

PART II

Time has got a little bill—get wise while yet you may,
For the debit side's increasing in a most alarming way;
The things you had no right to do, the things you should
have done,
They're all put down; it's up to you to pay for every one.
So eat, drink and be merry, have a good time if you will,
But God help you when the time comes,
and you foot the bill.
"The Reckoning"—Robert Service

9

_L_ight had just begun to sneak over the mountain when she woke. Sometime in the night, Evan had shifted and was now in his wolf. They were cuddled together like two puppies, and her heart fluttered.

It felt so right.

Less than twenty-four hours had passed, and already there was a place inside that couldn't imagine not being with him. And yet, she didn't know for sure what came next, because that kind of trust and belonging were for other people. Too many plans had been set in place that would have to be worked out one step at a time.

Like shoving a musk ox into a china shop, things were about to get complicated.

After extracting herself from their warm, comfortable nest, she slipped outside to get some fresh air before the crazy day began.

She'd barely made it to the edge of the trees when it registered. Something was wrong. No birdsong, only utter silence from the animals of the woods and her sentries. Amy listened carefully, concern increasing at the unexpected stillness.

The faintest of rattles warned her in time to turn and face the wolf who leapt at her. He hit her hard enough to knock her to the ground, his jaws snapping on air rather than on her neck as she put on a burst of speed and moved to the defense.

She scrambled to her feet to face her foe, growling displeasure at having been attacked on her own territory. There was no way anyone should have been able to sneak up on the cabin like this.

Either her sentries were in trouble, or they would be.

The wolf she faced was black-furred and vaguely familiar. Amy cursed, the sound coming out as a furious growl. She'd expected to have to deal with Shaun at some point. She'd considered the Beta of the Takhini pack as she planned her strategy for revenge on Evan.

But it was too early in the day for this kind of discussion.

He took another run at her. Even as she dodged to the side to avoid his paw swipe, the attack just made her angrier.

Fine. He wanted a lesson in hierarchy? She would oblige.

She leaned forward on her front paws, crouching as she bared her teeth. Shaun hesitated for a split second, obviously surprised at the amount of power she put behind the snarl. While he was distracted, she slashed out, claws raking his shoulder. Before he could go on the offense, she crowded forward, batting again, this time striking the side of his muzzle as if disciplining a baby.

Her body might be smaller than his, but when she rushed in and hit simultaneously with her wolf side and a physical blow, Shaun had no chance of maintaining his feet.

They rolled down the slight incline, claws scrambling as they fought for freedom. A series of growls and yips escaped into the morning air.

Amy hung on tightly as he attempted to roll her one final time and get his jaws around her throat. The momentum took them farther than he expected, and she thrust out her legs to halt their motion. She jabbed a paw at his eyes, and while he was temporarily blinded, caught his throat in her jaws, biting ever so carefully.

She didn't break the skin, but her grip and body position was solid enough he wasn't going anywhere until she released him.

A third wolf stood only feet away, observing. Amy had sensed his arrival, but thankfully Evan didn't move to interrupt. She was determined this first fight would end the way she needed.

Shaun finally relaxed, tilting his head to the side just enough to loosen her jaws. It wasn't a complete offering of submission, and Amy debated biting harder to make her point clearer, but something warned her to ease back.

She let him free. Shaun rolled to his feet, shaking his fur to shed the dirt and sticks clinging to him.

Evan chose that moment to pace forward, but instead of going to his Beta, he surprised her. He moved smoothly to her side, leaned in and brushed his muzzle against hers.

Shaun shifted. His hands were clenched in fists by his side, his eyes snapped dark with anger as he sniffed distastefully at Amy. "Dammit, Evan. *She's* the important business you had to take care of in such a hurry yesterday?"

Oh goodie, this was going to be entertaining.

Both she and Evan shifted to their human forms.

"Is something wrong with the pack?" Evan demanded.

Amy had to give Evan credit for asking about them first.

"Yes." Shaun jerked to a stop then kicked his feet like a little kid with a hand in the cookie jar. "I mean, no. Nothing that needs your attention this instant."

"Then why are you here when I told you to stay in Whitehorse and take care of everyone?" Evan's growing displeasure was clear, in both his tone of voice and posture.

Shaun didn't seem to get the message to back off. "Yeah, well, there's news. I thought it was important enough to track you down."

That raised an interesting question. "How did you know where to find us?" Amy glanced into the trees. "And what have you done with my sentries?"

The Beta of the Takhini pack looked far too pleased with himself. "They're a little tied up at the moment."

Amy moved without thinking. She had an arm wrapped around Shaun's throat, him on his knees before the man could blink. Evan cared about his pack mates? She cared for hers as well. "If you hurt a single one of them, I swear you will pay."

"Amy. Let him go. Please."

She had no intention of setting Shaun loose until she was satisfied he'd learned his lesson, but the fact Evan had said *please* made the difference. She relaxed her grip, but shoved between Shaun's shoulder blades at the final moment to send him sprawling to his hands and knees.

He mumbled something, and she rolled her eyes. "Working with you is going to be an absolute joy. Yes, I am a bitch, thank you very much."

Evan stepped forward as Shaun scrambled to his feet, brushing the dirt from his knees. "Where are the Canyon members?" Evan asked.

Shaun pointed into the trees. "When I realized I'd tracked you into the heart of Canyon territory, I figured I'd better make sure no one could make a move on us. I found some rope in one of the outbuildings then snuck up on the sentries. They're where I found them."

Bastard. "You go and untie them this instant," Amy demanded.

He rocked on his feet as her order slammed him, but the fool still had the audacity to cross his arms and glare haughtily. "You're not my Alpha. I don't take orders from you."

"You want me to kick your butt some more to prove you *will* obey me?" She leaned forward, ready to take another swing, but Evan raised a hand.

"You made your point. Shaun's being an ass like usual." Evan turned to the dark-haired man. "Let her sentries loose then get yourself back to the Takhini pack house."

"But, Evan," Shaun protested. "You need to hear me out. Justin's team called this morning, and they've got crazy news."

Shaun continued to glower at her, his gaze filled with suspicion and concern. Amy couldn't blame him for his misgivings. There were big changes coming in his life, and she was the cause of most of them.

Evan snapped his fingers in front of his Beta's face to get his attention. "You said there was nothing that needed my attention. Do you really want to do this now?"

"There's probably not much you can do about most of it," Amy offered. "Isn't that right?" she asked Shaun.

His eyes narrowed and his expression grew colder. Then he deliberately ignored her and faced Evan.

"I thought figuring out my mate was rough, but you picked an even worse woman than me to get stuck with." Shaun sighed as if the weight of the world were on his shoulders. "*Fine.* I'll go back and make sure everything is waiting for you. Come back as soon as you can. And, dude, I suggest you keep your wallet hidden while you're around this chick."

Evan smacked him lightly on the side of the head. "Go. And don't forget to release the Canyon wolves. We'll see you later."

Amy stepped forward before Shaun could disappear. "If I hear you've been unnecessarily rough with any of them, I won't be pleased."

"What will you do? Send me to my room without supper?" Shaun snarked.

He should have seen it coming. Amy gave him plenty of time to react, but he was obviously still figuring out who exactly she was. And while she would never have used violence on one of her own pack members, Shaun was Takhini. A few sessions inflicting unexpected pain were exactly what she'd anticipated would be needed to bring Shaun around to the idea she *was* going to be his Alpha. Whether he liked it or not.

Her sucker punch hit him in the gut hard enough he curled around her fist, air rushing out in a choking gasp. She patted him on the head as she pulled her other hand free. "I would never deny a growing boy his meals, but you might have to sit at the little table for a few weeks until you've learned some manners."

Shaun straightened, that look of distrust lingering in his eyes, but a hint more respect in his body language. "I'll see you at the pack house, Evan. If you bring the she-dragon, consider handcuffing her for all our safety."

He headed into the trees, shifting as he ran.

Evan draped his arm around her, chuckling softly. "That went well."

It shouldn't have felt so easy to lean against his body and

soak in his warmth. "You know he's right. Nothing will be simple in the coming days."

He turned her on the spot, his strong hands caressing her bare shoulders, an unexpected smile on his face. "He likes you."

Amy snorted. "Thanks for letting me deal with him. That was important."

"Oh, I understand completely. And I'm serious. I think he's very impressed with you, once he gets over the shock of how the hierarchy has changed. If he wasn't safely mated, I might even be a little jealous."

Now Evan was being ridiculous, not to mention he was doing this thing with his thumbs against the skin of her neck that made her want to lean in and lick him all over. The desire made her uncomfortable on all sorts of levels.

"I'm more powerful than him." Amy gestured toward the cabin with her head, the motion breaking the physical contact between them, which was sad, but necessary. His touch made it tough to think. "In the end, he'll acknowledge it. He just might not like it."

"He doesn't have to like it for it to be real."

That brutal truth applied to them as well. The mating urge was there. The yearning to wrap herself around the solid man at her side and never let go grew every minute, cancelling out the impulse that suggested she stomp down hard on his unprotected toes. She focused on a new topic before the sexual tension could build again. "I can't believe he tied up my sentries."

"I wouldn't be too upset with them. Shaun is awfully sneaky when he wants to be." Evan followed her back to the cabin. "You may not want to hear this, but the fact he got away with it kind of proves my point about how strong

Takhini is. Just think. One man, working alone. How many sentries did Shaun put out of commission?"

Amy stifled her rumble of displeasure bare seconds after it had begun, hiding her frustration by stiffening her spine as she paused in the hallway between the bedrooms to stare him down. "And I'll remind you again, there are different types of power."

He shrugged, not looking even remotely worried. "Wolves are wolves. Whoever is in control calls the shots."

She closed the door to her bedroom while she dressed. So. It seemed the next part was less about them as a couple, and more about the packs joining.

Maybe that was the only way for her to survive this crazy situation. Amalgamation seemed to be Evan's main focus, for all his talk of wanting to make things right between them as a couple.

The pack merger was going to be a huge event, with lots of delicate manoeuvering required. Did Evan realize that? Or was his method going to be as straightforward and blunt as Shaun's? Sneak up on the unsuspecting, and force them to either cooperate or shut up?

Her pack might seem quiet, but they weren't helpless, and they wouldn't take being overrun without a fight.

Three issues loomed. Finding closure regarding her brother, dealing with her and Evan's mating, and joining the packs. Solving all three came back to trust. She needed time to learn to trust him. And Evan had no idea how much he had to learn about her.

Her phone rang as her sentries checked in one after the other. She reassured them she wasn't hurt, upset or otherwise in trouble. They were all fine as well, although embarrassed at having been caught so easily. Shaun wasn't going to be able to pull off that kind of trick again.

A knock on the door interrupted her in the middle of pulling on socks. "Are you okay with us heading back to town? I have no idea what Shaun might do if I leave him unsupervised for too long."

Amy nodded. "Of course."

The sooner they got back to town, the sooner the rest of the story would come out.

"Can I take you for breakfast, though?" Evan asked.

None of this was perfect, but she had to work with what she had. "Sure. I know just the place."

Evan paused for a beat when she handed him her car keys. "You aren't serious. I get to drive?"

"Trust me, I have enough confidence in my abilities I don't have to always be the one behind the wheel." Amy gave him directions to where she wanted to go for breakfast, then pulled out a miniature computer and started working on it as he drove.

"I thought you took time off from work," he teased gently.

"This isn't work. This is fun."

Evan shuddered. "*Fun* and *computers* are not words that go hand-in-hand."

She blinked at him before shaking her head. "Oh, you sad little man. You have no idea what you're missing."

"Frustration and carpal tunnel?"

She worked for a while as he concentrated on driving. The logging road was twisted enough he had to focus forward instead of staring at her. At the silky smooth surface of her skin. At the strong neck he wanted to wrap his hand around before slipping his fingers into her hair. Fisting tightly so she couldn't move away as he took a long, deep taste of her pouting lips.

Fuck.

He wiggled in place in an attempt to ease the pressure on his rapidly increasing arousal. The dire need to convince her to take the next steps with him grew exponentially.

They were nearly back at the highway before she put the tablet to one side and twisted in her seat to face him. "Not all wolves are the same. Not all wolves need the same thing."

"I don't need Alpha lessons," Evan muttered, pulling onto the Alaskan highway between a couple of eighteen-wheelers. Yeah, he was being cranky, but he and his cock were still not on speaking terms.

She crossed her arms over her chest and deepened her voice in an uncanny match of his. "I'll make it right. I swear I will. I swear I'll find a way to prove I'm worthy to be your mate."

Okay, that was freaky. "You have that thing that lets you repeat word for word anything you've ever heard."

"Uh-huh. Total auditory recall. Doesn't work on things I've read, but if I hear it, I can repeat it. And that's *why* I was doing the little Alpha lecture. From things you've said, it's obvious you're used to Takhini dynamics, which is fine. That's what works with them. Canyon operates differently, and if we're going to work together, you need to adjust your attitude."

"Not all wolves are the same. Gotcha. Attitude adjusted."

She shook her head, concern creasing her brow. She took a deep breath then settled with her body turned away. Evan gave himself shit. He wished he could back up a few steps and avoid the conflict. What he needed was forward motion, not poking her already sensitive edges.

Evan pulled into the parking lot of the tiny, beat-down

truck shop, wondering why on earth she'd picked such a dump to stop at.

Amy spoke softly. "Some of my pack are always around here. Please be careful how you move."

It was a test. He hadn't expected that, but in a way, the challenge seemed a good thing. It meant she was at least willing to give him a chance.

When Shaun had showed up at the cabin, Evan had thought the fragile peace growing between Amy and himself would be shattered. Seeing her exert her dominance over his Beta had been an awesome surprise. A little early in the game, maybe, but the challenge would have happened eventually. Evan had been impressed.

Now it appeared he needed to do some impressing of his own.

Evan held the door for her, waiting as she stepped past. And...he had to do another mental adjust. The inside of the tiny highway café was sparkling clean, the heavenly scent of coffee and crispy-fried bacon strong enough to overpower even the addictive aroma of his mate. "Mmm. Already my taste buds are cheering, while my arteries cringe in fear."

Amy gestured forward. "Pick us a spot."

Three steps forward he froze, one foot damn near suspended in midair. The people seated at the table nearest the door had left so rapidly one of the glasses on the table rocked unsteadily before tipping and spilling the leftover contents over their abandoned plates. Escaping from the room with their eyes averted.

Shit. He glanced at Amy who pointedly avoided his gaze.

This is a test, he reminded himself. He had instinctively headed to a place of central attention—a place where his pack mates could find him easily and take comfort in his presence.

Amy's little hints earlier made him reconsider if perhaps that wasn't the best choice. He studied the room, checking faces and examining eyes for clues.

Most of the remaining occupants were human. Toward one side of the room, though, a wolf who was about eight years old stared straight at him. Not in fear, but perhaps with a bit of awe.

"How about over there?" Evan asked, the words coming out so quiet he could barely hear himself. Hell if he wanted to freak anyone else into running away.

Amy led him across the room and slid onto the bench next to the boy. "Hi, Dex. How're things this morning?"

The kid's jaw hung open as Evan took a seat opposite them, but even as he stared he answered. "Good. Mom says I get a new book today."

"Nice." Evan snuck into the conversation. "What's it about?"

Dexter turned to whisper behind his hand to Amy, the words loud enough everyone in a five-table radius could hear. "He's with Takhini."

"He is. You should still be polite and answer him." Amy picked up the menu and pretended to study it. Her gaze met Evan's over the top of the paper, a clear warning to tread carefully.

The little guy crawled up on his knees and leaned his elbows on the table. "It's the final book in the Goligal series. Have you read it? It's really good. They're dragons, and they can fly, and they take care of their tree houses, and then there was this fire, and they got moon thieved, and..."

Evan nodded, and continued to nod as information flowed in a nonstop stream for the next five minutes.

"Dexter, I swear someday you'll wear someone's ears off telling them about your stories." The waitress turned to

Evan, her smile vanishing between one breath and the next. She backed up toward where Amy and her son sat, protective even as her fear shone out.

"Laney, it's okay." Amy laid a soothing hand on the woman's arm. "He's with me."

Laney's eyes were still panicked, and she licked her lips nervously.

Evan considered ways to ease the tension, but he couldn't make a rational decision if his life depended on it. Which was stupid, crazy and so unlike him, but for some damn reason, his brain seemed to have frozen between one beat and the next. His mouth might be hanging open, his expression blank for all he knew.

Talking. Maybe talking would be good. "Your son is very smart. He enjoys his books, and I don't mind listening."

The woman swallowed hard and nodded, but it was obvious she was very uncomfortable. "The special today... umm. The special..."

"The special would be great. And a coffee, please."

"Same for me," Amy ordered. "Cream for both the coffees as well."

The waitress nodded, then fled.

Dexter's gaze remained glued on Evan. "Do you like reading?"

"I like that you like to read."

Good enough for the kid. He went back to drawing something intricate on the pad of paper before him.

Across the table, Amy folded her hands, calmness and serenity pouring from her as she stared at him, her expression unreadable. It was a damn good thing she was calm because that was the last sensation Evan felt. He couldn't believe how fucked up he was inside.

A meet-and-greet at a café with a woman and her son,

and he was tied up in enormous knots as if he were a baby all over again. Evan wanted to slap some sense into himself if nothing else. This wasn't him. He knew how to deal with people, how to offer assurance and a steady hand to wolves. But right now he felt totally adrift and lost. Why was Laney so scared? Did the wolves who'd left at just seeing him think he was some kind of monster?

Stupid, crazy mating urge—it was messing with his emotions and his understanding, and it was as unwelcome as it was unexpected.

Amy tilted her head and caught his attention, breathing with deliberate slowness. He took the hint and concentrated on relaxing. Three breaths later he did feel better, and he reached across the table to cover her fingers with his own as a thank-you.

Amy tensed.

Dexter stiffened.

Heck, the entire café went deadly quiet, and most of them were humans, for fucks sake. There was no reason for anyone to overreact.

"Uh, sweetheart, can you up the positive vibes again?" Evan forced himself to keep looking straight at her instead of swinging to watch his back. He was not about to get into a brawl when she was simply trying to make a point—a valid one—about leadership styles.

Slowly her fingers relaxed in his. "Sorry. You surprised me."

"Understood." He swept his thumb over her knuckles. "Looks as if I have a tendency to do that. I hope you get used to it."

He maintained a grip on her fingers until the coffees arrived. Laney filled their cups as quickly as possible, dropping a bowl of creamers onto the table. But her gaze was focused on their joined hands, and this time when she left, her escape was noticeably slower because she was looking over her shoulder to keep examining the scene.

"You realize my entire pack now knows something is up." Amy slipped her fingers free to stir her coffee.

"The more alert of my pack probably have heard as well. Well, the ones who are awake. If I know Shaun, he already made some kind of grand proclamation in the pack house."

"Chicken Little running through the halls screaming the sky is falling? Or maybe warning the dragon-lady is on her way?"

Evan grinned. "Hey, that's the kind of reputation that impresses my pack." Although, as he looked around, he had to wonder…

Dexter finished colouring the picture he was working on and handed it to Amy. He pressed a kiss to her cheek before scrambling over her to get to the floor.

He twisted to face Evan. "Be nice."

"I'm always nice," Evan insisted.

The kid planted teeny fists on his hips, his expression far too serious for someone that young. "If you make her cry, I'll get even with you."

Then he darted off, escaping into the kitchen.

Evan looked into Amy's face. "You have quite the admirer there."

"He doesn't trust a lot of guys. His dad abandoned them before Dexter was born, and the guy Laney was living with until recently made it clear he thought Dex was nothing but a nuisance." Amy took a sip of coffee, staring into the café. "After she left Mike the first time, he tracked her down, stole her savings and left her with a broken arm and fingers."

Anger rumbled in Evan's gut. "What the hell?"

"They were part of the Dawson Creek pack. The Alpha

gave the bastard a lecture, and that was that. So she moved south, and when they got here, she came to me. I helped her find a job. They live upstairs from the café, and there's always at least one of the pack around to protect her in case her ex shows up again."

Evan gave in to a momentary mental fantasy that involved ripping off the bastard's arm and using the bloody stump to beat some sense into him. "Good. If they need any more help, let me know."

She tilted her head as she looked him over. "You would be good at that part—providing defense."

"Don't know why she didn't come to me in the first place," Evan grumbled.

A furrow formed between Amy's brows. "Seriously? You don't get why an abused woman wouldn't seek you out?"

Indignation set in fast. "I'm not an ass like the Dawson Alpha. No one gets away with shit like that in my pack."

"I believe you. But Takhini is loud and—" Amy shook her head. "If you can't see it, I can't explain it."

Their meals arrived, Laney still moving cautiously, but at least not throwing the food at the table and running.

Evan worked even harder this time to display his usual charming-and-completely-not-scary self. "Thanks. It looks great."

She dipped her chin briefly.

Amy brushed her hand along the other woman's arm. "My thanks as well. Will I see you later this week?"

Laney nodded, glancing at Evan before focusing on Amy. "Are you still going to make it?"

"I wouldn't miss it for the world."

The food was good, he was sitting across from his mate, but at the same time Evan wasn't quite sure what was going on. Somehow in the last while he'd lost all control. It was more than uncomfortable, it was downright frustrating.

A reluctant smile twisted Amy's expression. She leaned forward to offer a whisper. "You did okay."

The faint praise shouldn't have thrilled him as much as it did. "I feel like I should get a gold star, or something, for that."

Her lips twitched harder. "Eat. You'll need your strength for later."

"I could misinterpret that so many ways." He allowed the heat inside to escape in his tone.

Her eyes flashed for a brief second with that incredible passion he craved to indulge in, then faded to sorrow. "We'll see if you're still interested in me after talking to your Beta."

She sounded convinced he was going to toss her aside. Evan shook his head firmly. "There's nothing he can say that can change my mind," he insisted. "You're mine, Amy, and I'm not letting you go."

She looked both pleased and nervous at his comment.

The tug of war between them continued.

10

___

There weren't a lot of people awake and moving around the Takhini pack house at this time of the morning. Evan pushed the front door open for her, and Amy marched boldly through the entrance.

"Shaun and the guys should be around somewhere." Evan followed closely, his body heat a security blanket around her shoulders. "The common area is just to the right."

She wasn't sure if she should confess this, but in the interest of total disclosure, it was necessary. "Evan, I already know the layout of the place."

"Amy, Amy, Amy." He clicked his tongue. "Have you been spying on me?"

"Do I really need to answer that?"

"Spying is the least of what she's done." Shaun stood before them, arms crossed over his chest. He wore a disgusted expression as if he smelled something rotten.

"Hello again, my sparkling ray of sunshine. I've missed you so." Amy patted Shaun on the cheek.

"Yeah? Well, I'm watching you. I'm watching you *closely*."

Shaun did that little pointing thing, aiming two fingers toward his eyes then directing them toward her. "Because you are one dangerous woman."

"Shaun, back down," Evan snapped.

"She started it," Shaun protested.

"I said, back *down*."

There were a half-dozen wolves in the common area and more trickling into the room, checking her out.

Since Evan didn't seem to be interested in introducing her, Amy ignored the questioning glances. Instead she turned her focus to the quiet, dark-haired woman tucked into the corner of the room. Her hands were folded in her lap as she perched on the very edge of a couch, as if ready to spring to safety at any moment.

At her side sat an enormous shifter Amy recognized as one of the bears who had remained after conclave had concluded. She nodded politely, but spoke to the woman at his side.

She held out a hand. "Hi. I'm Amy." Maybe not using her first name would hold off a few problems for a while.

The dark-haired woman slowly accepted the greeting. "Amanda."

Mr. Shiny Suit beside her leaned to the left as he extended his hand. "Justin. You have a bit of explaining to do, young lady."

"Hold that thought," Amy requested as she lifted a finger in the air. "Amanda, you okay?"

The woman seemed surprised at the question. "Of course, I am."

Amy stood silently for a moment before speaking gently. "Yes, you are. But if you'd like someone to talk to, I'll be free later."

Amanda got very busy looking nowhere, and Amy knew

she'd guessed correctly. From the questioning glances Justin was directing her way, a lot of her work from the past year was about to come to light. That didn't mean she could ignore a person like Amanda whose body language was all but screaming for comfort. Offering help was part of who Amy was, and as necessary as breathing.

Evan stepped behind her, his hand settling on her lower back. "Let's take this to my office."

Amanda excused herself and vanished into the back of the pack house, but the rest of them ended up crowding into the small room. Justin and Shaun…

Amy hung by the door. She didn't need to be around when the truth came out. "I'll wait outside while you talk."

"You're not going anywhere." Evan caught her by the waist and pulled her to his side. Already the contact was so familiar and strangely comfortable. She was sad that the coming minutes might tear it away.

He tucked her onto the chair next to him.

Instinctively, Amy eyed how far it was to the door in case she needed to make a quick getaway.

Evan glared at Shaun. "So. I'm here. What was so damn important you felt the need to break a direct order and track me down?" he demanded of his Beta.

Shaun gestured to Justin. "He's the guy with the goods."

Justin handed printed pages to Evan. "These are from the accountant I told you about. He faxed them over this morning."

Evan shuffled through them, clearly not seeing their importance. "What am I looking at?"

The bear shifter ran a finger down the summary page. "These are the names of the properties and investments you've been building up over the past year. This column shows the total value of each."

A low whistle sounded. "Looks as if I've done all right."

Justin cleared his throat and pointed. "And this column shows how much you own of the investment."

"What do you mean *how much I own*?" Evan rearranged the pages. "These properties were purchased by myself or the pack. Why do we not own one hundred percent?"

Justin looked straight at Amy. "It appears you had a silent partner. Someone else contributed money toward your investments. It's actually exactly what you were doing in some cases, Evan, working under secondary business names instead of *Takhini* or your own. But someone else came in after the fact and repeated your trick on you. In some cases, after making a purchase, you made investments sellable through shares, and your silent partner picked up as much as was available."

"Here it comes," Shaun warned, imitating the sound of a bomb plummeting toward the earth.

Evan shook his head. "But these numbers in the final column make no sense. How can I own only forty-eight or forty-nine percent of something?"

Might as well make sure he knew exactly what he was about to hate her for. Amy laid a hand on his thigh. "It means someone else owns a majority of the investment. They have control over it."

"Bullshit. That wasn't what my accountant was supposed to do."

"It was done legally, but very under the radar. I'm not surprised your accountant missed it." Justin's expression remained fierce. "Amy's got it right. Everything listed on that paper, you or the Takhini pack has an interest in, but someone else owns more than you. They are the ones in charge. They have the right to make decisions."

Evan's rising anger was apparent to everyone in the room. "Who the hell owns the other half?"

"Half plus a little bit," Amy explained again, her voice softer than it had been. "And that would be me."

~

It was a good thing he was sitting down, because Evan didn't think his legs would hold him. He dragged a hand through his hair and fought to keep from growling.

"How? *Why?*"

Amy took a deep breath. "Do I really need to tell you why?"

Evan stopped in shock. "You planned this? You planned this all along?"

"This is why I came to Whitehorse."

"Holy crap." Evan shot to his feet and stomped across the room. Okay, this wasn't something he wanted aired in public. Not when there was so much at stake. He needed everyone to get out *now* so he could have a heart-to-heart with his mate.

He rotated slowly, working to keep his voice below a roar. "Justin. Shaun. Leave."

He could tell Shaun wanted to stay. Tough. Fucking. Beans. Evan snapped up an arm to point at the door. His Beta and the bear shifter reluctantly left, Shaun tossing a final warning glare at Amy before he closed the door.

The click echoed in the silent room like a gunshot.

She leaned back in her chair.

"You want to explain?" Evan demanded.

"I think you figured most of it out." She met his gaze without fear. "When I did my research and discovered you were the one responsible for Philip's death and everything that happened afterward, I was upset. The most logical thing seemed to be to take everything from you, like everything had been taken from me."

He'd thought being hauled to jail was bad, but this? This was an entirely new dimension of out of control, never before experienced. Evan took a deep breath. "But you were wrong. And now you've potentially not only hurt me, but my pack."

Amy shook her head immediately. "Takhini will be fine. Just because I have control doesn't mean I want to tear anything away from them."

He struggled to understand. "This was about personally taking me down."

"Yes. That's all it was ever about."

Evan dropped into the chair on the opposite side of the desk from her.

"So now what do we do? You own..." He glanced at the list of assets, resisting the urge to swear because that wouldn't make the conversation run any smoother. "You own just about everything. The hotel, the bar, the pack house. How the *hell* did you do some of this? I'm no expert, but wouldn't I have had to put things up for sale?"

She looked sheepish. "You did. You just didn't realize you had."

"Dammit, Amy."

"Like Justin said, it's the same thing you did to some of the companies in the first place," she reminded him.

"But you did it to *me*." Which was...okay he was infuriated *and* slightly embarrassed by the fact she'd out maneuvered him at his own game.

He fought for control, refusing to shout at her like he really, really wanted to. No matter how fucked up this was, giving her hell for doing it in the first place didn't change the current reality. He stared at the table and took slow breaths until he was rational enough to speak. "I understand why you started this, but now that you know more about what happened in the past, I hope you think the situation has changed. My question remains, what do we do now?"

Amy stood and walked to the window, her body tight. She remained silent for a while before turning to face him. "We join the packs, like the plan was all along."

"But my plan was for Takhini to take over Canyon. From the looks of things, you've already joined the packs, and Canyon owns my ass."

"Is that a bad thing?" Amy asked. "The only difference is you're not the one in charge. Does that make it wrong?"

"Yes," Evan snapped.

"Because *you're* the only one who can lead the joint packs? That's a rather bold presumption on your part." She glared at him, but there was a touch of pledging in her eyes. "I still say I could lead Takhini, but you can't lead Canyon. Maybe that moment in the restaurant would give you a clue as to why."

This was getting them nowhere. "Are you really demanding I challenge you on a leadership level? My mate? Because that's what it sounds like."

"It's not a challenge to point out a gap in your logic." Her words came softer. Slower. "Look, *I* made a wrong decision, and I will do what I have to and make it right. But *you* made a wrong decision about joining the packs, and I'm offering to work with you make it right."

She was attempting to be reasonable, but Evan was so far gone from reasonable, it wasn't even funny.

"I need some fresh air." He was going to explode. He jabbed a finger at her. "Stay here."

Her expression darkened. "*Ha.* I don't think so. Ordering

me around is not working together. If you need to burn off some steam, that's fine, but I'm going back to work. You know where to find me when you're in control of your emotions."

A growl burst from his throat.

It was as if there were two of him, and one half wanted to get the hell out of here and run off his frustrations. The other half didn't want Amy out of his sight, and not only because he had no idea what else she had up her sleeve. "Look, I'm trying hard not to blow my temper, because I don't want to say something I would regret."

"Trust me, I understand what you're feeling," Amy snapped back before softening, her expression growing sorrowful. "I can't change what I've done, but I will tell you this. I'm sorry. I wish I'd found more information before I started."

"Revenge is always a fucking stupid move."

She seemed to stop breathing, regret and frustration shooting from her, and that was the final straw. His wolf backhanded him for sniping after she'd apologized. Whatever happened before, they had to move forward, and blaming was certainly not going to get the job done.

Evan crushed her against him, holding her tight to his chest. She remained stiff for the first moment before slipping her arms around his torso and allowing him to offer comfort.

"We'll get through this as well," he promised. "Yes, I made assumptions. There's got to be a middle ground that we can find. Because all the wolves who live in Whitehorse deserve to have strong leadership, and the reassurance they have a pack who cares for them."

"I want that too," she whispered.

He slipped his fingers under her chin and lifted her face.

"We're both fiercely independent. Coming together is going to take some work, and we have to learn to trust each other."

She stared at him silently then nodded. "I'm willing to try. I need to trust you more first." She laughed ruefully. "But I bet you could say the same thing."

"I'm in shock, yes." Evan confessed. She was nestled against him, though, and he couldn't stop a smile from escaping. "But along with the shock, I'm damn impressed. You kicked some serious butt. I like that."

The corner of her mouth tipped upward. "You would be happier if it wasn't your butt I'd been kicking, right?"

"Yeah, but this is still exciting. Who wants to turn down a grand adventure? And damn if we aren't going to have the best pack in the entire North, with the skills we bring to the table. Whitehorse is going to rule, just like I'd always hoped."

~

For a moment Amy had almost dared to dream. Evan had been so angry, and she'd understood that, and accepted it.

And then instead of being about *them*, he got excited about their packs—joining and leading them. Not another word about him and her as mates. Learning to trust, yes, definitely. They needed that.

What about learning to love?

You nearly tore everything from him. Don't expect promises of eternal love and devotion right away.

Don't expect them ever.

Sadness rushed in to replace her anger and hate. She wanted to reject that condemning internal voice. No matter how logical the realization, facts didn't matter to her heart. She still wanted what she couldn't have.

God, she wanted her mate. In a simple, basic way with no complications and no fall out.

Evan had continued to stroke her, his strong hands trailing over her back and arms. They were both craving physical contact, but she stared into his dark eyes and fought giving in.

An entirely different observation poked her as she stood within the circle of his arms. Amy examined him closer. "You don't seem that upset anymore."

"Anger isn't worth holding on to." Evan shrugged, the move making his muscular shoulders that much more apparent. "You had your reasons for what you did, and I have mine. Also, touching you calms me like whoa."

He stroked her cheek with the back of his knuckles, and suddenly Amy couldn't breathe. A decision needed to be made, and now. Did she pull away? Or give in to the craving?

His gentle touch on her face created devastating effects. The wolf's appetite returned, hotter and hungrier than ever, and Amy turned her cheek to rub against him.

He held her firmly, one hand pressed to the center of her back. The other cupped her chin and angled her face to the side. The first contact between their mouths was gentle, but the tenderness lasted for all of five seconds before the pressure increased and he took control.

Her wolf cheered in satisfaction as Evan took her mouth with wild passion. He swiped his tongue across her lips and demanded entrance, thrusting deep. They tangled for a moment before he pulled back and put his teeth to her bottom lip. Goose bumps erupted on her arms, and a trickle of electricity shot along her spine from where his palm rested.

Her head was filled with his scent, the need to consume him growing more urgent by the second. He grasped the back of her neck, cradling her even as he tightened his grasp and held her motionless. A low rumble of satisfaction started in the back of his throat, and Amy melted against him.

She dragged her nails across his back, finishing with her fists tangled in the front of his shirt. Evan caught her butt in his hands, pulling her against his body, the rock-solid mass of him tight to her softness.

He took two steps and pressed her against the wall of his office, pinning her in place with his strong, muscular body. She was tempted to rip his shirt open so she could place her palms against his naked chest. Still he kissed her, still he took the very breath from her body until she grew lightheaded, clinging to him, her legs wrapped around his torso like some sex-starved Gumby.

Somewhere in the middle of their raging passion, she remembered what had brought her to Whitehorse in the first place, and the fire was doused with a bucket-load of unanswered questions. She stilled and retreated.

He sensed it. Between one heartbeat and the next, he dragged their lips apart, staring into her eyes as their breath rattled on like they'd sprinted a marathon uphill.

"Is this the beginning of the next step?" She looked for the confidence she'd had so abundantly not even a day ago. Careful to word her next comment in a way that made no promises she couldn't keep. "We move forward?"

"As partners. Two Alphas finding the best way to provide for our people. Maybe Takhini will rule in the end, maybe Canyon. Those are simply names. It's the people who are the heart. It's the wolves we need to provide a home." He lowered her to the ground but kept her by his side. "That's who we serve, and that's who we care about. Agreed?"

Even agreeing with him left a bitter taste in her mouth.

For the pack. The focus wasn't wrong, but it wasn't what she'd hoped for from her mate.

So be it. She twisted another protective layer around her soul. "I still need to know what happened to my brother, Evan. I need to be able to put it behind me."

He pulled her in again for a hug, stroking her hair. "I'm going to ask you to trust me a little longer. When it's time, I'll share it all, but not yet. It's too much."

When it's time. In spite of the burning ache inside, Amy squeezed him tight, savouring the last moment of physical contact before letting him go and stepping away. She tilted her chin up.

"For the pack, then. What should we take on first?" She had her plan already in place, but she'd see what his take on things was first. She didn't have to be in charge.

He paused, considered. "Do you have a leadership team?"

She wiggled her fingers. "I have an assistant. Canyon runs a little differently than a typical pack."

Evan's grin returned. "Our first step is to get all of them on board."

Oh goody gumdrops. "Shaun will be thrilled."

A burst of laughter escaped him. "You feel the need to step on him, you go right ahead."

"Gee, I don't think you're enjoying this much," Amy deadpanned.

He rubbed his hands together. "You have no idea. He might be my best friend and Beta, but Shaun's still a pain in the butt." Evan leaned over and whispered in her ear as he pulled open the door. "I'm eager to see more of what my mate can do. Malicious takeover included, you've been pretty impressive up to now."

That much at least was a positive. Amy checked him

carefully, but he didn't seem to be putting on a show for her sake. He really had gotten over his mad in an awfully short period of time.

How important was it for her to show the same kind of boldness? Especially when it came to representing Canyon's best interests. Perhaps everything else was mucked up and foggy, but her devotion to her pack would never be questioned.

Her wolf pouted. The only thing currently on the beast's mind was how much longer the silly human side was going to postpone the time until she and Evan got naked.

It was an impossible question. Amy soothed the creature with a promise of a long run. That was the best thing she had to offer.

Which sucked. Hugely.

11

———

*E*van had always considered himself an observant man. He ran his pack with what he considered firm, but fair control, and overall he was a decent guy.

Being put into the situation of having to convince his mate of this fact was a rather bizarre twist.

It had taken a little wrangling, but they'd organized the first gathering. In the end the female Beta of his pack, Gem, with her easy southern charm, had risen to the occasion and offered to host a meal.

So now there were five. Evan on one side of the table, Shaun and Gem on the other. Amy led her second-in-command to a chair at the head of the table before stepping into position next to Evan.

Shaun was doing his stormy-face thing while Gem examined Amy with a great deal of curiosity. Evan didn't even want to speculate how much mischief the two women would get up to once they got to know each other better.

His mate and her hacking talents? Gem and her ability to sweet-talk the universe into going her direction? His and Shaun's gooses were well and truly cooked.

The thought made him smile like a maniac.

Amy elbowed him, and he blinked, dragging on a more serious expression.

She turned to the table and headed into introductions. "Sarah, I'd like you to officially meet everyone. Gem and Shaun. And this is Evan. I'm sure you've seen them around town."

It was clear the elderly wolf was strong, but Sarah still stared at him as if he were a monster with two heads. The urge to make a scary face was far too tempting.

"Okay. I met everyone, now I have other things to do." Shaun began to turn away, his nose wrinkling as if he smelled something funny.

Amy leaned forward before he could leave, a gentle smile on her face and insistent pressure blaring from her wolf side. "Shaun. *Darling* Shaun. Put your ass down in your seat or the next time you're in wolf I will grab a nail gun, pin your tail to the floor, and force you to shift to human."

Tension spiked briefly, easing as Gem sat, pulling Shaun down with her. By the time everyone else was seated, Amy had turned her attention to Shaun's mate. "Gem, I understand you found some work with the Yukon government."

Gem wore an expression somewhere between exasperation and admiration as she glanced between her mate and Amy. She laid a soothing hand on Shaun's shoulder and rubbed as she answered. "Yes, I'm working through some research projects and summarizing details for the records. Suggesting future projects that will fill in the gaps and fit within the environmental guidelines for the area."

"When you're done, I would love a copy of anything you can share for the library." Amy's friend nodded cautiously at

Gem. "With all the cutbacks, I've been struggling to add resources, and up-to-date research is always scarce. I've heard amazing things regarding your work."

Gem beamed. "I'd love to help you, Sarah."

"Be careful what you promise," Shaun warned. He pointed a finger at Amy. "This one—"

"—and I think it's time to put the meat on the grill." Evan shot to his feet. The ladies were working at getting along, but his Beta needed some sense smacked into him. "Shaun, you're with me."

"The steaks are on the counter. Please don't burn them this time," Gem ordered, her glare at Shaun sharp enough to cut.

Shaun stood, sniffing indignantly. "We don't burn things, we add a healthy dose of charcoal to aid digestion."

"Well, last time my digestion was squeaky clean for days. Let's not do a repeat." Gem blew him a kiss to soften the words. "We're good here," she insisted. "Go. Go make things smoke. You know you want to."

Thank God for smart, reasonable women. Evan winked at Gem, and she smiled, pushing Shaun toward the door.

Shaun glared over his shoulder, but he followed Evan outside. Behind them, the three women continued to talk, the discussion branching into online book shopping and resource acquisitions.

Shaun stood silently as Evan cleaned the grill. Evan waited, figuring it would take about ten more seconds before his Beta let it all out.

"I can't believe you're mates with that barracuda."

"Aww, you like her." Evan slapped the first steak on the grill. "I don't know what your problem is. She's just as sneaky and twisted as you are."

The other wolf snorted. "Sure, I like her. Kind of how I

like double pneumonia and hives. She took everything, Evan. Are you going to let her get away with that?"

"It's not a matter of letting her get away with it. She did it. There's no going back and erasing it. That's why we're meeting tonight, to move toward the next stage for Whitehorse and the packs." Evan closed the top of the grill and turned his full attention on Shaun. "I know it wasn't the best of beginnings, but tell me the truth. What do you think about her?"

Shawn hesitated long enough Evan smacked him in the chest.

A slow grin snapped free. "Fine. She's got balls, I'll give her that. And I suppose if she puts that same kind of effort into building the pack, I'll refrain from trapping her in an alley some dark and stormy night and burying her in rotting compost."

Evan nodded. "That's what I figured."

"Besides, she's cute, in a sort of 'willing to tear your throat out at a moment's notice' kind of way. And she's strong—damn strong—which is sexy even while it's freaky to have someone as tiny as her pack that much of a punch."

A rush of extraordinary anger slammed into Evan at the thought anyone, even Shaun, was looking at Amy with sexual admiration. He crowded the man, backing him toward the railing of the deck. "The word sexy never again comes out of your mouth along with her name. Don't even think it, do I make myself clear?"

The words weren't that frightening, but the threat was there in his tone.

"Someone's got an issue." Shaun gave him a look. "You don't have to warn me off. I mean, I'd never cheat on Gem in the first place, but I'd never in a million years go after someone you're mated to. You need to chill the eff out."

Evan squeezed the bridge of his nose. "Sorry. That wasn't about you."

"Your balls are turning blue, I get it." Shaun shoved him away. "But no matter how much I love and respect you, I'm not offering to help with that issue."

"Fuck off."

Shaun grinned. "You know, you teased me pretty unmercifully when I was figuring out this mate thing with Gem. It's very amusing to be on the other side of the fence."

Evan glared harder. "You're going to get that fence shoved where the sun don't shine if you're not careful."

"Just saying." His Beta opened the barbecue to flip the steaks. He glanced through the window at the three women who were now gathered around the main table, putting out cutlery and making salads. "When did we get domesticated, dude? I mean, I love Gem and all, but this picture is scary weird."

"The world had to change," Evan pointed out. "As much fun as it was being single, this is our destiny."

That is, as soon as he and Amy were truly mates. They were stuck in limbo. Not only was it physically frustrating, Evan hated not being in control.

Maybe he should take charge and make it happen.

Or maybe he should back off a little more.

Or maybe he should...

Jeez, he was being pathetic again. *Maybe* he should get rip-roaring drunk and not have to make any choices. He needed to screw his head on right and make a bloody decision. This going around in circles wasn't him, dammit.

Gem joined them, slipping her arms around Shaun's waist and settling in tight. She kissed his cheek then turned her smile on Evan. "I like her."

Relief struck. "Good to know."

"There's something different about her." Gem frowned. "I'm not sure what it is, but on the other hand, she's easy to talk to, and she seems to care. Whatever she's holding back doesn't worry me, since this was our first meeting. I can work with her."

Her assurances meant a lot. "Thanks."

Gem stroked a hand down Shaun's cheek. "And you, my darling, are being a problem child. Do I need to remind you to watch your manners?"

"I will be an absolute prince from now on," Shaun promised.

Gem laughed. "I'll believe that when I see it." She turned to Evan. "I invited a few others from the pack to join us after dessert. I hope that's okay."

She was brilliant. Post-dinner they would have had enough quality time as a small group for the first day. "That should distract Shaun so he doesn't do anything stupid. Any objections he's got to my mate need to get buried and lost, and soon."

"He's feeling a little threatened," Gem offered. "I'm sure he'll get over it soon."

"Still needs to behave, or I'll sit on him," Evan warned.

Shaun glared. "Hey, I'm right here. Don't talk about me in front of my face."

"Were we talking about you?" Gem draped her arms around his neck and kissed him soundly. "Oh, and here's motivation. If you do act like an ass? I get to pick all the movies we watch for the next month."

Evan whistled softly. "Man, I'd watch your p's and q's."

"You know it." Gem smiled as she backed away, waving farewell over her shoulder. "I've been saving every weepy chick flick I could find."

Shaun crossed his arms over his chest and frowned as

Gem closed the door behind her. "A guy could get a complex around here. You'd think I was an asshole or something."

"If the boot fits..." Evan sniffed, swearing as he realized what the strange hissing sound was. "Dammit, Shaun, did you turn the heat up?"

His Beta scrambled for the tongs, but it was too late. He held a sadly shriveled jet-black steak in the air. "You like yours well done, or well done?"

Evan rolled his eyes. Some things never changed.

THE MEAL PASSED without too many troubles, the emergency "back-up" roast Gem pulled from the oven going down easily. Shaun pretty much refused to talk directly to Amy, but the rest of them found enough to discuss that didn't involve major pack decisions. Just an open, welcoming time to get their feet wet and start new relationships.

Supper was barely done when there was a knock on the door. Amy paused in the middle of helping Gem clear the table.

"Oops." The beautiful dark-skinned woman straightened, turning to lay a hand on Amy's arm. "I forgot to mention. Some of the pack said they would be dropping in. I hope you don't mind."

"Of course not. It's your home."

"I don't want you to feel...rushed, or anything."

Gem bit her lower lip, and suddenly it was Amy offering a soothing reassurance the other direction. "I'll be fine, but could you warn Sarah?"

Amy needed to touch base with Evan to see how he wanted to approach the evening. That morning when she'd entered Takhini territory, people had been curious but reserved because she'd only been visible for a short while. Plus they'd been in the pack house, where all sorts of people could be expected to drop in.

Tonight's gathering? Questions would be asked, and if she'd done her homework correctly, she needed to be ready to make a show of power because Takhini respected strength.

Her Canyon members needed quiet. They needed plenty of space and freedom, allowing them to choose to come to their Alpha. They needed guidance, but many of them were damaged in some way, skittish and ready to bolt. The right Alpha met those hungers by being a deep, calm lake where they could refresh themselves.

Takhini were more like kayakers on a violent set of rapids in the moments before the river burst over the edge of the cliff, flinging them into free fall over a wild torrent. She had to be ready to throw herself off the precipice and prove she could guide their energy, same as Evan did.

She pulled Evan to the side of the room. "What's the plan?"

He slipped his arms around her, tugging her against his body. "Plan?"

God. How was she supposed to concentrate when her senses were filled with him? The heat of his body, his scent in her head? The lingering taste of the meal vanished until all she wanted for dessert was more of him.

The kiss earlier in the day hadn't been nearly enough.

She struggled back to her question as new voices rang out from the front door. "What are we telling your pack? Do I need to make a challenge?"

"Oh, no." He shook his head, skimming his knuckles over her cheek before tucking her hair behind her ear. "This is a social night with just a few of the pack. There's no need for any formal announcements."

Unease settled in hard. Amy glanced over her shoulder in time to spot Sarah disappearing, the elderly librarian vanishing into the night before any of the newcomers could even ask her name. "This looks like more than just a few. They're going to wonder who I am."

"They'd be pretty stupid not to be able to sniff out who you are to me. But you need to go with the flow." He leaned over and snapped his teeth beside her ear, sending a shiver racing over her skin as he lowered his voice to a whisper. "Trust me, and chill for a bit. Stop worrying about the details, and enjoy yourself for once without a computer in your hand."

"Smart-ass."

This didn't seem right, not with what she'd researched. But then...she'd made her take-over plans based on having removed Evan from the picture before fighting her way in to prove she could care for Takhini. Maybe with the unexpected mating on her side, things had changed.

Evan was staring at her, one hand cupped around her hip, his thumb teasing under her shirt along the waistline of her jeans. "So?"

Amy nodded slowly. "Okay. We'll do it your way."

He pressed his lips to her cheek. "Good girl. Now come, and say hello."

Evan brought her with him to the middle of the room, dropping onto the arm of the couch and tugging her onto his lap. She leaned against him for balance, loving how his body heat wrapped around her. Hating how sitting with him felt so natural. It had only been a day. How could she change her life in a flash like this?

Her wolf sighed contentedly, answering the question in the most basic of ways.

"*Evaaaaan!*"

The shout sounded from across the room a second before they were surrounded by half a dozen oversized male wolves, all over six feet tall and all loudly demanding Evan intervene in their dispute.

"Knock it off," he ordered, and the squabbling hushed in a surprisingly short time. "Lance, you first. What happened to your truck?"

While the man answered, Lance checked her out, his head swiveling between her and Evan. The entire group took turns poking their heads around Lance to stare at her with curiosity. Evan lifted his hand to her neck, stroking her hair to the side. His touch was driving her mad, and her physical reaction to the caress had to be obvious to everyone in the room.

Damn wolf senses.

Lance's complaints stuttered to a halt. "What the fuck is up with you two?" he demanded.

Evan's tone dropped. "Is that really what you want to say?"

The man stiffened, glancing again at Amy as he cleared his throat and spoke more civilly. "I mean, hi." He held out his hand.

She accepted it. "Hi, Lance. I'm Amy."

He squeezed her fingers a touch tighter than was polite.

Amy was good. So *very* good, which meant she resisted jabbing with her free hand and blacking his eye. Any other time, faced with his attitude, she would have reacted in an instant—attacking felt like the right thing to do.

But Evan had asked her to chill. So she was chillin'. Much to both her human and wolf's dismay.

Evan grumbled, easing her to her feet as he stood and faced Lance head on. It was no relaxed man but Takhini's Alpha who moved forward and crowded the other man. "Amy, go say hi to someone else. I need to chat with Lance and the boys for a minute."

Oh hell, no—

Chillin'. She was chillin'.

Amy stifled her anger. Lance's disrespect was a big deal, like she'd expected, but Evan was playing fix-it instead of them working together to set a firm foundation. But she refused to undermine his authority in front of his pack by calling him on it.

She pulled back as ordered, retreating to the sidewall so she could observe the entire room. It seemed watching was all she had done for the past year, but now a different perspective shaped her observations.

Not even five minutes later, Evan had an arm wrapped around one of the wolves' neck, rubbing his knuckles briskly against his head. She glanced at the man's face, but there was no discomfort, only satisfaction in receiving attention from his Alpha. Loud, physically aggressive and wild attention he seemed pleased with. Lance was in the middle of the melee, a broad grin on his face. In fact, the entire room was full of dynamic, eager-for-attention wolves.

Huh.

The situation had smoothed over rapidly. She'd been wrong, she guessed, and Evan had been right. But...Amy considered what Laney would do if plopped into the room, and she shook her head. No, she might have been wrong about some things, but she *wasn't* wrong about this. Her pack members would never feel comfortable in such a free-for-all setting.

And even here there was someone out of her comfort

zone. Like a fish out of the fishbowl, the delicate bear-shifter Amanda Ainsworth sat in the middle of the room. Her knees were pressed together, back straight, hands resting in her lap as she stared forward and avoided making eye contact with anyone.

This was worth coming out of hibernation for. Amy made her way across the room, putting herself between Amanda and the noisiest of the gathering. "Mind if I join you?"

Amanda blinked in surprise then forced a smile. "Go right ahead."

Amy made sure to leave space between them on the couch. She sat silently for a moment, glancing around to see what Amanda was taking in. Pretty much what had been apparent from the corner of the room.

Moving chaos. Energy and life bubbled around them, but for the quiet woman with the damaged soul, it had to be far too much shouting and questionable humour. "If you pick one spot just to the side of you, or one person, and focus on just that, it will seem as if there are less people in the room," Amy suggested softly.

Amanda turned toward Amy. She didn't say anything for a moment. Her wolf power wasn't useful in this situation, so instead Amy deliberately matched her breathing with the bear shifter. The tension drained from the other woman's shoulders. Around them, the crowd continued to move in waves, but they were safe in their little oasis.

"Thank you," Amanda mouthed.

"It's not always possible to avoid gatherings like this, so it's good to develop some coping strategies. I can teach you, if you'd like." Amy shifted her gaze into the room, giving Amanda more space. "You seem to be doing very well, though. You are strong enough to accomplish anything you want."

A small aching sigh escaped the other woman. "I'm pretending I'm strong, but each step takes so much energy."

"It does, I agree." Amy offered her hand. "It looks as if you'll be around town for a while. Any time you want, you call me. Ask me anything. I'm pretty good to talk to."

Amanda snuck her fingers into Amy's and squeezed. "These wolves have been nothing but welcoming since I escaped my abusive husband, but they are rather..."

"Rambunctious?"

A small nod. "I enjoy the energy, but at times it's overwhelming. And I want to move forward, but it feels as if I keep getting dragged backwards."

Oh boy, Amy could understand. "Is there one thing you'd like more than anything else?"

The other woman stared into the room for a moment, her gaze landing on the large imposing bulk of Justin.

Ah. That was an unexpected twist. "You like him."

Amanda shook her head in denial, before reluctantly turning it into a single nod. "It doesn't matter if I like him or not, I'm not falling into the same trap twice."

"Is he a trap?"

"He's a dominant male bear. He's demanding, and dangerous, and always looks as if he's ready to whip out a weapon or his checkbook to make his point." Amanda paused. "I don't need someone with that much power. A powerful man had me in his grasp, and it nearly killed me. The next person I let in will be someone who wants me for myself."

A rush of pain struck. Deep inside, Amy realized, that's what she wanted as well—for Evan to want her for herself. That's what they *all* wanted.

Fortunately for Amanda, her dilemma might be more easily solved than Amy's convoluted situation. "I think Justin's outside might not be showing you the real inner man," she hinted.

"Perhaps." Amanda brushed Amy's arm lightly in thanks then slipped from the gathering down one of the quiet hallways.

Evan was working the room. Patting people on the back. Hugging some, joking with others. The volume continued to rise, and someone turned on music. The dining room table was picked up and moved to the side and dancing spontaneously broke out.

Amy sat quietly for another few minutes as she debated. This was her life. All her planning and preparation had been taken out of her hands, and this was what was left. Revenge had been torn away. There was no agreement between her and her mate how to proceed.

She still wanted him with a craving that neared obsession.

Ever since she'd removed herself from her final foster home, she'd been in charge of her own destiny. Maybe she couldn't change some of what she'd been handed in the past twenty-four hours, but she would damn well take what she needed.

She was pissed off at how her life was proceeding? Fine. Angry sex was better than no sex.

She tracked her mate to the corner of the living room, standing to one side until he noticed her. The delay gave her time to ogle his strong body with an increasing determination to enjoy what she'd denied herself. His muscular arms flexed against his short sleeves, biceps and shoulders a mass of curves she longed to grab hold of and explore. That firm jaw she wanted to bite, the layer of scruff she wanted him to rub against her sensitive bits.

The wolves he was speaking to fell away as he moved toward her.

"You forgot to say goodbye." Amy accepted the hand he held out. "I was waiting until you were done."

He pulled her against his body and swayed to the music. "Are you freaking kidding me? They understand. You came looking for me, and the expression on your face says something other than you want to kill me or kick me. No way am I letting this opportunity slip by."

Amy allowed a laugh to escape. "I'm not confrontational all the time. Really."

He pressed his cheek against hers, fire flaring between them. "I'm not complaining. I've decided I like you the way you are."

Her frustrations unfurled a bit at the hint of praise.

Amy slipped her fingers into the hair at the back of his neck and stroked as she spoke. "You're good with your pack," she admitted.

"Stop analyzing for a bloody moment and dance with me, woman."

All around them, people continued to talk and drink and eat. Some joined the dancing while laughter rose from the corner of the room where someone had started a board game. The entire house rocked with energy, but Amy's world reduced to the man who was holding her. He pressed one hand possessively against her back, using his firm grasp to direct her where he wanted. And where he wanted her was locked tight to his torso, no distance between them. Only rising heat and need.

Her wolf had been sulking, but roused to agree that taking her mate for a test drive wasn't a bad idea. Amy wasn't nearly as upset at the beast's suggestion as she should have been.

Evan put his lips by her ear and spoke in a whisper, probably in an attempt to keep the other sharp-eared wolves from overhearing. "Come home with me. Let me make you feel good."

Lust was temporarily smacked down by another shot of guilt. "Umm, about your place. We need to talk."

He chuckled. "Don't worry, I noticed my apartment was on the list of things you appropriated."

"You can ignore the eviction notice when it arrives, okay? I mailed it two days ago."

His chuckle broke into full-out laughter, and he twirled her. Brought her feet back to the ground carefully then cupped her face in his hands. "You are the most perfect woman in the world."

Then he kissed her. Wrong place, wrong time for a gesture that might have appeared a claiming, but she was far too into what they were doing to complain.

To hell with it. All she was worried about right now was enjoying the way he tasted. The way his tongue tangled with hers, and the intense pleasure streaking through her entire body.

Some smart-ass wolf whistled, and Evan finally let her go, breathing heavily as he flashed the bird at his pack member. He grabbed Amy by the hand and dragged her toward the door.

Raging desire fought with the urge to do at least a few things to smooth her future with the pack. "We shouldn't vanish. We need to say goodbye, and say thank you to Gem, and all of that," Amy chastised him.

"You're right," he agreed without slowing one notch. He shoved her coat at her, jammed his arms into his leather jacket. He barely waited until she'd pulled on her coat before picking her up.

"Evan!"

He jerked the door open, shouting over his shoulder into the room. "Thanks for dinner, Gem. Goodbye, everyone. Don't do anything that gets you arrested, because I'm not bailing anyone out."

They were beside her car before she could protest again. She went for one desperate shot at regaining control. "My place."

His response was to grin like a maniac. "No problem."

Oh boy. Amy focused hard on not getting any speeding tickets on the way. The little internal argument with her conscience about keeping things platonic until she'd been told the full truth was over. Evan met her outside the driver door, scooping her up in his arms again and damn near sprinting to the front of her house.

If she hadn't been as eager as him, she would have laughed.

It was time. Her head and heart might regret this in the morning, but her body was currently the one in control. Damn the consequences, full speed ahead.

12

He needed to get his head back in the game, but with the scent of his mate filling his head, Evan teetered on the edge of losing the final link to his humanity.

He should be more concerned about how they were going to balance their differences, but he simply couldn't muster a single damn fuck.

She unlocked her door, and he pounced, every last iota of patience vanishing. Maybe she had other plans, but his were pretty direct and to the point. "Excuse me while I shred your clothes."

He kicked the door shut behind them before crowding closer. He picked her up and planted their lips together the way they belonged.

Amy wrapped herself around him like she had earlier in his office, fingers driving into his hair to keep their mouths connected. Her taste was mesmerizing, and he could've stayed there all night licking and tasting, and tasting some more. Nibbling on her lower lip as the air from their lungs mingled.

His shirt was already open as she worked to strip it away. She clung with her inner thighs to his hips while she jerked the fabric free, tugging upward to bare his skin. He leaned back, balancing her against his body so he could return the favour and yank her shirt off in one motion.

Their bodies made heavenly contact. He went back for another round of kisses, stumbling forward blindly. Amy moaned, and the noise went straight to his balls. His knees trembled, and the next thing he knew she was smack up against the wall.

Twice in one day. He could get used to this position. Oh. Hell. Yeah.

She pulled his hair hard enough to free their lips from each other, drawing in a deep breath. "Touch me. Touch me everywhere." She tilted his head until their eyes made contact. "Just don't mark me. Promise."

"Biting is okay though, right?" He snapped his teeth, and her pupils dilated further. "And nails. Please, dear God, tell me you like to use your nails."

She shivered and touched their foreheads together. "This thing tonight between us? It isn't a forever commitment, but I want you. So, yes, do your worst."

"You mean do my best." He twirled them, finally having identified where the couch was. The curtains hung wide open, and the sky was clear enough that moonlight slipped in. He dropped her and had the button on her pants undone, unzipped and stripped away before she stopped bouncing.

He snapped the fabric at both sides of her thong and tossed it over his shoulder. He picked her up and returned to the wall, only this time, he lifted her higher. Nudging his teeth against her breast.

Amy caught his head for balance. "I don't need a lot of foreplay."

"It's not foreplay, it's a conversation. And I like to talk in detail." Evan hummed happily as he examined one pretty breast then the other. "Oh look! Just what I ordered."

He licked in slow circles, sneaking in on the tip until he could no longer resist closing his lips and sucking. Amy squirmed, attempting to get more of her breast into his mouth. He was content to torment her, alternating sides until she was swearing at him, thighs squeezing his ribs so hard they creaked.

"I can scent how turned on you are," Evan gloated.

She groaned in frustration. "I think we've established that fact. Hurry up and fuck me."

Evan shook his head, pushing one hand down her body so he could slip his fingers between her folds. "I've waited a long time for this. No one gets to take away my toys."

He played her, stroking his fingers over sensitive spots. Every time he hit the right speed and tempo, Amy rewarded him with a gasp or moan. He had two fingers buried deep, his thumb working her clit when she stiffened, a long, low keen of delight echoing off the walls.

They weren't yet fully mates, but the absolute satisfaction of getting her off blew him away. He always made sure his partners had a good time, but this was different. He not only wanted her to feel great, he wanted her to know it was *him* who had taken her there. That no one else could possibly want as much for her.

He put her feet on the ground, bracing her against the wall as he fell to his knees. "Again. A little louder this time. I don't think the neighbours heard you yet."

She attempted to collapse to the floor with him, but he held her vertical, one hand braced over her stomach as he put his lips to her sex. Her full taste hit him, and for a moment he froze, absolutely rocked with delight.

Amy trembled. "If you stop right now, I swear I will duct tape you to the center of the street then organize a stampede of wild caribou."

"Hush. I'm savouring my dessert."

Her shaking turned to laughter. "Damn you, Evan. I need you inside me."

He nipped at her inner thigh, rumbling happily when she let out a little shriek. "Once I get in, I'm not leaving for a while," he warned.

He leaned forward, scraping his teeth over the sensitive spot at the apex of her mound. She buried her hands in his hair and stopped fighting to get away.

Evan lifted one of her legs over his shoulder to get more room to work, then slid back in to enjoy himself. Using long slow licks followed by deep plunges, he tormented her until her fingers tightened in his hair, pulling the roots as she shook and came.

Hmmm. His cock might be rock hard, but he was already satisfied at making his mate happy.

He scooped her up and headed down the hallway. "Where's your bedroom?"

"At the end of the hall, on the left. I can walk, you know."

Evan clicked his tongue. "Damn, I didn't do a good enough job then." He pushed the door open with his shoulder. "Oh, now that is nice."

He lowered her to the king-sized bed, staring into her eyes as he crawled over her, once again taking her lips. He was in the middle of a long, slow kiss when his hand touched something hard. He adjusted his fingers, and a click sounded.

Music burst out from nowhere.

Amy's lips curved into a smile against his. "So that's where I left the remote."

Evan tossed the small object aside. "Now we have the perfect ambience."

He supposed it was perfect. Classical music swelled around them as some guy with a deep voice bellowed in a foreign language. Evan was more interested in licking every inch of Amy's perfect naked body. He put his teeth together over the curve of her neck, lightly enough not to be a mate mark, but with perfect pressure. She just about levitated off the bed.

She curled upright, swooping in on his belt and jeans. "Naked. Now," she ordered.

"Eager." Evan evaded her grasp and slid to his feet, debating if he wanted to get naked as fast as possible, or continue to push her delectable buttons.

"Desperate." She scooted forward on her hands and knees, bouncing as she stared. "Hurry up, or I'll tie you to the bed first next time."

"That's kinky." He leaned on the bed and got his face right in front of hers. "Ropes can be added at some point, but I think you'll be the one wearing them."

"Too much talking, not enough fucking," Amy complained.

"Savouring, remember?" Evan dropped his clothes to the floor. It took two seconds flat.

His mate swallowed hard, settling back on her heels. Her gaze dropped to take him in, and her look of appreciation made him rumble.

This moment had been a long time coming, and it had been totally worth the wait.

~

AMY LET out a contented sigh as six-foot-something of muscular shifter stood before her in all his naked glory. He was sculpted and cut in all the right places. She'd finally gotten a good look at his tattoo, the words *Whitehorse Forever* waving on a banner that wrapped the rock-hard biceps. From his shoulders to his toes, she didn't have any complaints.

She wasn't even focusing on any sexual bits, but if she did...

"Whoa." Okay, the sexual bits were as fine as the rest of him. Although *bits* was too...small...a word for what she was looking at.

Evan laughed, and his abdomen and other parts of his anatomy moved in the most interesting ways. "You're drooling."

"You're gorgeous, and you know it. Now get your ass over here and stop making me wait."

He prowled closer, the predator clear in every step. "You're damned demanding."

"What did you expect when you put two Alphas in bed?" Amy stared up at him as he stopped at the foot of the bed, close enough she could drag her nails across his ass cheeks.

"Hell, yeah. Do that some more." Evan's head fell back as she leaned in and pressed her lips to his skin. He moaned as she kissed her way past his belly button, headed for her target.

She swiped her tongue across the head of his cock, enjoying the constant rumble of pleasure rising from his chest. She moved slowly, running her tongue along the underside of the heavy shaft. Licking and getting him wet. Taking in his taste, which was oh-so-right, and far too addictive.

Only when she went to wrap her fingers around him, he

broke free, grabbed her under the arms and collapsed onto the mattress with her on top of him.

The music station changed, this time to old-fashioned bluegrass. Evan dug under his back. "This thing is going to haunt me, I can tell."

"I'll teach you how to use it tomorrow. Just don't push—"

The dim lighting was shattered by neon glaring along the ceiling. Brilliant red and blue strobes alternated with green and yellow, turning the room into a bad disco setting.

Evan sat up, his jaw falling open as he looked around. He kept a tight grip on her though, refusing to let her go even as he laughed. "Do I want to know?"

Her cheeks were red hot. "It's a long story. Just give me the control."

Evan held the small object in his hand, lifting it away from her so she couldn't make any adjustments. "What happens if I push this button?"

"I wouldn't do that if I were you."

The bed started shaking under them. Evan collapsed back, clutching his stomach as he laughed. Amy joined him, because there was nothing else she could do.

Fiddles blared in the background, out of sync with the flashing lights. The bed switched from a constant shake to a slow undulating motion like the ocean.

"It's like being on the set of a bad porno," Evan gasped.

Amy crawled up his body and peeled the remote control out of his hand, pressing the stop button before collapsing onto his chest.

"Don't say another word," she warned.

Evan slapped a hand over his mouth, but his eyes sparkled.

Amy leaned down and bit his chest, hard. "One of the

pack wanted to experiment with decorating. It wasn't my idea, but I haven't gotten around to changing it back."

His hands settled on her hips. "Don't go changing anything on my account."

He shifted her higher, and suddenly all their important bits and pieces were lined up just right. He moved her again, rubbing her clit over his rigid cock. Laughter faded, but there was something a lot gentler between them now than even ten minutes earlier.

Amy reminded herself that great sex was fun and satisfying, and a good partner made a difference. She couldn't dare wish for more, or she'd break.

Evan sat up, rearranging her so they stayed in contact, but he could touch her. Smoothing his hands up to her breasts and teasing with his fingertips until her nipples were tight and aching. He slipped his tongue along her ear, and put his teeth to the lobe and bit.

Laughter had changed the moment from a mere physical act to a connection between two people who maybe could learn to like each other as well as lust after each other.

"Give me your lips," Evan whispered.

She set her mouth to his, rubbing back and forth. Sneaking out the tip of her tongue to trace the outline of his upper lip. He sucked her tongue into his mouth, pulsing in a way that made her heartbeat shoot skyward again.

She couldn't wait any longer. Amy rose to her knees and reached between them, pressing the rock-solid head of his cock between her folds.

She looked into his face as she slipped downward. So full, so good. He helped her, hands tight to her hips, fingers splayed over her ass cheeks.

All the while his eyes never left hers. They were connected, his body deep inside hers, but it was the expression on his face and the tender look in his eyes Amy didn't know how to deal with.

"If you don't move in about two seconds, I'm going to lose it," Evan warned, the words shaking as he spoke.

Moving wasn't a problem. Amy lifted just far enough to tease before sinking, pressing him as deep as possible. Evan's head fell back as she enjoyed the decadent sensation.

Suddenly slow wasn't enough, and simply speeding up wasn't going to cut it either. Amy pressed her hands on his shoulders, attempting to turn up the pressure even as she luxuriated in the wonderful pleasures enveloping her body.

Evan curled an arm around her back, bringing their torsos in line so that on every move they brushed. His lips pressed against her neck, sucking and biting, and the tension inside rose again in spite of her earlier orgasms.

He rolled them, dropping her to the mattress. He hooked his arms under her thighs and opened her wide. Then he leaned over and rocketed forward. Thrusting deep and hard. Demanding, and controlling.

Amy reached over her head, fingers clutching the quilt as she attempted to keep his name from bursting from her lips. She found herself holding the hard plastic of the remote, and as she tossed it aside she bumped the control button.

The music started again, a heavy drumbeat shaking the walls. Evan matched the music's tempo, as if following a ritual dance. He slipped a hand between them and rubbed in exactly the right spot, and Amy lost it. She screamed, the sound turning into another of the musical accents, and Evan shook. He buried himself deep, hips jerking as his release exploded from him.

The entire time he never stopped watching. Never took his eyes off her. It was too much, and as she shook under him, Amy closed her eyes to focus only on the pleasure flowing through her veins.

He wrapped her arms around his back and rolled her on top. She couldn't resist licking his neck, tasting the salt lingering on his skin and the passion of his wild wolf.

They lay in a heated tangle for the longest time. Evan stroking her cheek, Amy drawing circles on his chest with her nails. Somewhere in the silence they were connected, and neither of them seemed ready to break the tenuous bond.

It wasn't forever, but it had been pretty spectacular just the same.

13

Around three a.m. Amy woke, her heart pounding madly. The room was pitch black, silence surrounding her.

The warm body at her side was unexpected, but perfect. Evan had refused to give her any space in the enormous bed, and even now was plastered against her back. He had one arm curled around her stomach, his hand casually pressed against her breast. Between the two of them the temperature was hotter than a volcano, and they'd tossed the quilts to the foot of the bed sometime in the last couple hours.

She stared into the darkness and tried to rearrange her plans. She wasn't about to complain regarding the sex—she was no idiot—but how did this all fit in to her familiar reality?

People left. Whether they died or disappeared, it made no difference. The end result was the same, and there was no way she wanted to have to rebuild her life again. Once was enough.

His first focus might be her saving grace. Keeping their

focus on the packs was the only way she could survive. Pack would never abandon her, because she would never abandon them. Concern for their well-being was always there. Her first thought, and her last, every single day.

Evan's nose rubbed the side of her neck, and she fought the urge to roll to face him. He was dangerous, far more now than she had ever expected.

Still, she couldn't resist laying her hand over his, gently stroking his fingers and up his forearm as he breathed at a steady pace behind her.

He seemed mighty content. The two sides of her psyche battled—between the part that was pleased she had such a profound effect on him, and the lingering part that, while fading, still wanted to kick out his knees.

She might have lain there for an hour thinking before his breathing sped up. Otherwise he didn't move, but his heart rate increased, and small twitches shivered his skin. Another low rumble started in his chest, but not like when they'd been playing, or when he was sexually aroused. This seemed more frantic. As if an edge of fear had crept over him.

This time she did roll, examining his face. His eyes were closed, but his eyelids moved rapidly.

He was having a bad dream. Something horrible enough to cause him to shake, and his arms to tighten around her. Still gentle enough he wasn't hurting her, but Amy placed a warning hand against his chest.

Beneath her palm his heart fluttered wildly.

And then as quickly as it had begun, everything went back to normal. Except he moved them slightly, tangling his legs between hers and pinning her to the mattress. His groin tight to her hip, an arm across her chest and his face buried in her neck.

So much for sneaking out of bed.

Amy matched her breathing to his. She cautiously stroked his hair off his face. There was just enough light for her wolf-enhanced eyes to admire his strong jawline and his long lashes where they rested against his cheeks.

It seemed nearly impossible to hold back her longing for their mating to be real. Forever. The only thing she knew for sure was to enjoy the sexual side and guard her heart as much she could.

Even while falling asleep, she sensed her wolf's confusion at her decision.

Morning light brought no new changes. Other than Evan had finally rolled away, giving her enough room to sneak off the bed and into the bathroom. It was only five thirty, but she rarely needed that much sleep. She washed and dressed.

The entire time Evan slept, sprawled across her mattress. One arm flung over his eyes in a position of absolute relaxation and trust.

She left the television and computer off for once, grabbing a quick bite before leaving a note on the counter for him along with her spare key.

She hoped he didn't read anything too big into that gesture.

Stopping in the park was as natural as breathing, but she wasn't sure if today's pause was for her sake, or for the others. And when Matthias turned up again, Amy soaked in his comfort. Preparing her old friend for the coming storm.

"I found my mate," she announced, testing the words.

They felt strange.

Matthias sat with his haunches on the grass, his head resting peacefully on her thigh.

"We're still dealing with a few things. It's not as simple as

I hoped. But trust me, I'll take care of your pack, no matter what."

The old Alpha butted his head against her hand.

"You're right. My pack." She nodded. "Remember I told you I planned to join Canyon and Takhini? It's going to start soon. Not sure how—all my plans are kind of up in the air, but it'll work out," she promised.

And somewhere in that promise to him, she found hope. She could do this. No matter how much effort it took, she would make a way for her people to stay safe and have a home.

Matthias put his paws on the bench on either side of her legs, lifting his grey head until their eyes were level. He tilted his chin to one side, examining her for the longest time before nodding.

She waited until he'd returned to the trees before she left the bench.

Things were pretty chaotic at the shop considering she'd only been gone for a day. She didn't blame her staff for panicking when Evan had surprised them, but there was no reason they shouldn't have been able to pull it together and stock the shelves like they usually did on Sundays.

Amy spent two hours on the floor before the shop doors opened, stocking shelves and cleaning up. The work soothed her. Simple enough she didn't need to make any decisions, but detailed enough she had to concentrate.

"Sam? What are you doing here?" Tom stepped from behind the counter. "It's okay. I can take over," he offered.

She planted her fists on her hips. "Did you get anything done yesterday?" she demanded.

His sheepish expression answered her.

"Oh, Tom." She shook her head. "It's okay to get scared

and react, but once you've had a chance to think, you need to make the right decision."

"Are you closing the shop?" Worry creased his face.

What? "Of course not. Why would you ask that?"

He shrugged. "I don't think the Takhini Alpha likes computers very much."

"What would that have to do with Bytes Unlimited?" Amy narrowed her eyes as she examined her pack member. Oh dear, she knew what was up. She didn't even wait for his response. "No. I am not closing the shop, and it doesn't matter whether or not Evan likes computers. Trust me, everything is going to be fine."

The tension drained from his shoulders. "It was just with you taking off, and then you and Sarah heading over to…" He smiled, hesitantly, but with growing confidence. "I was just being silly."

"It's okay, I get it. But, really, Canyon is fine. And even though there are changes coming, I promise I'll take care of you."

The other half of her Tweedledee and Tweedledum popped out from behind the counter, Braden's smile shining like a beacon. "That's good enough for me."

Amy remained patient. "So. Is there a reason why you didn't get the stock put out yesterday? Decided to take Sunday off instead of your usual Tuesday Wednesday?"

The two guys eyed each other before Tom spoke for them both. "Well, there was this *bear*. He didn't do anything, but he sniffed around the entire store. When he left, I kind of might have locked the door and forgotten to open it again."

"And what with us hiding in the back," Braden confessed, "we got a little behind on our duties."

Amy laughed, letting her amusement wash over them

and soothe them. "I'm not mad at you, but I need to get some work done and I want you to promise you'll get your work done today as well. Deal?"

They assured her loudly everything was better than fine, and Amy headed upstairs to dive into her regular morning routine.

Only everything was different. She'd been gone for a day and a half, but she couldn't get comfortable behind her desk. It was as if her skin was one size too tight. And opening the computer just reminded her of her plans and all the changes that had to be made in the next weeks to join the past into some sort of cohesive future.

By the time she gave up and slipped back to the shop, there was one final box to be put away. She sent the guys for coffee and got to work, her back to the door as she bent over and lined up the small components where they belonged.

A pair of strong hands slipped over her hips, and she jerked upright, smacking the back of her head into the shelf above her. The metal pulled away from the supports and tilted toward the floor, packages and boxes falling around them like techno rain.

"Do you mind not sneaking up on me?" Amy took a deep breath to continue to scold Evan, when she realized it wasn't his scent. It wasn't his touch on her body.

She twirled, looking up into Colin's bright green eyes.

Oh, shit.

She opened her mouth to warn him off, but it was too late. He'd already curled himself around her, his lips warm and passionate over hers. She didn't want to freak out and blast him, but *holy moly,* this was not what she wanted.

Complications? With a capital C.

It took a moment's effort, but she got her hands on his chest and gently pushed him off.

His expression was one of complete confusion. "Did I read your signs wrong the other day? Because I don't usually go around kissing women who have no interest in kissing me back."

Where to start? "It's not you—"

"—but it's me?" Colin chuckled, dropping his hands to her hips. "Come on, now, you can do better than that."

Amy caught his wrists and pulled them away. "That's not what I was going to say. No, you didn't read me wrong, but things have changed."

"In two days? That seems odd." He inched back, his smile tugging the corners of his mouth upward. "Oh. You've been with someone else. I guess I shouldn't have been so patient."

Amy hesitated. She didn't want to blurt out what had happened, but there wasn't much else that was logical. She wouldn't have made a date with Colin for Monday, then taken another lover. She was trapped with the truth. "I might have run into my mate."

Colin's eyes widened. He looked around the shop, before leaning forward and taking a long slow sniff. He shook his head. "Still not buying it. You met your mate and yet you're here, working, at ten a.m. the day after it happens? What's wrong?"

"Nothing's wrong."

He shook his blond head in denial, and dammit all if he didn't inch forward again. "If I had discovered you were my mate, there is no way you'd be back at work as if nothing had happened the day after we met. So don't try that one on me. If you aren't interested anymore, that's more than fine." He moved in even closer and lowered his voice. "But if something is wrong, I'm here for you."

Oh, *brother*. Just what she needed. "Honest, I'm not

looking for protection. There are some things I'm working through, but it'll be fine."

"That's not a denial," he informed her. "*Things I'm working through* and *I met my mate* are not phrases that are supposed to be put in the same conversation."

Amy checked her watch. It was nowhere near the drinking hour. "Drop it, Colin," she warned.

He crossed his arms over his chest.

Amy tossed him a single bone. "Fine. If there's anything I need you to do, I promise I will let you know. But in the meantime, I apologize. I forgot to call and cancel our date."

A dangerous rumble sounded from the front of the store. Amy and Colin both twirled.

"Oh, shit." Colin put himself between Amy and Evan, who was wearing his angry face. "Is *this* what you're working through?"

"Get away from my mate," Evan snarled. He stomped closer.

Amy grabbed Colin's jacket, jerking him toward the back of the shop as she slipped around him to form a barrier between the two men.

"She's the one who makes that decision," Colin asserted firmly. "Sam, you can step aside." There was terror in his voice even as he insisted on standing up for her. Cute, and yet as close to a suicide note as he could write.

"Testosterone is making this entire place stink," Amy muttered. She raised a hand toward Evan. "Stop right there. Colin was just leaving."

Evan's eyes were wolf wild, and his body trembled as he tensed for attack.

"Are you sure—?" Colin began again.

This time Amy snapped. "Get your ass outside, or I'll let him eat you."

Colin darted along the farthest aisle and headed for the door. Evan turned on the spot as the other wolf ran, a roar of possession echoing off the walls of the shop.

Amy closed the distance between the two of them and swatted him on the arm. "Don't you *ever* do that again."

Only when he turned to face her, she wasn't talking to the human. Evan's wolf was at the foreground, and there was nothing she could do to pull him back until he was ready.

Evan caught her against him, lifting her feet off the ground as he clutched her tight. He took her lips with a ferocious kiss, one of ownership, and damn if Amy didn't like it.

And hate it at the same time.

She gripped the back of Evan's head and attempted to jerk him away, but all he did in response was bite her lower lip. The resulting flash of desire pissed her off as much as it heated her blood.

She was furious with him, and she'd never wanted to fuck anyone so badly in her life.

FROM DEEP IN the haze of his madness, Evan struggled to focus on the here and now. Finding some other wolf hanging off his mate was the last thing he'd expected when he walked through the door.

It was bad enough to wake in an empty bed and discover a note telling him nothing more than she'd see him later.

Things to decide or not, no one was touching Amy.

And now with her taste roaring through his system, he knew he needed to calm down, but damn if he wanted to. Pain exploded along his spine as she fisted handfuls of his hair and pulled violently. Of course, with the way he was feeling, that was just a lovely bit of foreplay.

She did manage to break the seal between their lips. "Damn you, Evan, there was nothing going on, and now you've freaked out one of my pack."

"He *kissed* you."

That was all the explanation he needed, which was good, since it was the absolute limit of comprehendible words he could manage.

Fortunately, she was as wild as he was, using her firm grip to jerk his head to the side. "You will not scare any more of my pack. Do you understand?"

"No kissing," he demanded.

Amy licked him. Started at his neck and went all the way up to his temple, before she put her lips by his ear. "You're such a *jerk*."

He had been considering putting her back on the floor, but after that? "Someone is looking for trouble. Like getting tied up. Or a spanking."

"You wouldn't dare." Amy had him by the ears, her gaze boring into his. They stayed still for one hesitant moment as a world of possibilities swirled around them. Something flashed in the depths of her eyes, dark and hungry.

"Lock the front door," she whispered.

Halle—*fucking*—lujah. Evan held on with one hand as he sprinted for the front of the shop, miraculously avoiding taking out any of the displays. She clung to him while he turned the deadbolt and damn near ripped off the cord controlling the blinds covering the glass door.

The next second his shirt was shred from his shoulders. Amy put her mouth to his neck, biting hard as nails scraped down his arms. Evan's cock went from zero to five hundred between one breath and the next.

She wasn't marking him or accepting him as a mate, but *fuck*, he liked that touch of pain from her, especially when he was at a feverish pitch to begin with. "Use your teeth again."

Amy caught him by the chin and kissed him madly, all teeth and delicious fire. He tore her shirt open, pushing her against the wall with his hips so he could get his hands on her perfect breasts. Massaging and playing, teasing her nipples to tight points so he could lick them again and again with his tongue.

By the time she was whimpering, they were both shaking violently. Tucked in the corner of the computer shop, broad daylight streaming in the front display window only two feet to the side.

Evan brought her feet to the floor, ripped her pants and underwear away and put his mouth over her sex. It was only a matter of seconds before she started swearing. Loudly. And creatively, especially when he slipped two fingers between her folds and plunged them into her while he worked her clit with his tongue.

"Oh, yes, right there. Right there. Right *there...*"

She screamed. Evan moved before she was done shaking. Pulled out his cock, twirled her and plunged in deep. He was bent over her, one arm wrapped around her waist, the other braced on the door as he pumped wildly. Her feet hung off the floor, legs swaying every time he buried his cock as deep as possible. The overwhelming sensation of being surrounded breaking him.

His orgasm surprised him, not only with its power but with how long it lasted. Every time he thought he was done, she squeezed, and he would jerk again, another layer of ecstasy breaking free.

By the time they had stopped tormenting each other, he

could barely stand. Amy had both hands clutched around the door handle. Evan had to lean on the wall as he helped her back to vertical. Bodies curled together, he reluctantly pulled his cock free.

He slid down the wall, drawing her into his lap and brushing her hair off her face. She wore a bemused smile, and he figured his expression must be pretty much the same.

"You will not freak out any more of my pack," she mumbled as she tugged on the remains of his shirt.

He kissed her cheek, working to catch his breath so he could respond. "I will not freak out any more of your pack, except if—"

"There are no exceptions, Evan," Amy challenged him.

He cupped her face, twisting her so he could nibble on her lips and press kisses to her cheeks. "I don't want to see that blond close to you again. Not for a while. I know it's stupid, and I'm sure there's a logical explanation, but my wolf wants him for a rug."

She sighed, looked as if she was going to say something, then changed her mind. And when she rested her cheek against his chest and relaxed, Evan took that as a yes.

14

———

Evan straightened himself up before following Amy into her office. His mate pulled extra clothing from the cupboard, tossing him a T-shirt.

He sniffed it.

"It's new. I occasionally get wolves in here who need clothes, so I keep some on hand." She straightened her own clothing then settled into one of the easy chairs. "Let's talk about dealing with the packs."

He pulled his chair close enough he could lay a hand on her thigh. The need to touch wasn't fading.

She stared at his fingers, a faint smile on her lips. "I did a lot of planning, and if we're careful, things shouldn't get too messed up. I have to warn my pack before I bring you around, so give me a couple days for that. But with the way Takhini operates, I should join you as soon as possible."

It was a great idea, but...

Something felt off. Dangerous.

What if Takhini rejected her? Or hurt her. Images of the Hudson Bay disaster flashed to mind, not just the fire and the explosion, but the screams. The crying.

No way was he letting her get into a situation where she could be hurt. He'd step on the hotheads before they could get out of line, which meant putting the fear into them before Amy starting hanging around.

Evan shook his head. "No. Let's tell them on our own. Sort of a heads up before the merge officially begins. You talk to Canyon, I'll deal with Takhini."

Her nose wrinkled. "You think that's the best way?"

"Straight-up shocking my crew isn't a good idea either. Last night worked great—no one was upset or worried with you there. It's a good start." Yeah, this was a plan. Evan patted her leg. "There we go. We both spend the day working. We can get together for supper, touch base on how things are going, and make plans for the next stage as the packs fall into line."

Amy hesitated. "I thought Takhini would need a bigger show of power."

"No." Evan insisted. He was *not* going to let that be needed. She'd done fine dealing with Shaun, but the entire pack?

Hell, no. Protective instinct demanded he not put her in danger.

"But—"

"*No*," he snapped. "Drop it."

She eyed him for a long time before rising to her feet and heading to the chair behind her desk.

Evan looked at the obstacle she'd placed between them. He watched as she turned on her computer and without another word went back to work.

Okaaay.

Evan moved his chair beside her. She seemed to have pulled on a mask. This was not the hot-blooded, enthusiastic woman he'd just fucked in the front shop.

"What's wrong?"

Amy blinked. "Nothing's wrong."

Silence returned.

Evan leaned back and watched her. The next fifteen minutes she kept her eyes glued to the computer screen. Every now and then her lips twitched, and she seemed to hit the keys a little harder than was necessary.

Something *had* gone wrong, but he was no super sleuth. Unless she gave him a clue, he wasn't going to be able to solve this mystery.

Finally she gave up her façade of being deathly interested in whatever she was working on, and faced him. "Can I help you with something?"

"Yes, you can talk to me."

Her exasperated sigh escaped in a gust. "I thought you wanted to talk to the packs on our own."

"I do. But I want to..." He wasn't sure what he wanted.

Amy shrugged, her gaze not meeting his. "Okay, I'm just sending off notes to my pack so I can visit them. It's going to take me a couple days, so I guess I'll see after that. Unless you want me to come with you...?"

"No. *No.*"

She sighed softly. "Then I think I need some space, Evan. To finish getting ready to mesh the packs. And to adjust."

"I have things to do as well," Evan reminded her. He leaned in and kissed her cheek, frustrated at the strange wall building between them.

She didn't say goodbye as he left the room.

JUSTIN AND SHAUN were both waiting in his office.

"I've got good news." Justin glanced up from the computer screen. "Amy sent an email with a list of the cancellations she had made that would impact the hotel and restaurant over the next two weeks."

"We've already gone through and updated the orders. No more having to shut down the restaurant because we have no supplies on hand." Shaun lifted his hands in the air and did a cheer. "You did it, dude. You got the evil she-dragon to cave."

Evan glared at his Beta. "I did not get her to do anything, she gave up that information of her own free will. And you will not shit-talk her again. Do I make myself clear?"

Shaun's eyes widened as he backed away to a safe distance.

A bit snarky, maybe, but Evan refused to apologize. Amy was his, and the sooner that sank in for Shaun, the better.

Justin stroked his chin thoughtfully. "There's a lot that needs to be dealt with. I checked her place yesterday morning, and it seems she knows plenty about running a business."

"So we let her keep ownership of everything? Is that what you're suggesting?" Shaun demanded.

"I'm saying it's not as big of a worry to leave control in her hands as it would be if she were incompetent. As long as Evan trusts her to act in a manner that doesn't harm Takhini, there's no need for immediate action."

Evan settled into his favourite chair, the worn leather upholstery nowhere near as comfortable as he remembered.

This was *bullshit*. Why was he hanging out in his office when his mate was somewhere else?

The big bear shifter excused himself with a comment about needing to meet someone. Shaun threw himself onto the couch across from Evan, propping his feet up on the coffee table. He examined Evan thoroughly, shaking his head.

"I hate to say it, but you don't look good."

"Shut your yap." Evan stared at the ceiling.

"Where's the...your mate? Is she coming the pack house soon?"

"No. Not for a couple days." *Because I told her not to.* God, he was so stupid.

Shaun gurgled. "What the fuck?"

"Seriously. She has stuff to do. And she...needs some space." Evan ran a hand through his hair. "She came to Whitehorse to track me down."

"Wait. What? You didn't tell me any of this yesterday." His Beta's eyes narrowed. "And that doesn't sound good at all. Track you down? Where the hell has she ever met you before, and if you'd met, why didn't you know you were mates?"

Evan swung his feet to the floor and rested his elbows on his knees, allowing him to brace his aching head in his hands. "She's from Hudson Bay."

"Shit." Shaun knew Evan's history, shared during late-night drinks. Over the past months, they'd become best friends as well as a leadership team.

"It gets worse. Remember how I told you things went to hell at the end?" Evan stared into the concerned face of his Beta. "Her brother was the innocent wolf who took the fall."

Shaun figured it out right away, swearing softly. "She tracked you down because her brother died."

Evan nodded. "All of the crap she pulled was because I'm responsible for his death."

Shaun's rejection of Evan's statement was instantaneous. "No, you are not responsible for his death. You told me what happened, and if she thinks—"

"I didn't tell her everything yet," Evan confessed. When Shaun looked as if he was about to protest, Evan hurried to explain. "Look, she just had something huge thrown at her, between meeting me in person and us being mates. I told her the explosion was for good reason, and that Philip's death was an accident, and she seems to have accepted that so far. Telling her anything more..."

His Beta's expression changed, no longer judgmental but incredulous. "That's bull. You need to go the whole way, dude. Half-truths aren't enough with your mate."

"But I don't want to make things worse."

"And her not being here with you isn't worse? I didn't know any of this yesterday when I gave her hell. Now I feel like a shit, and *you're* being a jerk." Shaun paused, his discomfort and irritation rising. "Wait. Why am I trying to get you to confess everything? I don't like her."

The most entertaining part of the whole fucked-up situation was watching Shaun shuffle around the change in dynamics. "She's got your number. She is the Alpha of the Canyon pack, which puts her a good boot print higher than you."

Shaun sniffed. "We'll see about that."

The phone rang, and someone knocked on the door, and he and Shaun got tugged in different directions dealing with a crisis around the hotel. Fortunately, a normal, ordinary, everyday crisis that could be solved.

Through all the work, Evan couldn't stop thinking about Amy. He hated not having her around, but he didn't want to crowd her. He fought the urge to drop everything and haul ass to the computer shop so he could stay on her butt as a bodyguard. She could go ahead and do the things she needed, and he would innocently tag along...

And then he remembered her comment about him not

fitting in with her pack. And remembered the pack members who had blotted just at the sight of him. He was stuck between two evils. Being without his mate, or being with her when his presence could damage delicate relationships.

As a wolf, he wanted to say screw everyone else. As a fellow Alpha, he understood her dilemma. Not to mention his insistence she not show up at Takhini. If he pushed her, she might push back and end up hurt.

If what she needed was space, that's what he would give her. He pulled paperwork forward to distract himself. The entire time, though, his focus remained on one petite dark-haired wolf who had already tangled her fingers around his heart.

AMY RESTED her head against the window to gather her strength. She hadn't lied to Evan about having work to do, but the biggest work she had was to avoid spending too much time with him. Familiarity was only going to make this harder.

Sex with him had felt so incredibly right. And then...all the doubts had returned. The confusion of those days after Philip went missing. The loneliness that had filled her life for the rest of her growing-up years.

Why was Evan refusing to tell her what had happened? He wasn't interested in listening to her suggestions, or talking about the best way to merge the packs.

Was this going to be her life? Having a connection to a man who her body and wolf craved, but her mind and soul felt distant from? Like the married human couples she'd seen who were used to being with each other, but that was all they had. Familiarity. Comfortable with a person who they loved once, but didn't really like anymore.

She would be better off never falling into that trap in the first place. Until he trusted her enough to tell her everything, trusted her enough to listen to her advice, she couldn't let her walls down again. She'd focus on her commitment to the packs.

Although, after she'd met with the first of her members, she wasn't sure what was going to be tougher, avoiding Evan or making Whitehorse one.

The couple she'd thought would be the most reasonable about the announcement stood in shock, faces reflecting their horror.

Terry pulled his saucepan off the gourmet stovetop so it wouldn't burn, a stream of faint curses escaping his lips. "Joining with Takhini would be like mixing cream and vinegar. You *can't* be serious," he gasped.

He should have been in theater, not culinary arts. "There are a lot of positive reasons for a merger, one of which is our joint powerbase would be expanded."

"We don't need more power," he complained. "We have everything the way we like it. A comfortable catering service where we get to cook but don't have to deal with actual people. It's a nice, quiet and orderly lifestyle. Which is the opposite of most of *them*. Noisy creatures."

Good grief. "Don't stereotype them all as hoodlums. There are good people in the Takhini pack. A few hotheads, yes, but we can deal with them."

A sniff was all she got in response.

Amy sighed wearily. "Look, I know it's not what any of us expected, but..." She had to confess it. "Their Alpha is my mate, and we are doing this."

Marie stepped closer and eyed her with concern. "You don't look thrilled at finding your mate. What's wrong?"

"Nothing's wrong," Amy insisted. "I'm adjusting. Giving myself time, like I expect all of you to give this merger between the packs the time and effort it deserves."

They still looked skeptical, but at least they weren't complaining anymore. Amy visited for a while longer before gathering her things and getting ready to go.

"I plan to bring Evan around so you can get to know him one on one before we try anything with mixed packs. I'll warn you ahead of time."

"So I can find a good hiding spot," Terry muttered.

His mate bumped him, and they both smiled innocently at Amy.

She shook her head. Wolves. "Behave, and that's an order."

"Yes, ma'am."

They ushered her from their kitchen with a hug, an enormous cookie in her hand as a farewell. She nibbled on the sweet treat as she paced back to her office, wondering how much more challenging the rest of her pack were going to be.

The familiar bulk of a bear approached the doors of the computer shop from the opposite direction. She waited until Justin had come to a stop, her head tilted so far back to meet his eyes she thought she might tip over.

"It's like going on the floor during a basketball game."

Justin smiled politely. "I'd like to speak with you."

Tom and Braden would crawl out of their skins if she brought the bear back into her office. She gestured to the nearby coffee shop. "Do you mind if we grab a drink?"

"Not at all."

She kept her curiosity at bay until they settled into

chairs, steaming cups of the locally brewed Midnight Sun in hand. Amy eyed the bear shifter.

Justin raised a brow. "Do I have something on my face?"

She shook her head. "I was just admiring your suit. I didn't know the Men in Black supplier carried big and ginormous sizes."

He chuckled. "Blunt."

"It's how you prefer it. I'm not that outspoken about shitty clothing choices with everyone."

The big man lowered his coffee mug. "Blunt again. Is this a wolf thing I'm unaware of? Upfront and in people's faces?"

Amy didn't hesitate. "I try hard to speak the language people understand. It saves misunderstandings."

"So, you up and confessing everything to Evan the other day was what he needed to hear?"

She cleared the knot in her throat. "That's kind of a special circumstance."

"I see." Justin looked her over carefully. "What type of language do you understand?"

Good question. "I think you can pretty much say anything you want, and I'll be okay with it."

"I have a business proposition for you."

Talk about out of the blue. "Whoa, okay, that was unexpected."

Justin smiled. "This is, of course, provided you and Evan don't end up whipping Whitehorse into a frenzy of bloodshed and scandal."

"Now you're being no fun at all," she teased.

He shrugged lazily. "I know, I know. Although, since my boss stopped the bear shifters from tearing the city apart, I wouldn't object to a little fireworks from the wolf side of the equation."

Bloodthirsty bastard. "I think Evan and I can find some common ground that doesn't involve ripping out entrails and leaving them strewn in the streets."

Justin leaned forward, elbows on the table. "Harrison Enterprises owns diamonds, but they have other holdings as well. I took a look through your computer shop the other day. It's pretty impressive for a small, locally run enterprise."

"I try my best." His compliment didn't make sense, though. "Surely you don't want me to set up a computer shop in Yellowknife."

"It's more your overall business savvy. We could use someone like you on staff. Tyler has extra work because of his position as head of the bear clans, but he wants to be sure Harrison Enterprises continues to advance."

She wasn't quite sure where this was leading. "You did catch the part where I'm an Alpha here in town, right?"

He nodded. "Yes, and I heard the rumour stewing about you and Evan being an item. That makes no difference to me, I mean, to Harrison Enterprises. We'd want you for consulting services. You could work from anywhere, including here in Whitehorse."

Well, now. She was always up for alternative sources of revenue. "Put together a business proposal, and we'll see what we can do."

He looked slightly sheepish for a moment. "You do realize if we hire you, I'll suggest we put in the tightest fail-safes possible. To make sure at the end of every transaction, we actually end up owning what we intend to buy. No offense."

Her amusement rose. "None taken. I wouldn't hire me without major supervision as well."

They chatted about the difference between living in Whitehorse and Yellowknife, until Amy interrupted. "I realize this might be out of line, but what are your intentions regarding Amanda?"

Justin sat back, obviously surprised by the twist in the conversation. "I'm not sure what you're asking."

"Remember my business about speaking people's languages?"

He nodded.

It was interfering, but Amanda seemed so determined to make the wrong decision. Amy didn't want the woman alone when a simple misunderstanding was keeping her from being happy. "You're accidentally speaking a language she doesn't want to hear anymore."

Justin frowned. "Could you be more specific?"

Amy tapped her fingers on the table as she pondered the best wording. She gestured toward him. "My comment earlier about your suit. You're a good-looking man, Justin, but you wear the trappings of civilization a little too hard. At least in terms of what Amanda is looking for."

"Did she say something to you?"

Amy tilted her head from side to side. "Sort of, but mostly it's in the way she watches you. Her body language says she's very attracted then she remembers something, and up pops a barrier."

The bear across from her nodded. "She does run hot and then cold. I couldn't figure out what I was doing wrong, but I suppose..."

Amy reached across the table and laid her hand on his. "She's been hurt, but she's not permanently broken. You can make a difference." She let her gaze run over his expensive clothing, and her nose wrinkled. "But you need to lighten up."

Justin cracked a smile. "Are you into psychiatry as well as computer hacking?"

"Being a shrink is part and parcel of being an Alpha." She tossed him a wink. "I admit this is the first time I've attempted other-species matchmaking."

He sat up straighter, fumbling with his coffee.

Amy grinned into her coffee cup. Awww, she'd never seen a bear blush before. He must have it bad for Amanda.

They rose to their feet and he escorted her out the door. "Well, I'm thankful for your suggestions. And I'll get that information to you as soon as I can."

"No rush. I have a fair bit on my plate to deal with."

Which was pretty much the understatement of the century.

15

wo days later Evan was ready to crawl out of his
skin. He'd done everything possible to honour
Amy's request, but not showing up at her house was getting
more and more difficult. The sudden flurry of activity she'd
buried herself under was frustrating, especially when he
had thought things were straightening out.

His pack was no help either. All of them were as
confused as his wolf. Those who had been at the
spontaneous gathering the other night knew Amy was his
mate. Word had spread through the pack, and now none of
them could figure out why there wasn't more action taking
place.

A few of the more aggressive males had made comments
regarding his leadership and strength. He'd dealt with them
sternly, Lance and Toby especially, but they were young and
cocky enough to continue to be pains in his ass.

Having to deal with an internal rebellion at the same
time as dealing with his reluctant mate was not Evan's idea
of a good time.

Tonight she had promised to get together with him,

bringing him as a guest to a concert her pack was involved in. As long as she didn't cancel like she had their previous dinner and luncheon dates. Evan was beginning to get a complex. He'd never had such trouble with any female before, and the fact his mate was the one avoiding him only made things worse.

So now he was standing outside Amy's house waiting for her to answer the doorbell, feeling like a complete ass. He'd wondered about bringing her flowers and rejected it as the act of a desperate fool.

Amy swung the door open, and Evan's tongue stuck to the roof of his mouth. He peeled it off and barely managed to keep it from flapping like a damn dog in heat.

She wore a clingy dress, its shimmering wintry-white fabric like a second skin. The neck scooped low and the skirt skimmed up, stopping at exactly the right moment to entice him to explore. Add in high heels that made her legs go on forever, and he was pinned in place for far too long.

"Did you want to come in?" Amy stepped back.

Evan sighed happily as he watched her move. "I'd love to."

It took an incredible amount of control to not make his forward motion become stalking. What he wanted to do was keep walking until he had her pinned to some flat surface so he could put his hands on that gorgeous body. Check out how soft the fabric she was wrapped in really was.

"Did you want a drink before we go?" she asked.

He shook his head, already intoxicated from looking at her. Just from the scent of her filling his head for the first time in days. He was tempted to skip the activity and spend the night devouring her. Tasting her skin and driving her mad.

Instead he'd concentrate on pack, like they'd agreed. "Want me to drive?"

She accepted his arm and he led her to the sidewalk. "Park around the side of the building."

He opened the door and watched with fascination as she placed herself in the passenger seat. It was impossible to look away from her legs as she pulled them into the car. Her shoes were held on with delicate bows, and visions of untying them with his teeth struck.

A cough snapped his attention back up to her face, and he sheepishly closed the door and came around to the driver's side.

"Tell me about tonight." He slipped into the traffic and headed toward the theater.

"Canyon sponsored the concert—this is one of the few cultural exchanges that includes musicians from all over the northern hemisphere. The performance typically brings in people from around the world. This is the second time we've hosted, and it's growing on an annual basis."

The event wasn't something that had ever been on his radar. "Good for business?"

Amy nodded vigorously. "The financial implications are huge. Investors considering setting up shop in Whitehorse like to know their people won't have to sacrifice the experiences available in the more civilized South."

"Makes sense." He supposed. Although the idea of sitting and watching people while they played music had never been on *his* bucket list.

"I also want you to meet two of my pack. Giorgio is part of a string quartet, and Tessa works the soundboard. They are both very good at what they do, but Giorgio especially might be hesitant to see you."

"On the shy side? That seems a little strange for a

performer," Evan wondered.

Amy shrugged. "Just because someone is talented doesn't change their internal character. Giorgio escaped from a pack in Russia that was using him for entertainment."

Evan thought for a moment, but couldn't figure out what she meant. "Entertainment? As in, he played for them upon request?"

"More like they kept him in a small room, and every time they turned on the light he was required to play. When they didn't need him anymore they left him back in the dark."

His mind reeled. "Sometimes I want to go back to the days when my job was to eliminate the stupid and the cruel in the packs out there."

She stared out the side window. "Eliminating people in charge who are horrid individuals is important, I agree. But it's dangerous to get so caught up in that side of the equation the actual people who need our help get ignored."

They were at the parking lot. Evan slid into a stall to the side of the building where she directed him. "If packs were run properly, and leadership did what they needed to do, wolves wouldn't feel they were trapped. What if there are others still imprisoned like your friend was?"

They were on the sidewalk headed for the main doors when she spoke again. "Giorgio is free from that room, but he's not necessarily free from his past. Going back and eliminating his captors doesn't liberate his heart. That's where I *can* help, so that's where I put my focus."

Only a moment later they were following a red carpet to massive doors that swooshed open as they approached.

Men in suits bounded up to greet Amy, gesturing her forward even as they eyed Evan with caution. She slipped her coat partway off before he woke up enough to assist her. The moment of contact between his hands and the bare skin of her shoulders was far too brief.

A neatly dressed woman reached for Amy's coat, and Evan passed it over. Even in his suit he felt out of place in the midst of the elaborate formalwear milling around the brightly lit area. His ignorance of an entire portion of Whitehorse population shocked him.

But Amy's fingers were wrapped around his biceps, so in spite of the discomfort in his gut, the night wasn't a complete write-off.

She leaned in, her lips brushing his jaw, and he swallowed hard to control the urge to pick her up and go somewhere private to switch the evening's agenda to ravishment.

"There are a dozen visiting CEOs we'll try to touch base with before we move into the auditorium. Are you okay with that?"

His discomfort flashed to anger. "I'm not a bohemian. I know how to behave in public."

Amy stiffened, her fingers cutting into his arm. "Of course you do. I'm...never mind. We just need to do the polite thing for a bit."

Great. Evan took a deep breath and pasted on his most pleasant expression.

She answered a wave from a couple and led Evan toward them. He fought the urge to do something outrageous, which was kind of annoying, since she obviously didn't think he belonged in this world and him being an ass would just affirm her belief.

The next twenty minutes were filled with banal conversation and polite nothings. Or at least that's the way Evan thought of it. He made sure he kept a smile pasted on his face although the edges got a little more ragged each time the conversation turned to employment. He'd announce his occupation only to be greeted with raised brows and almost sympathetic congratulations.

The current bastard pontificating in front of them was the fifth, and Evan's patience had been stretched thinner than a small order of wings at the pack house.

"I think that's *fascinating*. You must be thrilled to have so many opportunities to observe human nature while you're in that bar of yours." The behavioral-scientist expert, or whatever the hell his job had been—there had been too many letters and shit for Evan to be able to repeat it. The man wore an oh-too-familiar expression of "let's humour the peon" that was really beginning to grate on Evan's nerves.

Evan laid his fingers over top of Amy's to make sure she didn't run away as he spoke. "It is a great place to hang out and people watch. I've even analyzed exactly how the evening is going to go based on what people order to drink. There's a science to it, you know."

His opponent blinked. "Really? That's fascinating—"

"For example, the beer drinkers have a totally different objective to their evening than the ones who order fancy mixed drinks with names that are hard to pronounce after they've had three or four. But my personal favourites are the customers who are so pretentious they ask what years our wine cellar carries, and then go on to recite some memorized spiel about tannins and smoky apricots to show exactly how knowledgeable and classy they are."

The man's face drew tighter as Evan spoke, and he lowered the glass of red wine he'd praised only moments earlier.

Amy tugged Evan's arm, smiling sweetly as she made

their apologies. "If you'll excuse us. It was lovely to see you again."

They damn near ran across the room as Amy dragged him toward a door that said *Staff Only*.

"Oh, goody, do I get a new job?" Evan asked. "Maybe I should go back and tell that ass I'm moving up in the world. Now I get to use a broom instead of pouring drinks."

Amy shoved him through the door and jerked it closed behind them. "What was that all about?"

"He was being an ass. One of many."

"Oh, Evan." She shook her head. "Could you not hold your tongue for a couple of hours?"

Evan snorted in derision. "No, I think it would make it really difficult to tell that jerk off if I was actually holding my tongue."

The hallway lighting was dim, but it was bright enough to see her frustration. "You know what I'm talking about. Yes, I agree, Dr. Winston is an absolute jerk."

"Then why do you care if I let him know he's a jerk?"

"Because he's not a dangerous jerk, and he's a potential business opportunity for the pack. That's worth putting up with a little bit of jerkdom for. Plus, there's no need to prove I have more balls than everyone in the room. I already know I'm smarter than most of them, and that I'm nicer than most of them, and so I let the stupid things they do go."

Evan narrowed his eyes. "You're not making any sense."

Amy rubbed her temples.

Evan caught her by the upper arms, rubbing his palms up and down against her bare skin in an attempt to soothe her. "I'm sorry if I embarrassed you. I have no objection to being polite, but I do have trouble being polite when there seems no need."

"And sometimes it's not worth the fight. That's the point

I'm trying to make."

She crossed her arms, brushing his hands away and breaking the contact between them. Evan was more disturbed by that than by her words.

"Were you going to introduce me to this Giorgio of yours?"

"After the show. Right now I want to talk to Laney."

"The woman from the café?"

Amy nodded. "She plays the violin. Or, she did before her ex broke her fingers. She's still trying to regain her skills, but she loves coming to these concerts, so I bought her a pass. She'll be hiding down here until the lights go out."

She tilted her head to indicate the hallway. He followed her, mentally rearranging his plan of attack so that he could get through the evening without pissing her off again.

He was smart. He was strong. He should be able to be suave and debonair for a couple more hours, especially when impressing his mate was on the line.

Only he did miss his comfy chair and the game that was going on back at the pack house. But if this was what it took to bring him and Amy back on track, he'd make the sacrifice.

AMY'S HEADACHE HAD A HEADACHE. They were finally seated in the auditorium, and for the next forty-five minutes there should be no necessity to put out any fires or sit on Evan to stop him from offending anyone.

Up on the stage the string quartet was already into the second movement, and the peaceful sounds flooded the room. Perfect acoustics carried the gentle performance of a soothing melody.

Her soul needed a whole lot of soothing. At her side Evan slumped, totally relaxed with his hips forward on the seat, his upper body set against the chair back. His knees were wide apart, his entire muscular body seemingly too large for the delicate auditorium chairs.

He'd dressed up, and she had no complaints about the external packaging. In fact, everywhere they had gone, people's gazes had followed them as if he were a highly sought-after model. Whispered conversations from those in the room who were visiting made it clear they were all intrigued by the handsome stranger on her arm.

But the chip on his shoulder seemed to get bigger by the second. She had no issues with his job choices—owning the bar and hotel. Both were good solid positions and perfectly suited for his role in leading a wolf pack. Bringing him to the symphony hadn't been about making him feel inadequate.

His defensive responses every single time someone questioned him had gone from bad to worse.

She took a deep breath and let it out slowly. By the time the performance was over, she hoped Evan would have settled down enough she could take him for a brief meeting with Giorgio. They could escape before tensions rose again.

A few others of her pack were scattered through the auditorium. Laney had smiled hesitantly at Evan when they'd met, but the rest stayed away. Joining the packs was going to take a lot more finesse and planning than even she had expected.

The music swelled, and she closed her eyes in an attempt to soak in as much relaxation as possible. The biggest thing she could sense, though, was the man at her side. The scent of him filled her nostrils, his presence borderline overwhelming. She wanted him so badly, and she hated that she wanted him when he didn't seem to care about her in the same way.

Their knees bumped, and she jerked at the electric connection between them that remained as strong as ever. He reached over, and for a second she thought he was going to take her hand. She was already opening her fingers to accept his touch, kicking herself for wanting it. Craving contact with her mate desperately.

Evan ignored her fingers, and instead pulled the program from where she'd tucked it beside her hip.

He stared intently at the small brochure while she fought to get her pounding heart under control.

A set of lights on the right side of the room clicked on, the unexpected brightness drawing everyone's attention. An usher rushed forward, slipping out the side door. A moment later, everything was restored to normal.

Until a flash struck on the left as lights clicked on there. The musicians didn't falter, but the audience was distracted as, one after the other, banks of lights all over the auditorium flashed on and were hurriedly turned off.

A low beeping sound began. This time the base cellist turned her head toward the side of the stage.

An Energizer Bunny toy appeared, its little furry arms pounding in steady repetition on an oversized drum, the turning wheels of the toy bringing it toward where the quartet was seated.

A murmur rose, and fingers pointed toward the stage. At her side Evan was no longer in a relaxed slouch but seated upright, raptly watching the action. A a low curse rose from his lips.

Suddenly, from behind the curtain and the sides of the stage, more toys appeared. A wild assortment this time, not just bunnies, but leaping frogs and mooing cows. Battery-operated devices of every kind poured onto the platform with a whirling pandemonium of noise and disorder.

The performers gave up all attempts at continuing, the final notes dying off into a melodic dissonance that mixed in a strange way with the clattering toys.

She had never seen such a thing before in her life.

Evan had his head cradled in his hand. Amy dropped an arm around him in concern. "Are you okay?"

He cleared his throat. "I think we should leave."

There wasn't much reason to stay. Everywhere around them, people were abandoning their seats and heading back to the foyer. Up on the stage, one of the performers had retreated to the top of her chair as hundreds of wind-up and battery-operated toys milled around them, the volume increasing all the time.

Amy pointed to a side exit. "We can get out that way."

Evan caught her by the hand as they briefly fought people moving in the opposite direction. They pushed through the door, and Evan jerked her to a stop.

At least a dozen wolves were waiting, huge grins on their faces, all of them Takhini.

Understanding hit, and this time Amy was the one who swore. She pushed past Evan. "You're responsible for this?"

Lance sneered at her.

She was going to rip him apart.

Before she could take a swing, though, Evan had come between her and her target. "I don't know why you thought this was a good idea, but it wasn't. Get your asses back to the Takhini pack house. I'll deal with you there."

Evan continued to block her path, and before she could get past him, the group had vanished as silently as they had come in the first place.

"Those little *shits*. What the hell did they think they

were doing?" Amy was a second away from punching a wall since she couldn't punch the miscreants.

"They probably thought they were being entertaining." Evan dragged a hand through his hair. "Don't worry, I'll deal with them."

She was furious again, but maybe this was the final straw needed to make Evan see reason. "Let me come to the Takhini pack house with you, and *we'll* deal with them. That will help with this whole joining-the-packs issue. You and me, working together. Facing their concerns as a team."

He shook his head. "They're just feeling their oats. I'm sure they thought it was funny."

"It wasn't funny."

Evan wrinkled his nose. "Well, it kinda was, if you think about it. I mean it was wrong of them, and I will totally rake them over the coals for it, but you have to admit it was rather hysterical when that first bunny showed up."

This was a perfect example of what she'd talked about earlier. Another of those moments where it wasn't worth making her point because he obviously wasn't on the same page as her. Amy jerked past him, not even caring if he followed her or not. "Fine. Do it your way. But if they try something like that again, I will have something to say about it."

"Of course you will, and rightly so," Evan soothed her. "Let me drive you home."

She already had her hands on the exit-door release. "Don't bother. I'll get a cab. You have some brats waiting for you at home to discipline."

"Will I see you tomorrow?" Evan asked.

Slamming the door was the only answer she gave him.

16

The morning after the symphony had been disrupted, Amy's staff looked far too amused. She hesitated before heading up to her office. "Do I want to know?"

Tom and Braden exchanged glances before shaking their heads.

Which only meant she *had* to know. "Okay. Tell me."

They pushed a printout toward her. She picked it up to read an energy bill.

"What's this?" She rapidly scanned the page until she spotted something out of the norm. "Damn. You guys are a bunch of turkeys."

Tom shrugged. "An eye for an eye. We didn't do anything to the Takhini pack members who weren't involved. Just the select group who need to learn a few manners."

Amy shook her head. "It's not funny, and I don't want you to do anything like this again, do you hear me?"

"Is that a direct order?" Braden asked.

"Do I have to make it one?" Amy watched them for a moment, and when they slunk away, she left it.

She'd barely sat down when her phone rang. "Hi, Evan."

He was in a vile mood. "I thought you promised you were done messing with my finances."

"Don't look at me this time. Couple of my pack decided to be smart-asses in response to last night. What happened to you?" She paused for a moment, confused. "Hang on, they did something to *you*? That doesn't make sense. They told me they only went after the jerks who screwed up last night's performance."

"Well, it looks as if they're blaming me as well. Some of the pack have bills from the electric department for three months' back payments. Others got shipments of rabbit traps delivered to their door COD this morning."

"And yours?"

Evan sighed. "My cell phone bill just got delivered. It's for over thirty-two thousand dollars."

Poetic justice in a way. "They seem to be making the punishment fit the crime."

There was silence for a moment before Evan spoke. "Okay, I get the electric bill and the bunny traps, but why my cell phone?"

"As head of the pranksters, they probably figured you should be in better communication with them."

A low growl came over the phone, and not the type that made her heart rate pick up. This one was sheer annoyance. "What are you going to do about it?" he snapped.

That was polite. *Not.* "I've already spoken to them."

"I mean, can they get the charges reversed? I'm going to spend all day on the phone with customer service trying get this straightened out."

"Poor baby." Her snarky response snuck out before she could help herself.

"Amy. It's not funny."

Vengeance was sweet. "I don't know. It's actually kind of funny, if you think about it. I mean, I can just imagine what your face must have looked like when you opened that bill."

He must have accidentally dropped the phone, the clatter in her ear extremely loud.

Things just went downhill from there.

IT STARTED SLOWLY, the internal rebellions. Retaliation for one act was followed by another. Both she and Evan spoke to their packs, but it seemed there was no way to make them see reason. Everyone took what had begun as a childish prank personally, and in some ways Amy couldn't blame them.

For the first time Takhini and Canyon were in the middle of a huge change, and yet at every turn Evan blocked her suggestion that they work together. It wasn't like him, not from what she had observed over the past year, but his leadership style had changed completely.

It seemed Takhini and Canyon had declared war.

Takhini egged her house.

Canyon somehow figured out which pack members had been involved and wrapped their cars with three layers of egg cartons and chicken wire.

Takhini sent invitations to participate in the next Iditarod—as sled pullers—to all the Canyon pack.

Canyon sent flea collars to everyone.

Harmless pranks for the most part, but all of them annoying and disruptive. And yet every time Amy offered to come and talk to the Takhini pack with him, Evan turned her down. She felt as if her hands were tied. Between the once-again-denied mating urge and the continued chaos in the packs, frustration was her constant companion.

If only Evan would come and ask her to work with him, but it seemed that was beyond the level of trust he was willing to show. All she could do was hold on and attempt to keep order over wolves who were increasingly hard to control.

Nearly a week later her phone woke her. Amy picked it up, still groggy from a poor night's sleep. "What?"

"Damn vandals, and I bet anything I know exactly who the damn vandals are. Anyway, they took all four of my tires last night," Tom complained. "Sorry, I'm going to be a little late to work."

"No problem. Get there when you can."

The third time the phone rang in the next five minutes with one of her pack letting her know they'd had a theft, Amy knew Tom was right, Takhini had hit again. She walked past her front window on the way to the kitchen for some extra-strong coffee, and froze in place.

Her entire old front yard was filled with tires. They'd been stacked like rubber Inuksuk, their torsos made of black circles, winter treads extending out as arms. Shiny hubcaps balanced on top as heads.

Her lips twitched, and she snorted briefly with amusement before getting on the phone to let her pack know where they could find their tires. Inside, though, the icy sadness only grew.

It was just after lunch when Evan stomped his way to the couch in the pack house where Shaun and Gem were talking with Justin. "I'm going to kill them," he declared.

"Are you giving me a heads up so I can gather bail money again?" Justin asked.

"Very funny. I don't mean literally kill them." Evan paused. "Although, it's tempting."

"What's the latest?" Shaun asked.

"As if you don't know." Evan narrowed his eyes. "You're sure you're not encouraging the brats?"

"Dude. Of course not. I want the little shits to start behaving themselves as well. Okay, it was funny when they toilet-papered the Canyon pack houses."

Gem shook her head. "It wasn't so funny when Canyon arranged to have fresh manure spread on the lawns of the troublemakers."

"They're going to be the envy of all their neighbours come next spring," Justin pointed out, a huge grin spreading across his big bear face.

Evan offered him a death glare. "You're enjoying this far too much."

Justin shrugged. "There's no bloodshed in the streets, so yes, it is rather amusing."

"But it needs to stop, and soon." Gem looked as worried as Evan felt. "So far it has all been fairly innocuous and safe, but what happens when it goes beyond that? And there's the other trouble with the pranks. I thought the goal was to join the packs. This isn't helping. If anything it's forcing them farther apart."

She had a point.

Shaun obviously agreed. "Toby and Lance cornered me yesterday. I swear they were sounding out if I was still supportive of you staying in power."

This was a kind of chaos Evan had never expected. "I need to talk to you, right now."

Shaun kissed Gem, gave Justin a finger wave then

followed Evan into a more private part of the pack house. "What's up?"

Evan leaned against the wall and stared at his Beta. "What am I doing wrong?"

He expected nothing but the truth. That was why he had brought Shaun on as a Beta in the first place, but what he got was unexpected.

"You're not yourself." Shaun paced a few steps away before turning back, his face serious for the first time in… well, maybe in forever. "You've always been someone I've admired. I've lived a lot of places in the North, and we wolves tend to be a wild and hairy bunch. You've never been so full of yourself as an Alpha that your attitude pissed me off."

Evan nodded. "Go on."

"In fact, I might have to admit to a bit of hero worship when it comes to you. You care, but you do it in such an irreverent and casual way it fits this pack, and it fits me."

"You sound like a cheering section, and I know damn well something's wrong. Just give it to me straight."

Shaun smirked. "This is called a shit sandwich. That was the good part, here comes the crap. Ever since you met Amy, you've changed. I understand that whole unfinished-mate business is making you crazy, but it seems as if you're not interested in the pack anymore."

"Bullshit. You know the pack is important to me."

"Then why aren't you leading? Toby and Lance are doing more than pulling pranks now. They're eyeing your position, and mine, and if you don't get your ass in gear, we're going to be fighting for more than control. We'll be fighting for our lives."

The words might be logical, but they still didn't seem to register.

"It's like..." Anger and confusion mixed as Evan spoke. "It's like I've lost a piece of myself. Ever since I sniffed Amy, I can't concentrate. I can't figure out the right thing to do because every time I head in one direction, I'm tugged in another. I want her, and I'm amazed by her, but I want to protect her. It's so damn infuriating. You're right, this isn't me, and I know that, and that's another layer on top of the rest of the bullshit."

Evan scrubbed his hands over his face. It wasn't *just* meeting Amy. It was being reminded of the situation at Hudson Bay. Since that had been tossed in his face, he doubted all his decisions.

Back then he'd been pushed, hard, and Philip had paid with his life. Was he reacting to that mistake and choosing not to decide? It was fucked up and crazy-making, but it might be an explanation.

"If I could just move on and forget her altogether, I wonder if I would choose that."

Shaun didn't say anything. Just stood there and looked supportive. Shocked and cranky, but supportive.

"But the last thing I want is to give her up," Evan growled. "She's the missing part of me, but I can't seem to make us fit. She's a round peg and I'm a square hole, and all we do is keep butting into each other and never coming to any solution."

"Well, your confusion, and hers, is contagious." Shaun paced to the window, his shoulders stiff. When he turned it was with more determination than ever. "I'm with you, whatever you decide. I want you to be happy, but I also need you to be the Alpha of this pack. So get it together, or I will *make* you get it together."

It was a sign of how far gone Evan was that the blatant challenge didn't even get his back up. "I'm glad I've got you on my side. And I swear, I will find a way through this."

"Don't take too long, dude. The clock is ticking."

Then the fire alarms went off in the pack house for the fifth time that day, once again showing everything was not right in Evan's world.

17

————

Shaun left, claiming he had something important to do.

Evan needed to get his head on straight, and sitting in an office was not going to do it. Five minutes later, he was pacing down a trail in Riverside Park, fresh air in his lungs, but his mind still fogged over.

He'd reached the end of his rope. The increasingly bad pack situation. Amy shutting him out of her life.

He hadn't really needed Shaun to point out something was wrong. Evan knew it far too well, he just didn't know where to start to make it right. If there were some magical fix, he would have promised to wear pixie wings for the rest of his life in exchange.

Evan settled on a bench near the forest, leaning back and staring into the pale blue sky. He needed to think more about this idea he'd had—the one regarding being unable to move past Philip's death. Had he made the wrong choice back then? How many times since had he made mistakes and ended up hurting others in the process?

It was one thing to have confidence in himself, and another to be an ignorant fool.

The soft pat of a paw against his knee brought him to attention.

A lone wolf sat beside his feet. An ancient creature, his fur turned silvery-white with age. Even though he was older in years, his power remained. Bold and firm, he was obviously an Alpha.

Evan spoke politely. "Hi. Do I know you?"

The wolf shook his head.

Ah. "You're one of the Canyon pack, aren't you?"

Amy had warned him again and again her pack members needed something different than the Takhini bunch. He'd kind of thought she was pushing her point too hard, and too often. It wasn't as if he didn't know how to slow down and soothe an upset wolf.

But... Just to be sure, Evan took a really, really cautious approach. Held his questions, and instead, sat motionless.

"Please don't turn around."

Evan shot upright, shocked to realize someone had snuck up behind him.

"You're good. I didn't even hear you." Evan didn't sense any malice in the stranger at his back. "Are you a part of Amy's pack too?"

"Sam's pack? Yes. That's Matthias, our old Alpha. She took over for him last year. It was a good change. We love Matthias, but it was time to let someone else take care of us. He needed to rest."

Evan dipped his head respectfully. "Matthias."

The old-timer laid his chin on Evan's thigh.

"Don't worry, we're not here to hurt you." A new voice, female this time.

"That's reassuring." If he'd been impressed with Shaun

getting the jump on Amy's sentries before, he was even more impressed with how sneaky her pack were now. "By the way, I never saw either of you coming. Well done."

"Warn your Beta if he ever trespasses on Canyon land again, we have a roll of duct tape with his name on it."

Evan chuckled. They might be quiet, but Canyon still had a lovely wolf sense of retribution. "Are we doing this incognito for a reason?"

"It's not that we mind you knowing who we are, but our faces and our names are less important than what we came to say. When Sam told us the packs needed to join, we didn't like the idea. No offense, but most of us don't like you."

Evan stroked Matthias's head respectfully. "I've kind of picked up on that. But I really am interested in doing all I can to help you, and to be the kind of Alpha you need."

"The point is, we don't need you. We've got Sam. She knows what our problems are, and we trust her."

"But you've got me, because we're a pair. It's not up for discussion. The packs are joining."

A low murmur of upset rumbled behind him before a feminine voice scolded him. "That's why we're here. You say you and Sam are a pair. If you're talking about wanting to be our Alpha, you have to show us you know how to care for all the people under your watch. We'll agree you do a great job with the rowdies. But you're doing a crappy job with Sam. That doesn't give us much hope you'll be good for us."

Not much he could argue about. "I know."

His confession seemed to take them by surprise, and he waited for their response. The wind picked up, shaking the leaves. One detached from a branch and floated on the air currents, slowly spinning on its way to the ground.

Evan was spinning on the wind as well. Control out of his grasp.

A hand rested briefly on his shoulder. "Matthias wants to talk to you alone, but before we go, we want you to know we're willing to settle the issues we have with the Takhini crowd."

"We just want Sam to be happy. And you too, I guess. You need to be happy as well. Because while you're not nearly as scary when you're being Mr. Mopey, those adrenaline junkies from the Takhini Asylum need you to be yourself. They're running rampant."

No way Evan could keep a straight face anymore. "Mr. Mopey?"

No one answered.

He peeked over his shoulder, but there was no sign of anyone in the area. "Wow. Very impressive, indeed."

The weight on his leg lightened as Matthias lifted his chin. Evan faced him, wondering how on earth this was going to work. "You're not really going to talk to me, are you?"

A wolfie smile greeted him as the old-timer sat up straighter and grinned.

Okay, he'd done some strange things over the years, but waiting for a feral old wolf to "talk" to him ranked right up there at the top.

Why the hell not? Things couldn't get more fucked up than they currently were.

Like Evan expected, no words were exchanged, but he sat and listened with everything he had. Sensing the things the wolf wanted to share—mostly in bursts of emotion that were strong enough for him to pick up without any pack connection at all. Brief flashes of memory hit him, images and ghosts of scent and sound.

The timing was all wrong, but it was also perfectly right. With urgent issues begging for his attention, Evan calmed his soul, closed his eyes, and allowed the old man to reminisce.

Like an old-fashioned movie reel starting up, snapshots of the wolf's life emerged, mixed with the steady background beat of emotion.

Anticipation. Youthful vigor and hopeful dreams. Traveling north for the gold rush. Finding a home. A people. Settling into a pack. Day-to-day activities that made Evan smile as the young wolf's world moved forward, one adventure after another.

Contentment. A long life filled with responsibility he'd met the best he could. Joining the pack for a hunt, fur and fang and limbs in motion under a shining moon. Laughter and teasing. Hard labour followed by times of rest. A life lived to the max.

Joy. The strongest emotion yet. Full and satisfying and oh-so-deep. An image flashed of a pretty redheaded woman, and Evan smiled. It had to be the wolf's mate who had brought him such delight. Sensual pleasures mixed with more laughter, and for a split second Evan was blindingly jealous.

But then...*sorrow.* Waves of it. Heartbreaking in its intensity, like drowning in unending tears. Everything was gone. Every*one*. Evan gasped at the pain the man shared, wondering that carrying the burden hadn't killed him outright.

The wolf straightened slowly until he looked directly into Evan's eyes, paws braced on the park bench. The old-timer moved cautiously but brought his nose against Evan's for a split second before returning all four paws to the ground. His head and tail held high as he disappeared back into the bush.

Evan pushed to his feet. Shaking off the memories

before they could knock him to his knees. Instead, he embraced the realization that had flooded in with the message.

It didn't matter if he'd made a mistake years ago. What mattered was the here and now. Confusion and fear had snuck in, and he'd let them steal the joy he and Amy could have been sharing.

They had been apart for too long. There couldn't be more secrets between them, either. It was time the past stopped getting in their way. Time *he* stopped getting in their way.

Because only once he and Amy were truly mates could they find what their future was supposed to look like.

AMY LAY CURLED on the couch in utter misery. She reached into the cookie package, grumbling discontentedly when she discovered nothing left but crumbs.

The three containers of Häagen-Dazs on the coffee table were empty as well.

What a wonderful way to spend an afternoon. *Not.*

She laid her head on the back cushion and fought the urge to cry. This wasn't her. She was a strong, powerful individual—

Who was absolutely devastated and lonely.

None of it made sense. Evan wasn't paying *any* attention to her now, and while she understood part of it was her own fault, it also wasn't. She'd never once heard of a mate turning away from another unless they did it deliberately. She'd been hiding, and Evan had let her, and now she didn't know how to turn things around.

It seemed she knew how to speak everyone's language except his. The pain in her heart expanded a bit more.

The front door of her house jerked open, and Amy jumped to her feet. Shaun stomped across the room to get in her face. "You're an idiot."

It would've been funny if she weren't already on the edge of breaking. "Thanks so much for your unasked-for opinion. Close the door on your way out."

Shaun shook his head and finger at the same time. "Oh, no, you're not getting out of this that easily. You're making him miserable. So you decided not to destroy him financially. Great. Instead you'll just rip his heart out. That's so human of you."

Amy turned her back on him. "You know nothing about what's going on."

"I know nothing? Me?" Shaun laughed. "Maybe I don't have all the details, but if I'm a pot, you're the kettle."

"What am I being such an idiot about then? Since you obviously want to tell me."

Shaun glared. "You say you want what's best for the pack. That's all Evan has ever wanted his entire bloody life. Even in the past, before he should've had to worry about it, he gave everything for the pack."

"Not now. He's doing the things least positive for everyone. It's as if he sees one solution, and he refuses to try anything else. Hell, he was so out of line he scared one of my pack into moving away." Colin Wheeler had sent her a farewell note along with word he'd asked for a transfer to Ottawa.

His rapid departure from the area had hurt. She'd failed someone who had given her their trust. Frustration was too mild a word for how devastated her wolf had been.

"If Evan was this stubborn years ago, maybe that's why

he ended up killing innocent people." It was a shitty thing to say, but she was pushed beyond exasperation.

At her bitter words, Shaun froze. His fists were clenched tight at his hips, and he spoke slowly, attempting to maintain control. "Jeez. Has he *still* not told you what happened?"

Amy shook her head. "Every time I ask him he insists it's too soon."

"Ah, for fucks sake." Shaun dropped onto the couch, his anger cooling. "Don't I feel like the ass of the century. I thought he'd told you everything, and you were being an ice-bitch."

"Tell me," Amy begged, squatting in front of him. "I keep trying to think of a reason I can accept. It's killing me, being tossed between two minds. I want to trust Evan, but he's doing his best to frustrate me and, along with me, the packs."

Shaun shook his head. "I *can't* tell you. Don't get me wrong. Now I want to, more than ever, but that's his job. Only I agree, he needs to tell you now."

Amy gave a frustrated snort as she turned away. "Good luck with that. I've asked, and I've asked, but it seems I'm not to be trusted. Which I understand, but our discord is bleeding into the packs, and I can't seem to stop it."

When Shaun spoke this time, his attitude was quieter and less confrontational. "He trusts you on one level. I don't understand why he's not trusting you with this." Shaun looked her in the eye. "I'll talk to him. But I need to tell you something I know he won't share. Evan is all about pack. He's all about everybody else, and not himself. He told you he challenged Kirk a number of times?"

Amy nodded, the tightness in her chest still there. "He challenged his Alpha before he tried anything else. He said he tried twice, and then the third time he ended up..." She couldn't say it.

For the first time Shaun willingly laid a hand on hers. "He was only thirteen the first time he made that challenge. Kirk took it as an insult, but the fight was more than expected, and it took Kirk nearly an hour to break Evan's arm. Two years later when Evan tried again, Kirk had planned ahead. He knew he'd never win in a fair challenge. He had a group of his flunkies, all of them Beta level, beat the crap out of Evan. They left him for dead."

Agony ripped through her at the thought of a youth that age being so abused. "God."

Shaun nodded. "He kept trying, Amy. He didn't succeed in any of the normal ways, and in the end he did what he had to do."

The Beta rose to his feet.

"Wait." Amy took a deep breath. "Thank you for telling me."

"We all have history. It's part of what makes us who we are." Shaun shrugged. "I've had a pretty easy life of it, really. Sometimes I forget that. Take it for granted."

Pain hovered, only this time for different reasons. Her troubles, Evan's, her brother's lost opportunities. "It's never easy to leave the past behind."

Shaun was tugging the front door open before she could say anything else. He paused and turned back to face her where she stood only paces behind him. "For what it's worth, I don't hate your guts anymore. Maybe."

She smiled even though it hurt. "You're still an ass. But that's part of what makes you unique."

He slipped out the door, his laughter fading in the distance.

She stood there, trying to figure out the best thing to do

right here and now. She was to blame for some of the trouble. Evan had to take responsibility for some of it as well. But nothing was going to get accomplished if they weren't in the same room at the same time. She reached for the phone, her fingers shaking as she hit his number.

He answered on the first ring. "Amy?"

It might be difficult but it was the right thing to do. "Can you come over? I have something to tell you."

Tires squealed in the background.

"You okay?" she asked.

"No problem. I'll be there in five minutes." He hung up before she could say anything else.

Oh boy.

Amy looked down. She'd pulled on comfy clothes to have her pity party, and her worn flannel pyjamas and fluffy slippers made her look about twelve years old.

What the hell. He was coming to see her, not some slinky outfit. In fact, the last thing she wanted was to distract him.

This wasn't about letting the wolves take charge, it was about finally getting to the truth so they could move forward, or be brave enough to call it off altogether. Yes, they needed to get this done for the pack's sake, but more than that, this was their future happiness on the line.

The thought that it all came down to the next half hour made her more afraid than anything ever had before in her life.

PART III

Thy life is thine to make or mar,
To flicker feebly, or to soar, a star;
It lies with thee—the choice is thine, is thine,
I answered Her: The choice is mine—ah, no!
We all were made or marred long, long ago.
The parts are written; hear the super wail:
"Who is stage-managing this cosmic show?"
"Quatrains "—Robert Service

18

———

He stood on her doorstep, the world totally changed from the last time he'd waited for her to answer the door.

This was it. This conversation was either going to break him or turn things around.

The door opened, and Amy stuck her head around the corner. Her big eyes were as mesmerizing as before, but she had dark shadows under them, and everything in him hated the thought he was responsible.

"You have a key," she murmured.

"I didn't want to take anything for granted." He paced past her as she swung the door open and made room.

It was like walking on eggshells, and that was the last thing Evan wanted. "I know you said we should talk. I have some important things to say as well."

She headed into the living room, tucking herself away in a chair that was too small for him to join her.

How had things come so far, so wrong?

He ignored all the other places in the room he could have sat, instead choosing to kneel at her feet.

Moisture filled her eyes, and she swallowed hard. "Please, don't."

He reached for her hands, tangling their fingers. "Don't what, Amy?"

The utter misery on her face was breaking his heart. "Don't make this even harder than it's going to be."

"What's so difficult you needed to tell me?"

Amy's voice shook when she finally got the words out. "I came here for all the wrong reasons. My search for revenge has ended up bringing pain to the packs, and it's hurt you. I'm so sorry we started all of this wrong because of me and my assumptions."

He wasn't going to mess this up like he had done their other conversations. He *listened* to what she said. "Thank you, and I accept your apology. But we need to get past the mistakes. I'm more to blame than you are. I'm stubborn, and far too focused on what's obvious, when I should be thinking about more than what's right in front of my face."

Amy nodded. "So, we put the past behind us."

"We have to, which means one more secret needs to come out. I'm sorry I didn't share with you earlier. You need to know everything. About your brother."

She stared at the ceiling, blinking hard as if to stop tears. "I'd like to know. I don't want to, in a way, but I need to put it behind me and stop letting my imagination torment me."

Evan understood. "I have nightmares about it, sometimes."

Stillness grew between them, this time connecting more than dividing. Amy stroked his cheek. "I heard you that night, when you were having a nightmare."

He stood, their hands still joined. "Come sit beside me. I need you in my arms if I'm going to face this again."

When she didn't deny him, a flicker of hope flared.

He settled on the couch, and when she would've sat beside him, he directed her straight into his lap so he could physically close her in his embrace. She leaned her head against his chest, and for a couple of minutes they didn't say anything. Just sat and breathed together.

"Hudson Bay pack is smack dab in the middle of some of the best hunting territory in the world. Expeditions had always contributed to the pack finances. Only at some point, and I'm not sure exactly why it happened, Kirk Gatlann crossed a line that should never be crossed." Evan stroked her head and shoulders, drawing strength from the contact. "Instead of caring for the pack, Kirk did the unthinkable."

Amy leaned back, one hand resting on his shoulder as she met his gaze.

Evan took a deep breath. "One time the hunting party went to the airport and picked up visiting clients, took them on the hunt, then returned them to the airport."

She frowned. "That seems perfectly normal."

"It does, except afterward, one of the pack went missing. They announced he'd decided to move away, and there was no further contact. It was as if he had vanished. A young man in his late teens. It's not uncommon for people that age to leave the North and head into Toronto or Montréal, but they usually kept in contact. He simply vanished."

"Something bad happened?"

Evan couldn't say this while he was looking at her. "He was dead. I found him. There was a set of subterranean caves on pack land. They were useful for many things—that's where the moonshine still was hidden. Youth used the side passages as places to fool around. The younger ones played hide and seek. Dan was in the caves, in his wolf, and he'd been shot."

A gasp escaped her.

"The fact Kirk wasn't more upset with what I found made me suspicious, so I went snooping. The last hunting party he'd led had a special request. They wanted to hunt wolf."

She quivered in his arms.

"After I finished getting sick, I didn't even think about it. I went and challenged Kirk."

Her fingers tightened on his shoulders. "You were young."

"Too young to challenge an Alpha and win. The only good part of it was there were no more mysterious disappearances for a while, and then it started again.

"I was older now, and in contact with more pack. Nothing was being said in public, but you could tell things were going wrong on the inside. Those who were part of Kirk's inner circle felt overconfident, those who weren't in on the secret knew they were in trouble, but saw no way out."

"That's sickening." Amy's fingers stroked his face. "You challenged him again?"

Evan nodded. "There'd been three more disappear, this time a family. I still wasn't successful in getting rid of Kirk, but people knew things were bad. We just didn't know how to get rid of the sickness."

He held her close so he could finish.

"Did Kirk hunt down my brother?" she whispered.

Pain struck again. "Kirk came for me."

She froze.

No matter how much Evan wanted to stop now, he couldn't. "I'd already set a trap. I'd figured out how to blow up the still, and I was determined to take Kirk out when he was alone and running in his wolf. It was a simple plan, and the only one who'd be hurt was an animal that desperately needed killing.

"Only before I could act, he came for me. Told me to take my chances running in the hunt, or he'd shoot me where I stood. I had no choice. Philip must have seen me leaving with Kirk and guessed something was wrong. He followed us.

"There was a fair-sized group, all laughing and getting their guns ready. Kirk grabbed Philip and told him he was part of the hunting party and to act as a guide. I had everything in position to get rid of Kirk, but suddenly Philip was there as well."

The utter frustration of that day came raging back, and Evan shook his head.

"I led them to where I had set up the booby trap, the entire time debating what to do. No one knew what I had prepared, and maybe I could have waited for another day. But there were no guarantees, and when I got the chance I took it. While they were directly above the caves, I snuck down a side tunnel, shifted and lit the moonshine still to blow. I made it to the surface just in time for the explosion to go off and see the entire tabletop collapse. All the leadership, the group of hunters who had arranged the illegal hunt—the entire group fell in. Trapped or dead.

"Philip with them."

OF ALL THE horror stories he could have told her, she never would have expected this. It seemed unreal, impossible, and yet it made total sense in a terrifying, life-changing way.

There had always been moments when she had to make choices, deciding for the good of the pack. Many times serious decisions as well, life and death on the line for more than one person.

Maybe it wasn't the choice she would have made. But there was no way to know for sure, not unless she'd been in his position, dealing with the fear and anger Evan would have faced.

Was her brother an acceptable sacrifice? She didn't know.

Would her brother have considered his sacrifice acceptable?

That was an entirely different question, and somehow... she hoped he would have. If it had been her, knowing a terror like Kirk Gatlann was running the pack, she would've done everything she could to take him out, even sacrifice herself.

Evan hadn't said a word since he finished. He barely seemed to be breathing, holding motionless in anticipation of her response.

The only thing she could do was offer him comfort. She pressed closer, easing her forehead against his and holding him to her body. "I was wrong to make you a target."

His body shook. "Do you forgive me for killing Philip?"

She swallowed hard and hung on tighter. "There's nothing to forgive."

Something brand-new appeared in his eyes. Muted joy? Or maybe it was hope, plain and simple. "Tell me somehow in the next fifty years you can learn to trust me. I need you, Amy. I need you as my mate, and while I'm so sorry I broke your heart and caused you pain, I can't stand the thought of not being with you anymore."

"We need to trust each other. Not in the future, but now. That's the only way we can actually be together."

His eyes darkened, his breathing grew rapid. "We've

known each other such a short time, so filled with chaos, yet you're already a part of me. You don't believe that yet, but I'll show you. Whether it takes a day, a week, or longer, you'll know how much you are cared for. How much you belong to me, and I belong to you."

It was the time for sharing secrets, so she had to be brave. "I haven't belonged to anyone in forever. Any time I tried, people disappeared. My brother, my family. One foster home after another was ripped from me for reasons I never understood. My world was continually torn apart, and I always thought if Philip hadn't died, everything would have been different. I would have had a family who loved me and were always there for me."

He pressed his lips to her temple.

Amy pushed the past aside. "I won't blame you anymore. I needed to share that because it's part of what built me. What made me afraid."

He stroked her, both with his hands and the other part of himself that was so reassuring, so comforting. "I would've hated me too."

"I don't want to hate anyone anymore."

Evan cupped her chin in his hand. "You aren't alone. God, I've been such a fool, and made such mistakes. But we're going to fix this. This is not just about our pasts. It's about the fact I want to be with you, and I want to be everything I have to be so you're never alone."

"You want to be with me?" Inside, her wolf uncurled. Over the past weeks, the beast had retreated, upset and saddened by what she thought was rejection by her mate. "How do we move on?"

"The same way you start anything. At the beginning." He brushed his lips over hers. Infinitely tender before pulling back to stare into her eyes. "Yes, we have two packs that need us to unite them, but this isn't about them. This is about *us*. The stronger we are, the better we will be able to support them. It'll become a circle. The stronger they are, the more you and I will be happy. Because that's who we are, and what's important to us. But we need to come first."

Another crack split the ice around her heart.

"I can't leave them. I thought about it," Amy confessed. "I thought maybe if I did leave, Canyon would be forced to accept you as Alpha, but I can't do it."

Evan shook his head. "And you shouldn't. The truth is Whitehorse will be the strongest with both of us. The packs aren't independent of each other, no matter what they think. They need each other, and we need each other."

Something inside melted more, and Amy risked a smile. "Then it's a good thing we have each other." Fear was fading. It had no place when faced by such truth. She found her fingers tangled with his. "We serve the wolves."

"*We*," he emphasized. "We've only begun finding ourselves."

There was no way she could deny him.

Her head and heart were so full that when he leaned closer, she wasn't sure at first what he planned. By the time his lips touched hers, she'd lost the ability to protest.

Besides, they were past the point of protesting. This was what they needed, not as a frustrated way to deal with two wolves and two people who weren't sure what they wanted. This was a time for them to affirm they were mates, and that no matter what, they would face the future as one.

He held her tenderly even as the kiss grew more intense. Amy lifted up so she could straddle his body. She grasped his shoulders and held on tight as their mouths met. He sank his teeth into her lower lip, and a shudder rolled through her. Acceptance and trust building.

She got his buttons open, desperate to make contact with skin. Then one long, slow stroke followed another as she explored his pectorals, and up over his shoulder muscles. Dragging her nails down his biceps before repeating the move all over again.

He was busy as well, peeling away her top so he could tease and pet. Hands so gentle on her body even as she understood there was no escaping his touch.

He cupped his palms around her breasts, circling his thumbs over her nipples until they peaked. When he leaned over and licked the tight points, satisfaction rippled over her skin.

This was what she needed. Not just a mate she was attracted to because of fate and circumstance. This was a man who was totally connected with her and ready to take on the world at her side.

Evan brought her with him as he took them down the hallway to her bedroom. She smiled against his lips as he lowered her to the bed. "I disconnected the remote control. Sorry."

"I'm still seeing stars, and if this bed isn't rocking on its own soon, I'm doing something wrong."

It took ten seconds to get rid of the rest of her clothes while he was busy doing the same. There wasn't a frantic need for massive foreplay. Instead, it was all about connection. Being there for each other.

They lay naked on the bed, body and soul exposed. Touching gently, exploring and talking quietly at the same time.

"I wanted to wake up with you in my arms," Evan confessed. "That first morning, after we spent the night together. I missed you. Deep down inside my soul, I knew something was still wrong and I ached for you."

Amy understood. "That night you had the nightmare. I wanted so badly to comfort you, but I was so afraid. What if I opened myself up to hope, and you were torn away like everyone else in my world?"

He kissed her. Pressed his lips to hers, to her cheek, up and over her eyes. Brushing away tears that came involuntarily. Kissing her temples, and her nose, and her chin. As if he couldn't get enough of touching her.

"I'm yours. I'll never leave you, and we'll find a way to be together *and* serve the pack." He tucked her against his body so they were connected. Not like while making love, but every inch plastered together until neither of them could move without the other being totally aware of it. "If it ever comes to a choice, we'll work together to find a way. I promise."

Amy's heart was so full she could have exploded. He rolled her under him, opening her thighs to let his hips settle. The hard length of his heavy shaft pressed to her softness, and as she dragged her nails down his back he rocked, teasing her to a higher pitch.

Between one breath and the next, he slipped into her. Filled her completely, joining them the way they were supposed to be as mates.

Trust. Connection.

She held on tight as he convinced her they belonged together. For the next couple hours, he convinced her. Her loneliness and doubts finally erased.

19

———————

*E*van wasn't sure how he had survived before. It was as if he'd been asleep, and now woken up. He wanted to wax poetic about how the sun seemed brighter, and the air seemed clearer, but mostly he just wanted to hold Amy's hand and be with her.

His brain was playing every cheesy Beatles song imaginable, and he didn't even give a damn.

It was time to move forward *together*. Not only were they mates, but united they were powerful enough to accomplish whatever was necessary to calm the packs.

He knew it was his fault it had taken so long to get to this point. Amy resisted saying *I told you so*, and he appreciated it.

He expected no such restraint when he next saw his Beta.

"I want to do this." Amy rubbed his fingers absently as they walked from his car to the Moonshine Inn, headed to the bar. "Merging is going to be tough, but it doesn't need to become a huge war."

"Unfortunately, it might be too late. We're already doing

damage control. But since I've got a commitment from Canyon that they'll support me if I behave..." he gave her a wink, "...it's the hard heads at Takhini we need to work over, mine included."

"That's why I suggested dropping in at the bar. Just don't feel as if all of them need to fall in love with me today."

Evan had no intention of pushing things, but he was also immensely aware of what was on the line. It wouldn't do for him to be distracted or preoccupied.

"About time you got here, Evan. Oh. It's *you*. Hi, Amy." Shaun stood in the doorway, looking her over as if checking for lice.

Oh, hell no. Tonight was going to be about challenges, but Shaun should know better. Evan readied to defend Amy, but she beat him to it, grabbing Shaun by the collar. She whipped his Beta around and pushed him back into the bar. "Show a little more respect to your betters, brat."

Voices dropped throughout the bar as pack stopped in their tracks and turned their attention toward the door. Everyone wanted to see what Shaun would do, especially since he'd been pretty vocal about dissing her.

Then Amy stepped to Shaun's side and hip-checked him, rocking him hard enough to knock him off balance. She laughed, catching him before he could fall to the floor. "Oh, Shaun, don't you know women always arrive on time?"

Gem rose from where she was sitting, a real smile on her lips. "She's got you there. Or..." Shaun's mate raised a brow, "...did you have a comment to make regarding women and punctuality?"

Gem and Amy glanced at each other then burst out laughing, and the tension faded. Evan took his place beside Amy, slipping his arm around her and bringing her tight to his side.

Shaun wrinkled his nose, sniffed a couple of times, then rolled his eyes. "Great. This is what I get for being so smart."

"Yes, this is your fault." Amy glanced at Gem. The woman nodded in approval as Amy grabbed Shaun and gave him an enormous hug, kissing his cheek before she released him. Amy kept hold of Shaun's shoulders, looking up at him, her happiness shining bright. "This is your fault, and I don't ever want you to forget it. You wonderful man."

A flush spread over his face, and Shaun turned abruptly. Stomped to his chair and sat with a plop, scooping Gem into his lap and burying his face in her neck.

All around the bar, people eyed the situation with unease, and not a little confusion.

Someone sidled up to Amy and paused. Looked her up and down, then dipped his head before fleeing to the far corner of the pub.

"What was that about?" Amy muttered.

Evan had a bad feeling about it. "Going to snitch on us, I think."

He took a slow look around, examining everyone in the room. Taking in the rustic wood decorations on the walls, the pulsing beat of music in the background as conversations slowly resumed.

Moonshine Pub was his baby. This was something he had worked hard to make a success. In a way, it was very right that here was where he and Amy would make their first stand to prove they were more than Alphas of two packs. He couldn't fault Takhini for feeling confused, not after the way he had left them directionless.

But that was going to stop. Here and now.

"Come on, let's dance." Evan linked his fingers with Amy's and tugged her toward the dance floor.

A sense of normality continued to grow as people

observed Amy settling against him, their questioning expressions fading to smiles as they sensed Evan's contentment.

Soft fingers touched his face, and he looked at his mate.

Mate. A rush of happiness struck again. He could've been doing moonshine shots for the past five hours and not ended up as lightheaded as over one touch of her fingers.

"Heads up," Amy warned. "There seems to be some kind of *discussion group* headed our way from the far corner of the room."

Evan nodded, settling her hands around his neck before grabbing hold of her hips and continuing to sway to the music. "Until they prove otherwise, I'm going to assume the best."

One of her brows rose. "This isn't your fight anyway, right?"

She had him over a barrel. He'd promised to let her deal with anyone if it was appropriate, but that promise was about to drive him mad. He drove down his fears. "Fine. You spank them this time, but if they need any extra chastisement, I'm your man."

"I seem to remember hearing Caroline had to prove her worth when she started dating you. If anything, the expectations on me are much higher." She whispered the words, barely audible even from where he stood. "Trust me."

And that was the most powerful thing she could have reminded him of.

"Since when did Takhini become the play toys for Canyon?"

"Damn it, Toby. You got that backwards. Evan's found a new chew toy, and look, it's one of the little Canyon freaks." Lance stood behind Amy, Toby one step back. A small group of young male wolves clustered loosely behind them.

Amy rotated, leaning her back against Evan's chest. She was short enough the top of her head barely touched his chin, but somehow she seemed to tower over the annoying wolves standing before them.

"Were you talking to me?" she asked.

Lance and Toby glanced at each other before turning back with a smirk. "Not really talking *to* you. You're not going to be around for long enough for us to even find out your name. Evan has this bad habit of picking up strays. The last one had fleas. Had to fumigate the entire hotel after she left."

"I don't know, Lance. I think this one is worse than the last." Toby made a show of sniffing. "Think she's been hanging out too long with all those Canyon losers. She doesn't know how to handle real wolves."

Evan found stifling his growl of disapproval damn near impossible. He wanted nothing more than to knock Toby's and Lance's heads together, but he had to let her do this alone.

He sensed Amy's change of body tension, but kept himself out of the fight. Just stood like a wall as she wordlessly went into action.

She jumped upward. Caught hold of Evan's shoulders over her head at the same moment she kicked out her feet and made contact with Lance's chest. He flew backwards into the men behind him, knocking them over like a set of bowling pins. Before they had finished bouncing, Amy was back on the floor and moving toward Toby. She leapt forward at high speed, hooking an arm around his neck and using momentum to pivot onto his back.

Toby grabbed for the arm that was cutting off his air supply. Evan clenched his teeth to stop from calling a warning that Lance was back on his feet.

He shouldn't have worried. Amy maintained her chokehold while using her other hand in Toby's hair like reins to turn the man to face his buddies. Her timing was so perfect the blow Lance swung struck his friend instead of Amy, the sound of fist meeting face making a sickening crack against the lighthearted music playing in the background.

This wasn't Evan's fight, but it was.

He folded his arms and shifted his feet to draw attention to himself. "Not that I want to interfere in your entertainment, but just a heads up. Amy has full authority. If you want to beg for mercy, she's the one you kneel to."

Then he did the hardest thing he'd ever done. Evan turned and walked away.

He headed to the bar. Slipped behind the counter and poured himself a double shot of whiskey. The burn of the alcohol going down calmed his human side who hated having control out of his hands.

His wolf side wanted to watch his mate rip the disrespectful bastards apart.

But Amy had insisted, and she was right. This was the proper way. So, whistling lightly, Evan grabbed a cloth and wiped down the countertop.

The pack members seated on the barstools glanced back and forth a couple of times between him and the ongoing fight, their momentary panic fading as Evan's confidence screamed out.

Evan smiled at one of them. "She's okay."

The older wolf smiled back. "She's your mate, right? Of course she's okay."

The sound of wood splintering nearly made him look, but he resisted temptation and focused on the pack member before him. "She is, and she's not only beautiful and smart, she knows exactly how to take care of herself. And how to take care of me."

Heads nodded, one of the old-timers gesturing with his chin to the side. "You know it's okay for you to help," he whispered. "We don't mind."

Evan shook his head. "Waste of time. Some things she needs me to do, but fight her battles isn't one of them."

Someone shouted, and the noise faded to nothing but the pulsing beat of the music from the sound system.

"It's safe to look," the old-timer told him. The man grinned approvingly. "She's a feisty one. Reminds me of my mate."

Evan turned, leaning both hands on the counter as he hungrily took in the damage from the battle. For the first moment he couldn't see Amy, not by the broken chairs or near any of the bodies on the floor.

"Looking for me, sailor?"

She stood beside him, a thin ribbon of blood trickling from a cut on her forehead. Scratches and bruises marred her arms, but she showed a whole lot less damage than the pack boys pulling themselves to vertical.

"Do I need to call an ambulance?" Evan pulled her to his side and lifted her onto the counter.

Amy glanced over her shoulder. "I think Toby will be okay. Let me check about the other fellow." She raised her voice. "Hey, Lance. You want an ambulance, or are you going to shuffle home without a Band-Aid on your boo-boos?"

"Fuck off," Lance snapped, his lippy words sliding into a sharp scream of pain.

Evan and Amy watched Gem step daintily over the wolf she'd kicked. "If I told you once, I've told you a million times. I will not accept that kind of language around here."

She sniffed then approached the bar. "May I have another glass of white wine, please?"

Off in the background, the youth with the attitudes were helping Toby and Lance from the bar. Evan pulled Gem's favourite wine from the cooler, pausing to rub his cheek against Amy's.

Slowly the noise of conversation slipped back to normal.

"What would you like?" Evan asked his mate.

"Some of your moonshine. I hear it's pretty good."

He nodded, grabbing the slim blue bottle and gesturing into the bar. "Let's go sit. I have a feeling there will be a few people coming to chat."

Evan settled in his usual seat, Amy perched beside him like the queen of the wolves she was. Gem and Shaun joined them, the leadership sitting in state before pack who entered and left, checking out this new thing.

He tipped a little liquid into her glass, then his own. He raised the teeny tumbler in the air. "Whitehorse forever. To becoming one strong, united pack."

"Whitehorse forever." The toast was echoed by their Betas, and taken up by the pack. All around the room, glasses were raised and voices rang out.

Amy leaned against him, the warmth of her body against his so right and perfect. "That's not the last of it, but thank you for letting me take care of them on my own."

He looked into her eyes and smiled, glad to have put his fears behind him, although he still didn't like the idea of her being hurt. "Hey, you just about took my head off when we fought. I had no doubt about your physical prowess. I have even less doubts about your smarts."

Evan took a shot of his moonshine, cupped his hand around the back of her neck, and slipped her a kiss that was two hundred proof, and none of it from the liquor.

If the kiss went on a little longer than normal, he didn't give a damn. Tongues tangling, breaths mingling. She bit his lip, and Evan growled, hungry for more.

A cheer went up from one corner of the room, and he pulled back far enough to see glasses raised in their direction.

"People like to see their Alpha content." Amy caught him by the cheeks and smiled at him, bright satisfaction pouring from her in spite of the bruises and cuts.

"Their *Alphas*, you mean. Because we're doing this together, baby."

Evan tugged Amy into his lap, curling his arm around her waist and enjoying the sensation of being with her.

She nuzzled against his neck, the connection between them strengthening. "That was exciting," she confessed in a low whisper.

Evan laughed, his amusement rising. "Bloodthirsty little thing."

She shrugged, her smile twisting into something a touch more evil. "As much fun as it is to torment people via computer, there's something satisfying about beating the crap out of a person, isn't there?"

How had he missed seeing this? The perfect way they fit. Evan stared into her eyes, his attention focused on her. "I can hardly wait to see what comes next."

Amy put the rest of her extra sheets into a box, closed the lid and taped it shut. She glanced around the house, searching for more things she could get rid of before Evan brought his stuff over.

In the past week, her world had changed so immensely.

It seemed impossible, and yet she was a shifter. She knew impossible happened all the time.

This was her experiencing true happiness for the first time in her life, and that's what made it so unusual.

Her phone rang and she answered it cheerfully. "Hey, lover. What's happening?"

A low rumble sounded in her ear, raising goose bumps all over. "I've got everything in the truck, and Shaun tells me I'm allowed to take the rest of the afternoon off."

"How generous of him." Amy pulled open another drawer and dumped everything into a box. "I'd take him up on the offer if I were you. He needs the exercise in looking after things, anyway."

"Ah, he's got it easy. With the hotel shut down for maintenance and improvements, he gets to sit in state at the pack house. I don't think he's suffering too hard."

Evan was moving in with her. Changes were happening between the Takhini and the Canyon packs. A month ago she never would have dreamed this was where they'd come to, and yet it was real.

"Whenever you get here, I'm ready." She eyed the pile of boxes stacked against the living room wall. "Sort of. I've made room for some of your stuff. We can make decisions about furniture as we go. I know a few people in the pack who could use the stuff we don't need."

"Of course you do. I love that about you."

Another shot of happiness rang through her. "Hurry up and get your ass over here. I miss you," she confessed.

He hung up, and she went back to her task, nearly delirious at the changes. It didn't seem right she could be at this point in her life. A mate, a home. A place to belong.

All of it made even better because Evan went out of his

way every day to make sure she knew he wanted *her*, not just the pack.

Rapid knocking at the back door dragged her from her task, and she smiled.

"You don't need to knock. It's your house too," she said as she swung the door open.

Laney stood on the back porch, a haunted expression in her eyes. Amy automatically glanced around the yard even as she took in the trembling woman before her. Laney's hands were clenched, her face gone white, and her entire body shook.

Amy reached for her. "What's wrong? Come inside—"

"No. I'm so sorry." Laney jerked her hands free and took a step back. "I'm sorry, I didn't know what else to do. You have to help me."

"Of course I'll help," Amy assured her. "What happened?"

Laney motioned over her shoulder to a car in the alleyway, the engine still running. "It's Mike. He's got Dexter."

Fury filled Amy's veins. "Your ex?"

Laney nodded. "Dexter didn't come home after school, and I thought he might have missed the bus, but then I got a call. Mike grabbed him."

Amy reached for her phone. "Let me call—"

"It's no use. He's right there." She pointed again, her face a mask of misery. "Mike said he was sick of your interference. I'm sorry, but he's got Dexter in the backseat, and I didn't know what else to do."

Amy pressed her hands to Laney's upper arms and offered as much calming reassurance she could. "You did the right thing coming here. I'll take care of you and Dexter."

Laney shook her head. "No. Nothing is right. I'm so sorry."

Something blurred at the edge of Amy's vision a second before a sharp pain bloomed on the side of her head. Darkness rolled in as her legs gave out.

20

Coming back to consciousness hurt. Amy rolled onto her hands and knees, bracing herself against the nausea that struck. Complete blackness surrounded her, a low hissing noise the only clue she had to her location.

That, and the familiar scent of the Moonshine Inn.

During the year she'd been tracking Evan, she'd done all sorts of interesting research. Sneaking into the hotel and finding its hidden passageways had become one of her favourite pastimes. There was something fun about avoiding security cameras and casual patrols.

That meant even in the dark she wasn't totally lost. She was, however, in trouble. The room Mike had trapped her in was one of the least accessible in the entire building.

Amy patted her pockets to see if she'd been lucky enough to be left with her cell phone, or anything she could use to alert Evan.

Nothing. They had left her with nothing but the clothes on her back.

She took a long breath to calm herself. Evan would

come. In the meantime, she knew how to escape the room, and it didn't involve the door.

She did try the door first though, just to be sure. Her fingers slipped over the cold metal of the latch. It was firmly locked, the barrier itself hard and impenetrable.

Moving carefully in the absolute darkness, Amy orientated herself. The room held shelving, once filled with supplies, now mostly empty. The shelves made a dandy ladder to the roof. She pushed blindly on the ceiling tiles until one moved, then she stood on the top shelf and reached into the darkness to find a solid surface.

It was a good thing she wasn't any bigger. She could shift and change her size slightly, but for the moment she preferred to stay in her human form. Amy crawled up and sideways, inching forward toward a second room where she should be able to escape into the hallway.

It didn't take long before she had both feet on the ground, the light switch turned on. The second room held part of the mechanical system, and she moved quickly to the electrical box.

Damn. Original wiring. For what she planned, she needed a room that had been renovated recently.

Amy stood with her ear against the door, waiting silently. When two minutes passed with no footsteps or voices, she edged into the passageway and stepped forward.

In the bowels of the hotel, there were a million doors and pathways. From her earlier explorations, she knew which ones to follow, heading directly to where she should find computer access.

She didn't bother to turn on the lights in the room this time. Just left the door partially open, the hallway lighting giving her enough illumination as she spotted a control panel. She pocketed the keys hanging beside the box, jerked open the door and brought up the security system.

Damn again.

Someone had turned off the master control. Amy pulled the cover off the wall, going for the wiring, but it was too late. Noise rose behind her, and she barely had time to turn before she was struck, smacking into the concrete floor hard.

"I figured you wouldn't stay put for very long." Unfamiliar voice, familiar attitude.

Amy turned, preparing to fight. At least until she spotted Dexter trapped in the stranger's arms. "Don't hurt him."

"I wouldn't dream of it." The stranger patted the boy's head. Dexter squirmed, swinging his fists in a futile attempt to hit the man who held him around the waist. "Stop squirming, you little beast."

"I'm glad you're not my dad. I *hate* you."

So this was Mike. "Let Dexter go," Amy proposed. "You have a beef with me, we can deal with it all by ourselves."

She put as much suggestion into the words as possible.

Mike laughed, the noise nasty and dark. "You can't order me around. I'm strong enough, and I got people on my side supporting me. It's time for a shakeup in Whitehorse, and I plan to be the one standing at the end of it."

Amy got to her feet and brushed off her hands, not at all surprised to see Toby and Lance in the group.

She glared at Lance. "I should have ripped your throat out."

"Maybe you should have. Too late. We've had enough of you, and of Evan, and it's time for a change." Lance stepped closer to sneer down at her. "You shouldn't have felt so cocky the other day."

Amy lifted her knee and caught him between the legs,

hard enough he fell to the floor, hands clutching his crotch. "Who's feeling cocky now?"

"Enough," Mike ordered. "Take her and the kid, and tie her up in the room we prepared. We only need one more thing, and we're done."

"Kidnapping me and Dexter is a declaration of war." Amy struggled in the grip of four wolves, all of whom seemed wary of getting within knee range.

Mike grinned harder. "That's exactly what this is. And before the day is over, the war will be over. Whitehorse will have a new Alpha. Me."

In spite of the hands holding her, she was ready to fight as they were dragged down the hallway. Then Dexter whimpered softly, and the plan changed in a split second. "Hey, Dex. Chin up, buddy, we're going to be okay."

"Depends on your definition of *okay*," Toby joked, a ripple of laughter carrying through the group.

"Give me one minute with you by myself," Amy offered. "One minute, and you'll be joking through a set of dentures."

How could anyone threaten a child? She didn't care so much about herself, but she could sense Dexter's terror, and that pissed her off more than the attempt to take over Whitehorse.

They were brought into a room off the mechanical side of the hotel. "This is where I work," Toby bragged. "I know all the tricks how to make things work. The part that will impress you is that means I know how to make things break. And burn. And explode."

While he gloated, the others duct-taped her wrists to a chair, her ankles to the sturdy metal legs. "If you start running now, you might make it to the Alaska border before Evan catches you."

Toby shook his head as he reached for her, twisting his fingers in her hair to hold her still while he pressed a piece of duct tape over her mouth. "Evan? He's not going to run any direction except straight to you. Which is exactly what Mike wants. So you may as well stop with the threats and think about how much this is going to hurt."

She should have tried harder to bite him.

A moment later they were alone. She was secured to the chair, unable to speak or get herself free. A few feet away, Dexter was curled up in another chair, his back toward her as he cried softly.

Her only option was nonverbal. Even as she twisted at the bounds around her wrists, she reached out and comforted the boy, filling the room with as much peace as possible. Slowly his crying turned to sniffles, and he faced her, dashing tears from his eyes and lifting his chin.

"I'm sorry I was so scared." He crawled into her lap, touching the tape over her mouth. "I need to take this off, right?"

Amy nodded.

Dexter carefully peeled back the tape. Amy felt as if she'd been given some kind of horrifying facial. "That's much better. Thank you for helping me."

"Are they going to burn us up?" Dexter whispered, terror in his voice.

"They think they're going to, but they're not very smart." Amy tilted her head toward her hands. "They should have tied you up too. You're a very good ally in a tough situation."

The little guy worked to untangle the tape from one wrist. "He's not my daddy."

The kid might be scared to death, but that statement at least came out loud and clear.

Amy agreed with him. "No, he's not. He's a bad man who

needs to be taught a lesson. I think someone will be here soon to help us, but until then we have to work together. If that door opens I want you to hide." She looked around the room trying to spot a suitable place to hide an eight-year-old.

"I can't shift yet," Dexter warned.

"That's okay. There are lots of places for you as a human."

This room had more possibilities than the first one she had been stuck in, but it still wasn't a solution. Wolves would sniff Dexter out no matter where she tucked him.

As soon as Dexter got her right hand loose, she went to work on the left. "I think I see something that will help. Let me get my feet free, and I'll get you set up."

"Is my mommy okay?"

Amy nodded. "But she's going to be very happy to see you once we get out of here."

It was a matter of timing. Out in the hotel, there was a group of wolves she needed to stay away from. She had Dexter, and she needed to get him to safety.

And somewhere out there was Evan who she was certain was doing everything he could to get to her. If she could wait long enough for him to show up, that would make all the difference.

But until he showed up, she would just have to prove she was a worthy leader for the joint packs.

It took Evan five minutes flat to discover Amy was nowhere in her house. He paced the living room, following her most recent tracks, and ended up on the back porch, totally confused.

There was another scent along with hers. Something must have happened.

His phone rang, and he slapped it on.

"I'm so sorry, I had no choice."

The voice was somewhat familiar, and Evan struggled to place it. "Laney?"

"My ex showed up. He made me grab her, and now I think it's a trap for you." Laney's words increased in speed as her terror became more apparent. "Sam and Dexter are somewhere in the Moonshine Inn. Mike said he's taking over the pack here in Whitehorse. He said he's heard you'd lost control. Someone from your pack was helping him, and I'm so sorry."

Dammit. Evan was back in his truck and headed for the inn. "Don't panic, just tell me again what happened."

"We went to the inn. He said he would let Dexter go, but when we got there, they grabbed Sam, and tried to grab me as well. I got away. I think they didn't expect me to—" her voice broke before she forced herself on, "—they didn't expect me to leave Dex. But I had to. It was my only choice, and now they have my son, and they have Sam."

He should have expected something like this to happen. "Laney, I need you to do something. Contact everyone you know in Canyon. Whatever they can do to help, tell them to do it. I'm going to the inn, and I'm going to get your son. But I need backup. Can you do that for me?"

"You would save Dexter for me?"

"You're pack. Amy and I promised to take care of all of you, and that's what we're going to do. I bet right now Amy is looking after Dexter. I want you to remember that."

Wavering sniffles came over the phone.

"But you have to be brave and help as well. Contact Canyon."

"I will. Please, save my son."

Evan hung up and hurriedly made another call. "They've made their move," he told Shaun. "I bet it's Lance and Toby, but they've hooked up with some troublemaker out of Dawson City. I'm headed to the Moonshine Inn. Meet me there, and be ready with emergency services."

"Do you want me to call them in already?" All Shaun's usual joking had vanished.

"It's pack related, so we need to make sure this stays secret, at least for now. But let's not take chances." Evan pulled to a stop around the corner from the hotel. "I'm there. Don't let me down."

He jammed his phone into his pocket and headed to one of the service entrances. He paused, reconsidered and instead found a fire exit ladder, jumping up and grabbing the bottom rung so he could quickly ascend to the roof.

Stealing into his own hotel. He always figured it would come to this, but he never thought it would be Amy's life on the line as well. Someone kidnapping her and making a challenge for pack—this was more than discontented rumbles. This was going to end in blood.

Now he had to make sure it wasn't his or his mate's.

He eased open a ceiling vent. Sneaking in would be slower than rushing down hallways, but less risky in terms of running into any bad guys. He lowered himself into the dark space and closed the vent to hide his presence.

And then he forced himself to slow down. To sense where he was so he could reach out with the other part of him. The strong mental link between him and Amy had to make a difference. Somehow, he needed to be able to contact her, even from here.

He kicked himself that he'd mucked up so much in the first place that they'd never made it to the point of marking each other. This entire rescue would have been a lot easier if they already had that connection.

There was only so much that he could go on, but somewhere in the building below him she was waiting. A sense of peace came unexpectedly, even in the midst of his blind fury. She was smart, very smart, and he remembered something she'd mentioned about discovering everything there was to know about the inn and the pack house during her *recon* days. That gave him the first inkling of which direction to look for her.

Evan stole his way to the service elevator, using the cables and sidewall to travel. He had to force his way past the actual elevator, grasping hold of the cables with a set of gloves he found tucked into a service box. The heavy leather protected him as he slid downward at a rapid pace.

He reached the bottom floor and pried the door open an inch, freezing as a wolf paced past farther down the hallway. Low conversation carried from beside the elevator before moving farther away.

Evan followed silently, thankful for the lack of air currents that kept his scent from those he was tracking. As soon as he made the main hallway, one deep breath was the only clue he needed, and after a cautious wait he took the first door.

Amy whirled silently to face him, hands up and ready for attack before she straightened and smiled. Fingers going to her lips as he stepped toward her.

He caught her in his arms and squeezed briefly, needing a moment of physical touch to anchor him.

She returned his hug then moved back, gesturing with her head toward an open duct. Dexter stared from the metal boxlike opening, surprise and hope in his eyes.

Amy squatted and pushed the little boy's bangs from his

eyes. "This is my mate, Evan. Do you remember him?" she whispered.

Dexter nodded.

She turned, slipping a hand around the back of Evan's neck to draw him closer so she could speak quietly. "I need you to get Dexter out of here."

"We can all get out of here." Evan motioned toward the door.

Amy shook her head. "You have a better chance if it's just the two of you. Plus, if I can get to the main panel, I can lock the hotel down and trap them. If we all take off, they might burn the inn then hide. We don't want them to show up again later and keep tormenting us."

"You're not going to go wandering around the inn when they could kill you."

Her expression sharpened. "Dexter can't escape by himself, and you can't talk to the computer, can you? I know it's asking a lot, but this is my pack as well. I need to defend it, and this is the best way I know how."

Evan's heart fell as the seriousness of what she was asking hit.

He had said he trusted her, had even given her space during the fight in the bar, but this was their real world. This was a challenge not only to her leadership, but for the entire pack.

If he turned her down, he was as good as saying she wasn't worthy of leading. He had only one option if they were going to make it as mates, as sick as the choice made him.

"I'll take Dexter." He caught her by the chin and forced her to look him in the eye. "But you leave a trapdoor so I can get back in."

"Evan—"

She was about to argue. Forget that noise. He spoke firmly. "I trust you, it's not that. But don't ask me to stand by and do nothing to defend the pack. More importantly, I need to help *you*. I want to stand at your side while we do this."

She didn't hesitate. Just pressed up on her tiptoes and planted her lips against his. A fiery kiss full of desperation and passion. The two of them together, even though for a time their skills were needed in different directions.

Evan put everything he could into the kiss before pulling back.

"I'll set the side service door on a code block," Amy promised, sneaking her hand out of his pocket and holding up his cell phone. "I need to borrow this as well. The password for the door will be 'united'."

Evan nodded then turned toward Dexter. "Okay, buddy, it's time for you and me to do a little sightseeing inside some secret passages. Hold on, and we'll get you to your mom as fast as possible."

A set of arms wrapped around his neck as Dexter settled in tight. Evan spared one last glance over his shoulder at Amy, then crawled into the ductwork and headed for the roof.

21

Evan vanished with Dexter. The lovely sense of certainty her mate left with her washed away the urge to worry. It wasn't cockiness, but confidence. Even while they were apart, they were working together to get the job done.

Amy closed the panel and turned her back on the duct, focusing on the task ahead.

She opened Evan's phone, made a couple of adjustments, then turned it on. She used the 3G connections to access the main computer she had hacked into so long ago.

She had been using illegal access to the system as part of her revenge. Now it looked as if having the cheats in place might save them.

One after the other, she checked the systems for ways to give Evan time to get Dexter free. She turned on alarms in three different sections of the hotel. None of them connected to outside authorities, but hopefully the clanging would be bothersome enough that Mike would send someone to check them.

Her thumbs flew over the teeny keyboard as she accessed a direct line to the security cameras. It took her thirty seconds to find her targets, figuring out not only where Mike waited, but where Lance and Toby were setting up mischief.

Mike had taken over the bar. All the curtains to the outside were closed—no prying eyes could spot what they were up to. It also meant she'd have to go through the side hallway and take the back door into Evan's office.

Toby concerned her more. He was in the mechanical room, a soldering iron in his hand. She wasn't sure what modifications he was making, but in reference to their discussion about explosions, it didn't look good.

The entire situation had a deadline, and she had to make sure she was in the right place at the right time to get out alive.

With Evan's phone set up to show multiple camera angles, she risked opening the door and scooting into the hallway. It would be far faster if she could take the direct route rather than crawling through ducts. She snuck forward, placing each step to avoid making any noise, moving to the emergency staircase like a ghost. She ducked through the door seconds before two wolves passed where she had just left.

By the time she reached the top of the landing, her thighs were burning from lactic acid. As she moved, she kept one eye on the shifting camera reports, the phone clutched in her hand like a lifeline. That's how she saw the roof grid open, and Evan's head and shoulders appear. He glanced around quickly, but none of the rebels were on the roof.

Evan sprinted to the fire escape, checking over the side

of the building before crawling out of sight, Dexter clinging to his back like a monkey.

If things went well, Evan would be on the ground in less than fifteen seconds. Amy paused for long enough to set off a new series of alarms, all of them on the far side from where Evan and Dexter were descending.

Now it was her turn. She ran the length of the hallway, fiddling with the set of keys she'd taken from the maintenance room. A group of wolves were approaching, and she used the master key to access one of the larger suites.

She closed the door silently behind her, leaning against the door. Mike's wolves paced past, unaware of her presence only feet away. Incompetent fools. They should have been using their noses. But, she was glad their skills at espionage were as bad as they were. It meant she and Evan could get the jump on them.

Amy looked around as she got her breathing under control. It wasn't her final destination, but the room she was in was a good second choice. One of the fancier suites in the hotel, this one had an Internet connection along with the television. It was like Christmas, Hanukkah and every birthday wish she'd ever made. A couple adjustments later and she'd hacked into Evan's system again.

Now more than one security-camera view was visible at a time. Her alarms had worked, and outside the building Dexter was in Laney's arms, just barely visible across the street in a gathering of familiar faces.

There was no sign of Evan.

Amy took the time to trigger a program she'd written ages ago during her revenge-planning days. The one that would set off alarms at random intervals. She added in the power grid, which would set up the lights to fail in a random series. She hit start, then headed back to the door ready for the next stage of the adventure.

Down one more set of stairs, around the corner, she slipped into Evan's office and stood motionless against the side wall, waiting for her heart rate to slow before she risked opening the mainframe.

Mike was only a dozen steps on the other side of the door from her.

She checked Evan's phone again, but it only confirmed what she had suspected. While Mike seemed in no rush to burn things as he'd threatened, Toby was no longer in the mechanical room. Instead, he and Lance were both on their way back to the bar.

She bet anything they were hoping Evan would show up.

Which meant she couldn't wait any longer. She tiptoed across the floor and opened the computer in the corner. Evan had crashed all the Moonshine Inn laptops at one time or another, and Amy had slipped remote access codes into all of them.

But the big old mainframe was the jackpot for taking control of the final touches.

She opened the master control and stared for a moment at the flashing command box. All of the doors in the inn had an electronic safety lock. When given the order, the doors would automatically swing open to allow visitors to exit in a rush during an emergency.

If she reversed the command codes, the opposite would be true. None of the doors would open without her specifically setting them to release. She only needed the password, and the change would be complete.

So. What would Evan pick for a master password? She

was sure he would have chosen it, even if Caroline used the controls one hundred percent of the time.

No hesitation. There was only one thing Evan would have selected before anything else. The one thing always on his mind, at least when he would have set up the code.

She typed in "whitehorseforever".

The screen she needed popped open. She did a happy dance silently in her chair as her fingers flew to input commands.

One set of commands locked the doors.

The next set primed the service entrance with the access code "united".

The third shut down all programming access again.

Amy turned away from the computer and rushed to the main door of Evan's office. She hesitated briefly, but it had to be done. The wolves on the other side of the door had made some big mistakes in staging a rebellion, but they didn't know they were trapped. They didn't know the game had changed, and unless they were told, they couldn't change their mind and give up.

She stepped through the door and into the immediate attention of the rebel wolves.

EVAN THRUST Dexter into his mom's arms, spinning on the spot to head back to the building.

"Hey, where do you think you're going?" Shaun was at his side, sprinting forward and matching his pace.

"Amy is still in there. I'm going to get her." Evan attempted to jerk the door open, but it was firmly locked. "Shit, that's right. The code."

"Takhini has the place surrounded," Shaun reported as Evan opened up the control panel and entered the password. "And those geeky computer dudes from Canyon who work for Amy did something they said would override any calls from inside the inn to the fire department or police department until we give the word. I hope you know what you're doing."

"I hope so too." Evan tried the door again, but it still didn't budge. "I need you to stay out here and keep things under control. If anything explodes, call the fire department. I'm going in and getting Amy."

Shaun rested his hand on Evan shoulder. "She's a smart woman, your mate. She'll get it done, and then we can kick some butt and get those rebels to smarten up."

Evan tapped in *united* again, hit enter and sighed with relief as the door swung open before he even touched it. "She is smart, and I have no idea why she's willing to put up with me. But I'm so glad she is."

He stepped through the door and pulled it shut behind him.

It was déjà vu. So much like a few weeks earlier when he'd walked into the darkness, only this time he knew somewhere ahead of him, his mate was waiting. He'd found her, and damn if he'd let anyone take her away.

She'd been in the hall recently. He followed her trail all the way to his office, getting in without any trouble. That's when he realized what she'd done.

The door on the bar side of the room was open a crack, and laughter poured through. Nasty, mean laughter, followed by the sound of skin smacking skin, and the faint cry of pain from his mate's lips.

Fury enveloped him. At that moment he had no desire whatsoever for the authorities to come and pick up the bastards. He wanted to tear them apart one piece at a time for daring to touch her.

He slung open the door and stepped through like an avenging angel, infuriated by the sight of Amy held tight between two wolves. Toby stood before her, his fist raised for the next blow.

"Touch her again and you die," Evan promised. His words soft, but deadly.

"The guest of honour has arrived." Another wolf rose to his feet, throwing the drink in his hand to the floor where glass and liquid splashed up over his flunkies. "We can do this so many ways, but the old ways are sometimes best. I challenge you for this territory. You're not worthy to be in charge."

"Let her go, and you and I can dance." Evan stepped closer to Amy, keeping an eye on the wolf he assumed was Mike.

For some reason, Toby didn't get out of the way. He opened his mouth to say something, but Evan had zero tolerance left by this point. He simply raised both fists, catching Toby under the chin with his rock solid hands, sending the wolf crashing into the others.

Evan turned a cold eye on the pack members who'd betrayed him and were now holding Amy's arms. "Are you deaf? I said, let her go."

He wasn't sure who they were more afraid of, him or Mike. They glanced in both directions before opening their hands and stepping back.

Who they should have been afraid of was Amy. The instant she was no longer restrained she swung, one fist flying in an uppercut that crushed a jaw even as she followed through the opposite direction with a kick. The second wolf's head snapped back as his feet lifted off the ground, and he flew backwards a good three feet.

Evan smiled at his mate. "Nicely done."

Amy gingerly touched the swollen corner of her mouth, wiping away the blood. "Toby's swings were getting a little boring. I'm glad you could join us."

"Why, this is all so lovey-dovey and friendly-like." Mike picked up the chair next to him and threw it across the room. He roared before setting himself squarely to face Evan and Amy, big fists rising to the ready. "Enough. Take the challenge, or get on your belly and crawl."

"Hold that thought. Even though it was a touch too melodramatic." Evan faced Amy. "Your choice."

She looked confused, watching Mike out of the corner of her eye. "What are you talking about?"

"Do I fight him? Or do we let the authorities take care of him for everything he's done? I'm pretty sure we can get him locked up for quite a while. We don't have to take the violent solution."

In spite of the bruises on her face, he'd never seen her look more beautiful. "You would do that for me?"

"Anything. Because you're my mate."

"I'm just going to kill the both of you," Mike snapped, picking up another chair and smashing it on a table. The wood shattered, leaving him with a long, deadly weapon. He lofted it in the air, stomping toward them.

"Kick his butt," Amy ordered. She got out of his way, headed for the side of the room where the rest of the rebels were moving uneasily. "Any of you even *think* about interfering, and I'll pull your lungs out through your eye sockets."

That's my girl, Evan thought, but he was too busy ducking Mike's attack to say it out loud.

"We need to get out of here," Toby groaned from his fetal position on the floor. "There's no time. There's no time."

The deadly chunk of wood swung over Evan's head again. This time he darted forward under the attack and into Mike's space. He slashed out with an uppercut, following it immediately with a vicious jab to the man's throat.

Mike jerked aside at the last second. Evan's knuckles grazed his neck. They were too close together for the piece of chair to be effective, so Mike tossed it aside, the wood clattering on the solid floor of the bar.

Their dangerous dance continued, the physical battle somewhat reassuring. Amy had skills Evan could only dream of, but this? This was his area of expertise.

He jabbed again, making contact with the man's temple before he scooted out of reach, headed for the bar. He grabbed a bottle of whiskey, smashing the glass over Mike's head seconds before the brute ran into him, driving him back against the solid rock lining the bar.

Somewhere below them an enormous explosion went off, the reverberations echoing through the hallways and changing the pressure in the sealed building. Evan's ears popped, but he was too busy diving from Mike to worry about what was happening elsewhere.

Lights flickered overhead, the fire alarms going off in a strangely musical sequence all over the hotel.

Inspiration hit. He caught Mike by the shoulder, using momentum to drop his arm around Mike's thick neck and put him into a chokehold. At the same time he brought his knee in sharply, smashing it into Mike's kidneys. The man's legs buckled, and he fell to his knees, Evan a heavy weight on his back.

Another explosion sounded, and this time Toby

shrieked. "We've got to get out of here. The gas line is open. The whole place will go up around us."

"I'll let you go," Amy promised, her volume rising to carry over the shouting and distant rumbling. "Just give me your word that you're done with this foolishness."

Evan jerked backwards, taking Mike with him. He twisted at the last moment to slam the other man into the floor first, once again driving a knee into his back. Mike groaned loudly, hands scrambling on the floor as he struggled for air.

"There's no use in fighting any longer," Amy snapped. "Take a look at the leader of your rebellion. Any of you want to fight Evan once he's done? Any of you want to fight *me*?"

The struggle on the floor continued, but in the background his mate was fighting a different battle. Evan grabbed Mike by the back of the head so he could repeat the face slam into the floor. In the meantime, Amy continued to give the others hell, forcing them to make a decision which way their loyalties would lie. The exit doors refused to budge, and the windows were shatterproof.

He was a little busy with Mike, but still admiring the hell out of his mate's evil sense of justice.

"You're in charge. I swear I'll follow you and Evan," one of the rebels shouted. "Now, please, for God's sake, let us out."

One after the other they affirmed the decision. As the crackling sound of fire encroached, panic rose.

"I shouldn't make you decide while you're under such duress." Amy clicked her tongue. "It's not fair. Maybe you're saying something you don't mean. I need to think about this for a little while."

"You're so demanding," Evan teased. He concentrated as Mike made one final attempt to rise. Evan squeezed harder, his biceps bulging as he closed the man's airway as tightly as possible.

"You think?" Amy stepped beside him, squatting to tap his arm. "Hey, you used my move."

"It seemed appropriate. And effective."

She grinned. "He's unconscious, by the way, so you can come and help me with these other guys."

Evan dragged his arm free. "You seem to be doing fine on your own."

She pulled his cell phone from her pocket and smiled past lips that were puffy and swollen. "If you escort the guys to the side door off the bar, I'll unlock it. That's the safest route."

"You can open the rest of the doors," Evan told her. "There's a fire truck standing by."

What followed was a rush of activity. The half-dozen men who had been with Mike, Toby and Lance raced from the building. Evan reached the door in time to see the Takhini pack, headed by Shaun, surround them and lead them off.

Which left Mike's unconscious body to be dealt with. Evan whistled at his Beta. "Hey, come take out the trash for me."

Shaun jogged over, patting Evan approvingly on the back as he slipped past. "Oh, look. Bad guy on the floor. Colour me shocked and dismayed."

He slung the man over his shoulder with surprising ease, heading out to safety.

Evan held his hand to Amy, both of them rocking on their feet as another alarm went off directly overhead. "Come on, let's get out here," he shouted.

"Just a second. I can shut off the gas from the master control."

And damn if she didn't turn around and go back into the hotel.

Evan swore, pausing only long enough to gesture to the emergency crew standing on the sidewalk watching patiently. "Get everyone away from here."

He twirled and headed for his office, yanking the door open. It was the work of seconds to drag her from the computer and scoop her over his shoulder.

"Wait, wait," Amy protested. "There're other things I can do. Stop it, you Neanderthal. Put me down."

He was beyond waiting. Evan marched out of the room. Heat was already pouring through the doors on the front-hall side. "It's not worth your life. It's only a building."

She relaxed, dragging her fingers up his back. "You just wanted an excuse to carry me around. Admit it."

Evan didn't stop until they were across the street and safely away from any further explosions. He lowered her to the ground and tucked her into his arms. "I'm glad you're my mate."

Her eyes shone, and that alone made everything perfect. "Looks as if you're still in charge."

"*We're* in charge," he emphasized.

Sirens joined the noise around them. The inn was definitely burning, smoke rising from the upper floors as the ambulance crew popped Mike into the ambulance. A police car waited to accompany them to the hospital. One of the pack who worked as an RCMP caught their attention then nodded. His chin dipped low as he affirmed his connection.

"Mike will be charged for kidnapping, and everything we can think of related to destroying the inn." Evan turned to see Amy's assistant, Sarah, standing with her clipboard in hand. She eyed the crowd nervously, but held her ground. "Evan will not be charged for assault or anything, obviously, since he was acting in self-defense and defending you."

"Well done," Amy praised her. "Anything else?"

Sarah pointed into the crowd. "The rebel wolves are in the care of Shaun and the Takhini pack. They're probably the best ones to deal with that side of things. In the meantime, I've got a bunch of our people looking into insurance and researching contractors so we rebuild as soon as possible."

Okay, that one came as a surprise to Evan. "You want to rebuild the Moonshine Inn?"

The woman blinked. "Of course. It's a great source of revenue, plus it gives the Takhini hooligans something productive to do. Keeps them out of mischief." Only she winked as she spoke, lowering her gaze respectfully before backing away.

It was too much to take in at once. Evan shook his head and nearly fell over. "Whoa."

Amy snuggled under his arm and helped hold him up. "I think everybody seems to have the situation under control."

Almost everything. "Take me home."

Her smile lit up the area. "I thought you'd never ask."

22

———————

They slipped back into her house, and a million years might have passed since she'd been there last. Maybe in a way the sensation was right.

Her world had changed.

Evan crowded her all the way to the shower, pausing to turn on the water. By the time he'd finished stripping off her clothes, steam billowed around them.

The aches and pains were there, but every bit of the punishment she'd taken was worth it, especially when he slid in next to her. Nothing but naked skin, his biceps flexing powerfully as he grabbed her buff puff and the soap.

"Close your eyes, and let me take care of you."

It seemed selfish to simply take. She closed her eyes as ordered, but reached out to slide her fingers over his body. Touching him while he scrubbed and cleaned, moving tenderly over the bruises and cuts she'd received.

"You're not supposed to do that," he breathed unsteadily, the words trembling as she traced her fingers over the delicious muscle between his thigh and abdomen.

"Try and stop me," she whispered. "You need some tenderness as well."

"What I need is to care for my mate. You were incredible back there." With his lips pressed to her temple, he turned her, settling her against his chest. The circles with the soap continued, his hands rising from her waist to her breasts.

Amy arched into his touch. "We work together. Oh, yes, right there."

He'd transferred the sponge to his opposite hand and was playing with her nipples. "Don't scare me like that again. When I got into the office and realized where you were, I was ready to take them all out for hurting you."

"It wasn't my idea of a good time, but it had to be done." Amy draped a hand around his neck, twisting her head to one side so their lips could meet for a slow, careful kiss. The taste of him sank into her very cells. "And you're still the one who fought Mike."

"I have every confidence if you had needed to, you would've handled him just as well."

The warm water and the comfort of his body helped release the remaining tension. "We work together," she repeated. "And while it's sad it came down to having to face a rebellion, we should have expected it."

He nuzzled her neck, the scruff of his chin like erotic sandpaper against sensitive nerves. "Stupid people always make the stupidest move, but I wish I hadn't fallen down on the job in the first place."

"I'm sorry about the Moonshine Inn." Amy twisted in his arms, rubbing her fingers through his hair as she tugged him under the showerhead. "I'll do everything I can to help make the new hotel construction go smoothly."

Evan smiled as he settled his hands on her hips. "It sounds as if Canyon already has our back."

"You'll find there are a lot of things that will go much smoother with their skills behind you."

His eyes burned brighter as he looked at her, ogling her body. "Same goes the other way around, but I think we've had enough pack discussion today. Don't you agree?"

Amy hummed happily. "You look as if you have something else on your mind."

He hoisted her upward, twisting far enough to pin her to the wall of the shower with his body. Slick heat and rising passion growing between them. "I'm about to have something on my cock."

She laughed, and it felt so good to release the stress. To have a whole new type of tension spreading through her system, driving her mad with entangling sensual tendrils. Evan adjusted her so the heavy length of his shaft rested over her sex.

They'd been going slow up to this point, but it was time to move. Amy wrapped her legs around his hips. She dragged her nails up his back, enjoying the rough response as he thrust forward, knocking her clit and sending shivers up her spine.

Things kind of got a little crazy from that point. Between his mouth and his hands, there wasn't a whole lot of her that wasn't being teased to a hot, quivering mass. He caressed her ass, fingers floating sensually over the curves. He stroked under her thigh, lifting her knee to one side so he could slip his fingers into her. He pumped languidly at first, then with increasing speed until she dug her nails into his shoulders and gasped for air.

A satisfied rumble filled the shower stall. "My mate. Perfect for me, exactly what I need."

Evan pulled his fingers free. Made one adjustment, and suddenly she was filled with the full, hard length of his cock. She rested her head back on the tiles and stared into his eyes. "You like this position, don't you?"

He held her with one arm, the other braced on the wall beside her head. She clung to his biceps, scratching her free hand down his chest as she used her legs to help him pump deeper, harder, until they were both shaking, teetering on the edge.

Evan paused, and the mood changed. No longer desperate, but fully engaged. All she wanted at this point was to give to him. He deserved so much, and she was going to spend the rest of her life showing him that.

She kissed his chest as his touch became more possessive, the blinding sensation of pleasure rising, tension growing. Evan caught her chin, and there was no looking away as he moved within her, one long, languid stroke after another until she tumbled apart, satisfaction carrying away all emotional baggage. Every moment binding them closer.

Then she broke eye contact. Not to deny him the intimacy, but to finish this. To offer the final moment of trust. She put her teeth to his neck and bit hard enough to make him gasp. Accepting who he was to her. Giving him all of herself.

Fiery passion roared through her as he came. The taste of him in her mouth. The sensation of being joined and completed shooting in a mad rush through her veins.

She let him go after marking him, savouring the intoxicating connection. And when he returned the favour, marking her and making her his, Amy shouted his name. Shaking as she luxuriated in being whole.

"I'll never let you be alone again."

His voice in her head. Amy swallowed hard, shivering as Evan licked the mark on her neck and then continued upward, playfully tasting her.

"Am I your personal ice cream cone?" Amy teased as delight swirled through her.

He pulled her to a vertical position, sheer joy on his face. "It's true. You're in my head and my heart, and it couldn't be more perfect."

Amy nodded. This was what she had always hoped for, but hadn't dreamed possible. "I never want to do anything to make you doubt me. I will always choose you, I promise."

They ended up on the bed, cuddling for the longest time. Evan stroked her hair and held her against him. It was the strangest of sensations, having given her heart, and yet it was the most right thing she'd ever experienced. *"I can sense you. What you're feeling, what you're hoping."*

Evan snickered. "Does this mean you know already what I plan to get you for a mating gift?"

"I would never dream of spoiling a surprise. I'll stay out of those parts of your brain." She pulled on an innocent face —the kind that usually meant someone was up to no good.

For a moment he looked absolutely horrified. "Oh God. Tell me this isn't like a computer, and you know exactly how to break all the codes? Because I wouldn't have a chance at keeping anything secret, not from you."

Amy laughed, and in spite of her bruises and swollen lips and all the aches and pains, it felt so good. So good to leave behind the heavy weight she'd been burdened under, not just for the last month, but for a lifetime. "Don't worry, if you break anything, I'm pretty sure I can figure out how to fix it."

He rolled onto his back and collapsed, arms overhead as if he'd given up. *"I'm in so much trouble."*

Amy crawled over him, staring contentedly at the man who was her mate. *"Then we'll be in trouble together. Because that's what mates do."*

EPILOGUE

"No, no. Don't put that there. It'll end up in the picture. And you. You, over there. You need to stand closer." The photographer shook his head in frustration at the lack of cooperation. He left his place behind the camera in an attempt to once more put everyone back into the proper position.

Evan tugged Amy closer to his side and waited for the rest of the pack to get their shit together.

She turned to smile up at him. "Happy?"

"Is this a trick question?" Evan squeezed her fingers. "Yes, I'm happy. I'll be even happier once we get permission to leave the building site and go enjoy the party."

She gave him a wink. "You know they couldn't do the groundbreaking without you. The head contractor insisted. He didn't care if Shaun, Gem or I were available, it was all about *you*."

Over the last month Evan had found a special kinship developing he hadn't expected with some of the quieter members of the joint Takhini-Canyon pack. "Yeah? Well, the party we're headed to is all about you. Did you know...?"

He slapped a hand over his mouth, partly because he'd just about let a secret spill, but mostly to tease her.

Amy's eyes narrowed. "Did I know what? What?"

She would have twisted to face him and demand more details, but Evan held her still. "Don't move. We're ready for the picture, and if you mess it up, you'll be in big trouble."

Amy laughed softly, but listened to his warning. They leaned on the shovel they'd been given, pretending to push it into the soil of the cleaned-up building site that by the summer would see the opening of the brand-new and expanded Moonshine Inn. Construction was due to start the following Monday.

Evan took hold of his mate's hand and didn't let go throughout the entire tour and the journey back to the pack house. He couldn't get enough of touching her, and he didn't think that sensation would ever go away.

They were barely through the door when he lost her to some of the more exuberant members of the pack.

"Look! Look what we got you." They tugged Amy into the common room and promptly handed her a control.

Amy whistled, then broke into a celebratory dance, hands raised in the air, her hips shimmying from side to side as she took in the giant screen on the wall and the enormous Call of Duty logo filling the screen. "Sweet. Who wants to get their butt kicked first?"

That was it. Evan lay odds he wouldn't see his mate for the next six hours as the pack took turns getting whomped. So far, the only person who had come close to beating Amy at any computer game was, surprisingly enough, Shaun.

Evan wandered over to where his Beta was holding up a wall, fingers wrapped around an oversized hamburger as he kept an eye on the festivities. "Good grief, how many patties did you put on that thing?" Evan asked.

Shaun swallowed his mouthful before eyeing the thick mass in his hand. "This one? It's only a pound and a half. The chef-dude said it had to tide me over until the steaks are ready."

"You're lucky you're a wolf. I would hate to see your cholesterol levels otherwise."

"No doubt." Shaun grinned. "But I am a wolf, therefore I have no worries about the twenty-four-ounce tenderloin I ordered with blue-cheese crumbles and extra fries."

Evan's mouth watered. "Damn, it's good to be a wolf," he agreed.

Shaun's pleased expression only grew bigger as he nodded. "And yes, I did order you the same thing as me."

"Good man." Evan thumped him on the shoulder, then made his way farther into the room. He passed Justin, blinking for a moment at the man, who instead of his typical suit and tie was now attired in faded jeans and a flannel shirt. The mystery made him pause until he spotted Amanda shyly motioning the bear shifter forward, patting the open spot on the love seat beside her.

Oh, *really*? Amy had bet him something was on the horizon for those two, and he'd insisted she was crazy. Looked as if he owed her twenty bucks.

Everywhere he looked the pack was enjoying themselves. At least, the rowdy part of the pack. He observed for a moment, smiling happily, then slipped through the doors and into the back section of the pack house where Amy had instituted a few changes in the layout and house rules.

As he expected, there were a dozen wolves curled up in easy chairs, the seating arrangements organized to allow for privacy even while in the midst of a large crowd. People dipped their heads politely as he passed, gentle smiles and waves that warmed him as much as the enthusiastic thumps on the back he'd gotten earlier from other members.

Laney rose from her corner and offered a hug, and Evan had to force back the tightness in his throat. He held her gently, but the fact she didn't pull away meant a whole lot.

He kissed the top of her head. "Are you having a good time?"

She nodded. "Dexter is playing with some of the other kids. He's so happy, and I'm so grateful for everything you've done to make us feel welcome."

"It's what pack does. Thank you for being a part of it."

She crawled back into her chair, pulling out her book and breathing a sigh of contentment as she fell back into the pages.

Evan had to move quickly before he ended up bursting into tears or some such bullshit. There were still moments when clashes were inevitable, but for the most part the combined packs were cooperating and finding ways to have fun, and those were the most important things.

It was neat to see the longer they worked together, the more often previous Takhini members went straight to Amy for help, while the Canyon folk slipped into Evan's office for a quiet moment of conversation.

Evan's phone rang about the same time a deafening cheer rose from the common room—Amy must have pulled off some wild and crazy move in the game, and the shouts of encouragement were loud enough to shake the walls. It amused him that some pack still called out *Sam*, some *Amy*. She didn't seem to mind, simply answering to both names.

She would always be Amy to him, though.

He stepped onto the outside deck into the cold October weather to get some quiet. "Your dime, spill it."

"Hey, boss. I talked to Amy earlier, and she told me to

call you now. How's the party going?" Caroline's familiar voice on the line brought him nothing but a smile.

"Well, hello, world traveler. The party is going well, but I don't suppose you know where we stored the beer mugs?" Evan teased.

"I'm so thrilled to tell you I have absolutely no idea." Caroline's joy was more than obvious. "We're headed to Germany next, if you want me to send a few steins your way."

Evan laughed. "Just a joke. Send a few mementos of your trip if you feel like it. I'm glad you're having a good time. How's that overstuffed teddy bear you married treating you?"

She sighed happily. "Oh. My. Word."

That's what he'd figured. "Enough said. No more details needed. You know that kind of discussion makes me uncomfortable." Evan ignored her snort of disbelief. "You're lucky you ended up with a shifter, because no one else on earth could keep up with you."

"Yeah, you're right." She paused for a moment. "I was happy to hear from Amy. We must have talked for over an hour, catching up. She thinks you're pretty incredible, by the way. Sounds as if you and her are a perfect match. And I'm so, so pleased for you. Really."

"She's my mate. That says it all." Evan looked over Whitehorse, the hills to the east that were dusted white with snow. "How did we get so lucky, Caroline? How did we end up in the right place, at the right time to find the perfect people at our sides?"

"I have no idea, but I have no complaints whatsoever with what fate handed me." A deep voice sounded in the background, and Caroline laughed. "Tyler says to say hello, and he hopes you're behaving yourself. But that if you're not behaving yourself, tough luck, I'm still not allowed to bail you out of trouble."

Evan's world was filled to the brim with people who cared for him and, as hokey as it was, people who he had to admit he absolutely adored. "Tell him I'm looking forward to the next time we fight, but in the meantime have a great time in Europe, and we'll see you in the spring."

He put his phone away, continuing to look over the city that had become his home. Running the merged Takhini-Canyon packs just made it that much brighter.

But the brightest part was having a pair of strong arms slip around his waist as Amy cuddled in tight. She was the absolutely perfect cherry on top.

"You looking for some alone time? Because I can come back and find you later."

"Now is perfect." He leaned his back against the railing and settled her between his legs. "There's another thing I've learned from your pack. How to slow down and smell the roses."

Amy caressed his face. *"Our* pack."

Evan kissed her, ignoring the city and the pack members who trickled onto the deck before silently leaving to give them privacy.

When he pulled away, her face glowed with happiness, just the way he liked. "I thought I wouldn't see you for days. Who's playing the game?"

She tilted her head to one side, the result damn adorable. "I gave the control up to Shaun. Made him my master-at-arms, and told him I was relying on him to set a new record. He acted as if I'd knighted him or something. He might not be available to fly any sightseeing tours for the next week."

"He's eager to defend your honour."

Amy made a rude noise. "He wanted to play, is all. Well, plus he hopes to impress me enough I'll teach him the backdoor secrets on Halo so he can set a new high score."

A burst of laughter escaped before he could stop it. "I'm glad you two are getting along."

She draped her hands over his shoulders and leaned back slightly, swaying gently from side to side to some unheard music. "We got a call from Shelley and Chase. They wanted to let you know that come the spring, they plan to bring a couple dozen trees out from the bush. A contribution to the hotel. Shelley will send the details later so the designers can work them into the landscaping. It's their gift to us. To the biggest pack in the North."

More people who Evan cared about, and who he was glad to have in his life. As much as he needed to give to the pack, the fact *he* was personally loved in return brought him to his knees.

And yet... "I'd give it all up, you know."

A crease appeared between her eyes even as she continued to stroke his shoulders. "Where did that come from?"

Evan shrugged. "Just had to be said. I love that we've established a strong, new pack, and there are a shit-ton of good people around Whitehorse, no matter if their party style is quiet or loud."

"Or as it seems right now, quiet or ear-shattering."

The cheers had grown shriller, and they grinned at each other. Contentment flooded his soul, but he didn't want to miss making his point.

"But at the root of it all?" He cupped her chin, bending his knees until their eyes were on the same level. "At the center, and right here where it counts the most?" He pressed her fingers over his chest. "Right here is where you are. I don't care if we've got the biggest pack in the North, or the smallest, as long as I'm with you."

Her eyes sparkled. "Ditto."

Evan pulled her against him, and they gazed over their domain. Hand in hand and heart to heart.

"I love you, Evan."

Her words whispered through his head. The ultimate intimacy.

He looked into her eyes again and saw his world reflected there. *"I love you, Amy. And I always will."*

United. Whitehorse forever.

~

New York Times Bestselling Author Vivian Arend
brings you a series of light-hearted,
stand-alone novels filled with shifters of all
kinds—bears, wolves, lynx.
Whether they're fated mates or falling
head-over-paws, there's always a happily-ever-after.

~

Black Gold
Silver Mine
Diamond Dust
Moon Shine

~

ABOUT THE AUTHOR

New York Times and *USA Today* bestselling author Vivian Arend loves to share the products of her over-active imagination with her readers. She writes contemporary, western, and light-hearted paranormal romances. The stories are humorous yet emotional, usually with a large cast of family or friends, and a guaranteed happily-ever-after.

Vivian lives in British Columbia, Canada, with her husband of many years—her inspiration for every hero and a willing companion for all sorts of adventures.

Find out more at www.vivianarend.com.